# The Miniaturist

*By the same author*
The Opium Clerk

# The Miniaturist

*Kunal Basu*

Weidenfeld & Nicolson

London

A PHOENIX HOUSE BOOK

First published in Great Britain in 2003
A Phoenix House Book

Copyright © 2003 Kunal Basu

A CIP catalogue record for this book
is available from the British Library.

ISBN 0 297 82926 2

Typeset in Minion by
Selwood Systems, Midsomer Norton

Printed and bound by
Butler & Tanner Ltd, Frome and London


Phoenix House
Weidenfeld & Nicolson
The Orion Publishing Group Ltd
Orion House, 5 Upper St Martin's Lane
London WC2H 9EA

For Susmita

Allah's Messenger (may peace be upon him) said, thou who draw pictures will be punished on the day of resurrection. It would be said to thou, breathe soul into what you have created.

HADITH

# Naqsh
## patterns

*

Arise, o cup-bearer, arise!

HAFIZ

'Rise early,' the Khwaja whispered, bringing his face close to Bihzad's ear, spraying his cheek with yesterday's wine. 'Then you'll see the true mischief of the sun!'

Father and son sat under the night sky. From the top of the watchtower, they faced the river – the Jamuna – and the neat rows of cannon poised over the fort's boundary wall. Behind them lay the city. The damp air made them shiver. The Khwaja had woken the sentry, who had bowed to them and let them in through the gates. Climbing the narrow flight of stairs, they had chosen their favourite spot, sitting with their heels tucked into their robes, holding tight to the railings. The Khwaja smiled at his boy, yet to recover from the sleep of the new moon, pointing up at the fading constellations.

Beyond the horizon, the sun hesitated. Lurking behind clouds, the invader appeared unwilling, like a horseman unused to darkness. Then, in a flash, a single ray leapt into the heart of the river, grew flat like the absent moon, and turned its face to the stars. A beam landed among the shrubs like a spear. Floating on the purple dew, it struck the first note of foliage. Breaking free at last of the clouds, a whole shaft of light attacked the row of poplar and cypress on the far bank of the river, and the stonecutters' camp nestled among the trees.

'Look!' The Khwaja nudged a sleepy Bihzad. What was white before sparkled with a fine glaze of crimson, smearing the ashen tents that housed soldiers and animals inside the fort's walls, lighting up the city of palaces and mosques, casting a halo over the silent fountains and the imperial boat. One by one, the great doorways of the fort gleamed like mirrors, reflecting the sun, now a spear's length over the horizon. Marble palaces breathed free of the crisscrossing beams, managing to stand aloof from common homes. The intruder, satisfied by the result, turned an effortless gold – a gold coin floating on the river, at its still centre.

A bird called, flew across, reflecting the world on its tiny wings – the lapis sky, the turquoise river, the crimson fort and the golden sun.

'Look!' The Khwaja whispered into Bihzad's ear, tracing its flight with his raised finger. 'The finest artist in all Agra!'

*

And so on Saturday the twenty-seventh of Rabi, year 975 of the Hegira, 1568 of the Christian era, the sun lit imperial Agra, blessing every moment and delighting every one of its subjects. It rose for the ten thousandth time since that dawn when Babur, the Mughal invader, had woken after a restful night to find himself the conqueror of Hindustan. Under the western wall of the fort, his grandson, the emperor, was about to rise. Rise and begin his favourite sport – racing elephants when they are at their frightening best. In heat.

The Khwaja frowned. Sitting before his visitor, his imposing frame fitted his title perfectly – 'Khwaja,' the chief artist of Agra's royal workshop, the kitabkhana. To a few close friends he was known by the name with which he had left Persia more than a decade ago: Abdus Samad Shirazi – born in Shiraz to a family of illustrious artists. But among the courtiers of Agra, he went by another name given to him by no less than the emperor himself. *Shirin Qalam*. Sweet Pen. The only one privileged to sit face to face with the master of Hindustan for as long as it took to paint his royal portrait.

The Khwaja's face bore the traces of a long night. A painting lay on his lap. Squatting on the floor of his haveli, knees raised, he turned to catch the light that streamed through the window, a worn tunic tight around the belly straining a set of feeble buttons. He avoided meeting the gaze of his visitor, the Darogha, the chief clerk of the kitabkhana.

It was curious, the Darogha sighed. He spoke softly, stopping from time to time to straighten his long moustache. Years at the kitabkhana had given him more than a neatly combed white beard. He could recite the name of every artist, calligrapher, illuminator and border painter, binder, gold beater and lapis washer. Of the hundred, he knew which one was an expert in setting a complex tale to a simple pattern, who could delight the emperor with the most eye-pleasing scenes, whose portraits drew the highest reward. He could tell by the strokes of the pen if a face had been drawn by more than one artist – who had painted the eyes and who the lips. Years at the kitabkhana had given him the eyes of a hawk. But this …

The Darogha pointed to the chess players in the painting on the Khwaja's lap, sitting in the garden of a palace. His finger came to rest on the turbaned head of the younger player.

'This,' the Darogha glanced nervously at the Khwaja, 'is yours …' The Khwaja nodded gravely.

'But this,' his finger moved to the older player, a Mughal cap on his bald head, 'can only have come from the pen of the Great One.'

Both looked each other in the eye. The Great One? Did the Darogha mean the absolute master of *all* artists of *all* ages – from Persia to Hindustan?

'You mean …?' The Khwaja continued staring at the painting.

'It *is* from the pen of Kamal-al-Din Bihzad, the jewel of Herat and Tabriz.' The Darogha muttered the many titles of the great master under his breath … *Hazrat-i-Ustad* – The Exalted Master. *Nadir-al-Asar* – The Rarity of the Age.

'But that's impossible! I never even met Kamal-al-Din Bihzad. How could he and I have worked on the same painting?'

The Darogha agreed. For a moment, neither spoke.

'And *this* …' The Darogha moved his finger to the marble balcony, to the face of the young princess who, prying through her latticed window, cast a fond glance at the chess players.

'*This* is the work of an unknown. By a future master perhaps, but not from the kitabkhana.' In his mind, the Darogha had gone over the hundred artists at the royal workshop. None could have painted that exquisite face.

'Who …' the Darogha sighed. 'Three masters in one!'

'Who?' the Khwaja grimaced.

The sun was in mid heaven; it was time to leave for the kitabkhana. Bidding his visitor away, the Khwaja climbed the stairs to his private chamber. But first, he glanced around the small terrace and down the row of rooms facing the stone passage. The boy was nowhere to be seen.

'Bihzad …!' he roared.

'Bedaulat ...!' he cursed.

With his fists he banged on the door of the attic, a short flight up under the roof, the buttons of his tunic on the verge of rupture. Then, he calmed himself and spoke, his cheek pressed against the closed door.

'Who taught you to draw like me?'

Laughter came from within.

'And who advised you to imitate the Great One?'

'You!' his son replied.

'Me?' The Khwaja was astonished.

'Don't you always say *better to serve a dead master than a living fool!*'

The Khwaja sat down before the door. Laughter shook his body, the buttons of his tunic popping one by one.

*

Little Bihzad. A grand name for a small boy. His father, the Khwaja, had left his native Persia a few years before Bihzad was born, summoned to the court in Hindustan by its emperor. He was one among the many – judges, generals, artisans and merchants – immigrants lured by the wealth of the new empire and its emperors, the Mughals, immigrants like themselves from the vast plains of Central Asia, welcoming men of talent with open arms, unlike their suspicious neighbours. From Tabriz he had journeyed to Kabul, crossing the fearsome Hindukush and the even more ferocious Afghans. From Kabul to Agra. In Agra they knew the Khwaja by his Persian turban, hanging low in a single fold, unlike the four-fold turban of Hindustan. He had charmed the emperor, it was said, by drawing an entire army on a grain of rice.

Soon after arriving in Agra, the Khwaja had lost his Persian wife, but not before she had presented him with their only child – a rare flower, just like her, plucked from a heavenly garden. In his grief, the Khwaja had named the boy after Kamal-al-Din Bihzad – after the greatest of artists – praying for a Persian flower to take root in the soil of Mughal Hindustan. Even after the Khwaja's second marriage, Bihzad remained the only child of his father's household, his most precious possession, shining like a pearl in his father's eye.

From the day he could hold a pen, the boy drew fluently. He chose to draw from the stories read to him by his stepmother. Stories about birds without wings, about Hizabr the lion, and the monster wolf Karkadann. When a tutor arrived to instruct him in the Koran, as was the custom, the Khwaja turned him away. He would not even have Bihzad taught to read and write. He blamed his strange decision on the fits. During every new moon a violent trembling would seize the boy, make him sweat even on the coldest nights. He would lie with his eyes closed, foaming at the mouth, bellowing like a young camel. As the fit passed, Bihzad would spring up, jump on the Khwaja's broad shoulders, clasp his bull-neck with his palms.

His friends struggled over the classics – read and reread passages from Sadi and Hafiz. Young artists at the kitabkhana, as young as five, would rise early to copy page after page from manuscripts under the watchful eyes of the chief clerk. But the Khwaja refused to allow his son to join his friends, casting a mere glance at his drawings of the lion or the wingless birds.

How strange, the other courtiers whispered. And how strange for a man of the Khwaja's rank to be happy with just one wife and one illiterate son. Truly unusual for someone so close to the emperor and fortunate enough to have been granted his own palace in the fort, near the royal quarters.

'He was born almost on the steps of the kitabkhana,' the Darogha reasoned time and again with the Khwaja. 'He is a child of the workshop.' It was customary for the powerful to prepare their sons to take their places. Generals presented their sons to the emperor as soon as they could hold a weapon in their hands. Governors, judges, even poets and executioners, did the same. And so the rivalry between men was passed on to their sons. But the Khwaja refused to listen.

He instructed Zuleikha, his second wife, to read to the boy. But he chose the books himself: *Tales of a Parrot, Adventures of Amir Hamza* – fables from Persia and Arabia reputed to be the emperor's favourites.

'Better to teach him to fly pigeons!' Zuleikha laughed. The Khwaja ignored his young wife. Ignored everyone.

'The house of Shiraz will wither on the banks of the Jamuna!' They warned. The Khwaja ignored everyone.

*

Bihzad drew fluently. He surprised his stepmother by drawing a clever miniature showing her sleeping beneath a tree with squirrels dropping an apple on her head from above. He startled the Darogha by presenting him with his portrait, as he arrived at the Khwaja's haveli with a request from the emperor. Bihzad had drawn the Darogha on a throne wearing a crown, his long moustache straight, a court of sea dragons around him. He drew continually in his attic room, sitting on the floor, one knee raised, like a true child of the kitabkhana.

At seven, he drew the likeness of Wasim Mirza, a senior courtier. A dying Wasim Mirza. The Khwaja had taken the boy with him when he visited the old man at his home. Bihzad drew him, just as he was, lying on a carpet, head raised on a silk pillow. A crumbling face. The tunic, open at the neck, revealing a stark set of ribs. Sprouts of limp hair. Lips parted in prayer. The skin deathly yellow, stretched over bone.

Holding up the painting, the Khwaja spoke, his tone measured. 'Why is Wasim Mirza's face dark on one side and light on the other?'

Bihzad bit his lips.

'Did he forget to wash one side properly?'

'It's his shadow.'

The Khwaja looked at him sternly. 'His shadow?'

'Yes. Just like your nose is dark now! Darker than your beard!' He jumped up and down.

The Khwaja cleared his throat. 'A shadow belongs to your eyes, Bihzad. It doesn't belong to a painting.'

*

Some days, his mischief would anger the Khwaja, on others it made him roar with laughter. Unlike other boys of his age, he didn't hide from the servants, or chase around the marketplace knocking over stalls, or secretly visit gamblers and dancing girls camped on the dry tracks of the Jamuna during the winter months.

His mischief was different. More often a matter of words – some overheard, some that he made up by himself to startle his audience. For instance, there was the time when the Darogha arrived one morning at the Khwaja's haveli to show him paintings by some junior artists. The Khwaja had been sick, unable to pay his daily visits to the royal workshop, half-reclining on the floor of his room, given to a vile temper. Just as the Darogha was about to make his entrance, Bihzad darted into the room before him, holding up his hand ceremoniously as if he was announcing a royal visit.

'The litterbearer, your majesty,' he proclaimed, bowing low.

The Khwaja frowned. The Darogha's face grew grim. He hesitated before taking his customary seat, after the Khwaja had banished Bihzad from the room.

'Why?' The Khwaja demanded later, holding Bihzad by the neck and pulling his right ear sharply until the veins by his temple started to throb. On the boy's congested face, he saw his Persian mother – the same strong brows meeting at the forehead, the same dark lashes curling over fawn eyes, a perfect oval face and half-mocking lips. Just a hint of the Adam's apple under a firmly drawn chin. Fearing the onset of a fit, the Khwaja released his hold.

'Why?'

Sitting on the floor before his father, Bihzad seemed unrepentant. 'Didn't you say those students are worthless? That their paintings are no better than horse litter, dog litter, cow litter …'

Once again, the Khwaja sighed and raised his eyes skywards.

Growing up alone in his father's haveli, without brother or sister, without any companion of his own age, not even a servant, Bihzad was apt to find his perch on the roof, watching the bustling affairs of his neighbours. When not in his own attic, bent over his paintings, or hiding behind the door of his father's room listening to him chat with his visitors, he'd follow his neighbours minutely as if they were figures in a miniature. Sometimes, he'd call down to them, offering his comments in a loud but childish voice. Later, once their complaints reached his ears, the Khwaja would demand proper explanations for Bihzad's comments: Why had he called the recently-widowed general a peacock, reciting a verse that besmirched his reputation? Why had he rhymed the name of a head concubine with something rude? Why?

The Khwaja has spoilt his son, the neighbours said. Illiterate, unskilled in sport, barred from mixing with boys his age. Only words and busy fingers. A lonely imp, beautiful as a flower but sick, not afraid even of his father, afraid of none. Perhaps it was the Persian way of raising a child – pure but worthless.

Then there was the business of the kites. And suddenly the boy seemed just like all the others, spending more hours on the roof of their haveli than locked up in his attic. They heard his squeals and screams, cutting the breeze with his line, raising his kites from the horizon till they were specks in the sky. He seemed hardly strong enough to hold down the fluttering kites, as he battled larger ones flown by bigger boys on neighbouring roofs. The neighbours felt sorry for him, left alone in the haveli all afternoon, with no one to help him as his ten-year-old frame struggled with the wind. But just as with words, the little Bihzad seemed unafraid to take on a stronger rival, any rival.

The mischief, as the neighbours came to realize, was in Bihzad's kites themselves. Once they saw what was painted on them, they no longer felt sorry for the boy. These were not the usual bazaar-bought kites. Floating above the row of havelis, they saw the craft of Bihzad's fingers. He had drawn pictures on the kites, painting them delicately, as delicately as he did his portraits. He drew the faces of his neighbours, in immaculate detail. Then he added a touch of mischief. The widowed general prancing around with the raised tail of a peacock. The head concubine of a neighbour devouring a rabbit. A boy, almost Bihzad's age, stealing a smoke from a water pipe. The recently betrothed daughter of the house next door winking lewdly like a bazaar woman. The more his neighbours howled, the more Bihzad laughed, his unbroken voice rising deliriously like the kites. They ordered him to pull the kites down, but he ignored them. He didn't even seem to mind losing the kites, cut by the lines of his rivals. As his pictures floated away, chased by alley urchins, he seemed even more delirious.

'Why?' At first, the Khwaja tried to bribe Bihzad with a stack of new kites from the market, already painted. 'What fun do you have ridiculing others?'

He warned Bihzad. One day, the kites would land in the emperor's palace, perhaps land at the emperor's very feet as he strolled in his garden.

'The emperor will punish the mischievous artist.'

'Even if he sees his own face among them?' Bihzad bit his lip, smirking at his father.

'Bedaulat...!' The Khwaja raised his hand to strike. It was forbidden, everyone knew, to portray the emperor without his permission.

The next kite that Bihzad painted showed his father's face. Asleep. Snoring. Then he turned his attention towards his stepmother and her favourite maid. This time the neighbours didn't seem to mind, roaring from their roofs as the kites went up one after another. 'Show the next one! More...!' Gasps followed as his stepmother unfurled, then fluttered in the breeze.

'What's the use of a veil if your son decides to expose your wife publicly for all to see?' A wicked laugh bubbled in Zuleikha's throat. The Khwaja glared at the boy.

'Why don't you stop him before he spreads our secrets all over Agra?'

The Khwaja threw up his hands in despair.

'If only you wouldn't hold him prisoner, let him play with the other boys...'

'For what?' the Khwaja growled. 'To become worthless like them? Like their fathers?'

'If only you'd let him learn to read and write...'

The Khwaja kept silent.

Sitting between them, Bihzad held up his new kite – a portrait of himself, dancing among revellers on the dry tracks of the Jamuna.

'If only you'd let the kiteplayer become a proper artist …'

*

And so the Khwaja sent his boy to learn his trade with Mir Sayyid Ali. His genius was reputed to have few rivals among artists, the only one the Khwaja regarded as his equal. He too was an immigrant, arrived from Persia to the Mughal court. The emperor had rewarded him with a title as well: *Nadir-ul-Mulk* – Wonder of the Kingdom. Older than the Khwaja, he worked outside the kitabkhana, visiting the workshop only to receive commissions for paintings or to collect his pay. The Darogha did not dare to judge the contents of Mir Sayyid Ali's albums. He was also known as a strict teacher, more severe than the Khwaja or the chief clerk. His students, the few he taught in his small studio, shamed the apprentices at the much larger kitabkhana. Although the Khwaja had reigned uninterrupted over the royal workshop ever since his arrival in Agra, there were some among the courtiers who thought the older artist rivalled him in the emperor's favour. Mir Sayyid Ali always dressed in white, a soul in quest, his tunic pulled tightly around his armpits, revealing just a trace of a wayward bulge. He courted not the applause of the vulgar – severe in private and monosyllabic in public, a simple nod was all he needed to convey approval. A rosary made from the soil of Karbala twirling around his fingers confirmed he was a Shia among the Sunnis of Hindustan, scrupulous in observing halal and haram, studious too in avoiding fish bare of scales.

When Nikisa, Zuleikha's maid, first brought Bihzad to Mir Sayyid Ali's studio, he was rolling up the right sleeve of his tunic to whip one of the few students who sat around him. He struck thrice, pausing to inspect the effect of each lash, and to utter a sentence of warning. The culprit had been caught with a charbah – the transparent skin of a gazelle. Stretched over a painting, it would make copying easy. All the student had to do was prick the charbah along the outline of the image he wanted to trace.

The tracing could then be placed over a fresh sheet of paper, and powdered charcoal poured through the holes to make a blurred copy. It was a well-known routine – common among the uninspired, essential for thieves.

'Do you think Allah has created you in jest!'

A fearful Nikisa tried to leave the room quietly, drawing on Bihzad's arm. The teacher motioned her to go, but ordered Bihzad to sit behind the ring of boys.

Mir Sayyid Ali's students dressed, like their master, in white. A lace cap and a tunic buttoned to the right, the right sleeve pleated back to avoid an accidental brush with the ink-filled oyster shells.

He demanded more from his students than other teachers – the discipline of a true disciple. Mir Sayyid Ali had himself learnt the secret of the perfect form from his forefathers – an oval face with narrow eyes, arched eyebrows, a short chin in three-quarter profile. Well-modelled hands with fingers opening like a flower, a gauzy shimmering robe with intricate folds covering one shoulder and sweeping down to the ankle. Pious and elegant. Women of astonishing beauty. Convicts and rulers – both sublime.

He painted in two styles. One fit for viewing in the morning – glittering and meticulous, imperial scenes of the durbar – and those fit for the night – haunting dervishes, lovers, poems of death and unrequited dreams. His students learned his secrets in time.

'If dust ascends to heaven, it still remains worthless!' Mir Sayyid Ali finished the last lash, then returned to his students. It was his day to teach a special technique, that of painting in simple black and white. But first he banished the oyster shells filled with colours from the studio and looked sternly at the four faces in front of him, including Bihzad's.

'Be careful!' he warned them. 'Beware of the temptation of colour. Remember, colour to an artist is like love to a fool! She can capture you easily. You must be a master before you approach her, and even then, only as a hunter approaches an injured beast.'

With a speck of ink on the tip of a fine brush, Mir Sayyid Ali drew Bihzad's face in black and white, then gave it a gentle wash. On the egg-white board, his face appeared, just as it was, pale eyes under dark lashes, rosebud lips parted in amazement.

As the other students began their work, a book was brought from the library for Bihzad. The *Shahnama* – the classic of Persian fables. Mir Sayyid Ali turned the pages of the book, stopping at the story of the Sasanian king Khosru and his lover, the beautiful Armenian princess Shirin. The tragic story of love and separation, of tears and reproaches, of love triumphant in death, lay open before Bihzad. With a flourish, Mir Sayyid Ali placed a thick sheet of ivory tone before his new pupil, then pointed at the book.

'Begin!'

Bihzad sat silently. Around him, Mir Sayyid Ali's students practised the new technique he had demonstrated. The whipped boy, wiping his tears in the pleats of his tunic, sat in a far corner, sentenced to repeat the same line of verse over and over again in calligraphy. The teacher stared out of the window towards a train of mule and camel carts drawing up in the street, full of sandstone. There were men following the animals. Stonecutters and masons, wood carvers, those with the rare skill of inlaying precious gems into marble. Some horsemen rode busily by – trusted court officials and their attendants. Elephants and their keepers kept a safe distance, passing two abreast under the western gate of the city. Up ahead, Mir Sayyid Ali could see a row of bowed heads – prisoners, chained to each other, eyes downcast, marching to the beat of a drum. Labourers, many thousands, were needed for Sikri, a mere twenty miles away. Sikri, chosen by the emperor to replace Agra as his capital, the ghost town soon to be born again and renamed Fatehpur Sikri – The City of Victory. Nervous laughter rose from behind him. Mir Sayyid Ali pulled his gaze back to the room, followed the boys' eyes to Bihzad's page. Blank. The ivory sheet still unblemished. Bihzad was laughing with the other boys, as if they had all discovered a new game. He was laughing and pointing at his blank page.

'Bedaulat ...!'

Veins throbbed on Mir Sayyid Ali's temple. Raising his right hand, he made as if to strike his new pupil.

Everybody stopped laughing. Except Bihzad. He gurgled on merrily, pointing at the open page of the book and shaking his head from one side to the other. Mir Sayyid Ali frowned, his arm frozen in mid air.

'He can't read!' One of the boys squawked.

'Can't read?'

And so on his very first day, Bihzad was sent home with an ancient copy of the *Shahnama*, the book of fables from the land of his fathers. Sent home to have read to him the story of the Sasanian Khosru and his exquisite Shirin, and to return with his own drawing for the next lesson.

*

'Once there were souls but no bodies.' Mir Sayyid Ali wetted his lips. 'Then, artists drew the soul.'

The paintseller Salim Amiri smiled. An attentive listener, his hand moved deftly over the thick parchment, polishing it with a crystal ball, eyes fixed on the elderly Mir Sayyid Ali. To the artists of Agra he was a trusted friend, known as the 'open ear', known too for his flowing tongue. 'He has all the gossip of the world from creation till today on the tip of his tongue', it was said of Salim Amiri.

'The ones denied entrance to paradise drew it in their minds. They became teachers to other souls ...' Mir Sayyid Ali went on.

It was Mir Sayyid Ali's custom to visit the kitabkhana every week, to hand over his paintings to the Darogha, and to pick up his commissions. He would pretend deafness, forcing the Darogha to shout his requests into his only good ear. Some days, the list would be long. A request from a senior official to depict the imperial court in its first session after the new moon. A request from a visiting general to draw his favourite horse. An offer from the harem's head eunuch to describe a veiled lady so that her portrait could be drawn for a secret lover. Sometimes the requests came from the emperor himself – to illustrate his favourite stories, such as that of the mythical bird Simurgh and its flight to paradise.

The Darogha spent much of the time in arguments with Mir Sayyid Ali. As usual, the old master would offer one excuse after another. 'But there are so many students to teach ... Why don't you ask the Khwaja? Horses would be better coming from his pen.' And, as for the veiled lady: 'How can I steal her modesty?'

On his way back from the royal workshop to his studio near the western gate, Mir Sayyid Ali would sometimes stop at Salim Amiri's haveli for a grumble.

'Then, artists weren't just artists. They were precious, more precious than a kingdom. Even the barbarians – the Mongols and the Afghans – showed respect, carried them off to Samarkand and Kabul as bounty. Demanded a fat ransom to return them to their owners. Swords were crossed over a simple pen!'

It was the paintseller's turn to speak. 'Had it been then, the emperor would've sent his elephant to fetch you. He wouldn't have allowed your feet to suffer from the coming and going. Even the barbarian Darogha would have had you weighed in gold, my friend!'

Mir Sayyid Ali complained about everyone. Even the emperor. Art was respected in the olden days, he'd say. Not like now, when artists had to wait on emperors like servants. In those days, astronomers and astrologers would determine the suitable hour for an emperor to sit for his portrait. The rulers of Herat and Tabriz would invite poets to recite while they posed – to tinge their faces with the fragrance of verse. And that's not all. There were kings who took to art themselves – to forget war, to heal the wounds, ask forgiveness for their sins.

'And now?' Salim Amiri prompted a tired Mir Sayyid Ali, lost in his thoughts.

'Now, anyone with gold wants to be drawn in gold. Every little sarkar, subedar, fawjdar, every khan, shaikh and umra, pretends to be a patron of the arts!'

Mir Sayyid Ali rose to leave. To return to his students he'd have to jostle through the men and beasts marching to Sikri. He

17

cast a nostalgic look back at the paintseller sitting in the ruins of his ramshackle haveli.

'Even the artists were different then.'

'Yes…'

'There were just a few of us then. Not hundreds. Not like stonecutters and masons. Or labourers. Not like this lot of impure idolaters and faithless infidels…'

Salim Amiri nodded. He knew Mir Sayyid Ali's distaste for the burgeoning kitabkhana. Distaste for the artists who weren't pure any more, pure Persian that is, but an odd mixture of natives wrested by the emperor from the defeated kings of Hindustan. And their art, not sacred like that of the god-fearing early masters. Unbelievers were ruining the true spirit, the immigrants whispered among themselves.

Mir Sayyid Ali sighed. 'Today? Today even illiterate boys pretend to be artists.'

*

The Khwaja reassured Bihzad. From now on, his stepmother would read him the stories chosen by Mir Sayyid Ali. He should plan the scene in his head first, then draw it before his teacher.

'Memorise, Bihzad,' the Khwaja advised. He advised him also to recite the story to Nikisa as he walked with her to his teacher's studio, in case he should forget.

Zuleikha, his stepmother, spent her days making perfume and selling it to the ladies of the royal harem. Unlike the neighbours' wives she didn't act like a true mistress of her household, scolding the servants, minding her children and guests. She was much younger than the Khwaja, but strong-willed. When the matchmaker had arrived at her home, her parents were unwilling, it was rumoured. The groom was a foreigner. Perhaps he'd disappear with their daughter to Persia. But Zuleikha had fancied the artist, shown no fear of the older man. It was *she* who had married *him*, neighbours said. But in Agra, her dreams had soured. At the Khwaja's haveli, she saw less of the Khwaja, more of the empty stone corridors, then moved over to her private chamber farthest from father and son, living much like an artist herself, surrounded by her perfumes. Only rarely would the neighbours catch a glimpse of the Khwaja and his wife together – usually quarrelling, or seated together with Bihzad between them, scolding the boy for his pranks.

Whenever he visited his stepmother in her private chamber, Zuleikha received Bihzad in a cloud of fragrance. A furnace roared on her balcony. Wooden vats stood in rows in her room. Her maid darted in and out, busy with her mistress's experiments. Drying, extracting, fermenting, distilling, straining. Rare flowers were her speciality, plucked from the valley of Kashmir and dried carefully under orders. She demanded the blue jasmine in the white jasmine season, when it was still in its bud. Or the rare sandalwood whose flower resembled a rose. Like wreaths, the dried flowers lay around her bed. Some days, her skin smelled of civet, or musk, or the common gul-i ja'fari – the marigold.

Bihzad would look for Zuleikha in the afternoons, but her door was frequently locked. Like the other wives of senior courtiers, she acted as the eyes and ears of the emperor's harem. Experts in trade, they'd buy the most precious goods from Agra's bazaar – gems, silk, magical potions – and exchange them for a handsome profit with the begums, the royal wives, who were forbidden to appear before the sight of strangers. Some said the courtiers' wives were richer than their husbands. Richer or not, free they were. Free, at least, to enter and leave the royal quarters at will, requiring no other explanation than the mere sight of carefully wrapped bundles over their maids' shoulders. None, though, was more popular than Zuleikha – the merchant of beauty. She dealt in hope. A touch of a rare herb could turn the fortunes of a forgotten wife, make her the emperor's favourite once again. And unlike the other merchant women, she didn't hurry to leave the harem, but spent long afternoons in the Chamber of Dreams – bathing and anointing the emperor's women, escaping in the summer to the cool vaults dug underneath the palaces. The kalmuk guards of the harem knew her well. Hilal Khan, the head eunuch, was fond of her perfumes. She entered and left through the heavily guarded doors as if she was a begum herself – the dark-eyed begum, quick-tempered and aloof. The one who truly belonged in the royal harem, not in a kitabkhana artist's home.

Bihzad would see her dressed for her royal visits in her full-length jaguli gown with tight sleeves and an opening at the breasts. She did not wear the married woman's kerchief folded crossways and tied under the chin, but the stylish taq, the cap she had worn in her native Multan before she had married the foreigner, the Persian master.

She would tease Bihzad – her pet – the boy who would peel off her veil and run away when she was still new to the Khwaja's household.

'Shirin and Khosru!' she exclaimed, then placed a finger under Bihzad's chin. 'Too young for love. Someone must tell Mir Sayyid Ali not to spoil our children!'

She made him sit on her bed, poured a drop from a bottle onto his palms, then rubbed them together. Many rosebuds bloomed at once. She forbade him to wash his hands.

*

By the time she returned from her visits to the royal harem, the Khwaja would have left for the kitabkhana. He returned home late, usually in the arms of the paintseller Salim Amiri, after a stop at Satan's Palace – the infamous brothel of Shaitanpura. They would stumble home, sensing their way back by instinct, holding on to each other in the dark alleys, the Khwaja urging his friend to recite one more from his favourite poets.

They hid the love marks inflicted by Satan's mistresses under the long folds of their Persian turbans. The paintseller would deliver the Khwaja to his door before falling to his own.

Climbing the stairs slowly at his haveli, the Khwaja would find Zuleikha's door firmly locked. He'd sit outside and whisper, spraying the wood with a fine mist of wine.

It's the emperor, not Zuleikha, who has driven the Khwaja to Satan's Palace – the neighbours said. The emperor was the more hungry of the two, drowning the ageing artist with request after request. First, it was *The Tales of the Parrot*. Fifty-two stories, fifty-two paintings. Now, the *Hamzanama* – even more sizeable, requiring fourteen hundred paintings in fourteen volumes to illustrate it fully. The elderly Mir Sayyid Ali had at first agreed to draw the Arabian fables, but changed his mind later. Not one or two, but hundreds of artists were needed, some to draw, some to apply colours, a few to illuminate the portraits, many more to apply titles in fine nastaliq-style calligraphy, burnish and border. Running the workshop required not simply an artist's but a general's skill – leading a whole army, or a governor's, minding a whole province.

The Khwaja had accepted the emperor's challenge to lead his artists in the massive *Hamzanama* project. In exchange, the emperor had showered him with gifts. A grand haveli inside the fort in place of his small studio next to the western gate of Agra, a new kitabkhana to shame all the imperial workshops from Samarkand to Isfahan. A score of students bloomed overnight to a hundred, artists and sons of artists drawn from all the lands conquered by the emperor.

The Khwaja has drowned under the paintings, the neighbours said, not the cups of wine he drinks every night in the comfort of his friend Salim Amiri. The envious spread rumours. He has forgotten how to draw, dares not present the emperor with a portrait in his own hand. He has taken to signing the works of others. He is but a clerk of clerks, who has exchanged his pen for a courtier's robe.

Then there were those who hinted at darker secrets, painted a tale of woe between the Khwaja and his much younger wife, gossiped over her empty cradle. A few even doubted his wife's honour. Wine and roses don't mix, they frowned.

*

From the fort to the western gate, Bihzad walked with Nikisa to Mir Sayyid Ali's studio, memorising the story of Khosru and Shirin. Then he took his place before his teacher, a sheet of ivory paper on his raised knee.

Yet, he drew not the lovers. Not the scene, favourite among artists down all the ages, of a besotted Shirin admiring Khosru's portrait hung from the branch of a tree. Seated on a cushion of fragrant leaves, as was the custom, under the vivid whiteness of the blossoms in sharp contrast to a fastidiously drawn sky. Nor the forbidden glimpse of a bathing princess. Shirin, naked to her waist, a lotus floating on a lake. Mir Sayyid Ali's students had pried open his old album. Breasts half-submerged in silver – how did their teacher's strict gaze behold his own creation? they had sniggered. How could his gnarled fingers have added a touch of blush to the secretly open bud?

One of Bihzad's fellow students, asked to illustrate the same story, had seated the lovers, united at last by fate, on a throne lit by lamps, listening to the rebab of a wandering musician. He had followed the right way, taught by their teacher.

Bihzad drew the lovelorn Farhad, the peasant desirous of Shirin till the very end, a haughty Shirin indifferent to all but Khosru. He drew a great mass of rock, a dark monster rising from the ocean. The peasant was carving a face on the jagged stone. The face of Shirin. With fierce rage striking the immovable, shattering with demonic might, showering his subject with blows. His face full of anger. As if he was rescuing his love from the dark veil of the rock, setting her free.

Mir Sayyid Ali studied the page for a long while.

'Why didn't you draw the lovers?'

'Because,' Bihzad bit his lips, then spoke in the voice of Zuleikha, 'the brush hasn't the tongue to speak the secret of love.'

A rare gleam entered the elderly teacher's eyes.

*

Till 1570 when he was almost fourteen, Bihzad drew continually, never missing a lesson. He drew, mastering the pattern of stories, scenes of great importance – majestic courts, famous battles, giant fortresses. Word came to the studio that the emperor was tiring of seeing fables. It was time for his artists to record the glory of his conquests.

'He is illiterate, just like your son!' The Khwaja frowned at Zuleikha's words.

'The prophets were all illiterate. You mustn't speak ill of the emperor.'

'He needs your stories to amuse his wives. The emperor is the chief storyteller of the harem. He needs your pictures to keep them happy.'

But now he needed more. He needed portraits to present to those vanquished rulers, his vassals, around Hindustan, and to emissaries from far-flung Goa and England. He had called on the finest artists of Agra to mark the inauguration of his new capital, The City of Victory, with a fitting tribute: a grand portrait of himself – the twenty-eight-year-old emperor seated on his new throne.

After decades of war, Hindustan basked in the shadow of peace. Agra itself seemed secure. The city, rebuilt in the image of each of its conquerors, was a citadel of red-hewn stone. It is written in the books of Hindustan that the invaders were drawn not to the city but to its river, the Jamuna, to quench their armies after hard campaigns over mountains and deserts. It is written that the river came from a mountain too cold for humans. It blessed the soul of Agra, but brought with it lassitude and melancholia, favouring only those of like temperament.

From the eleventh to the fifteenth regnal year, the emperor was in ceaseless campaign. After five years of relentless war, invaders were repelled in the north. A rebellion was suppressed in the west, and forts put to siege one after another. The heads of enemies were piled high to erect columns, fugitives gibbeted and put on display. Kettledrums reverberated with each surrender, smoke rose steadily wherever he visited. Splendid palaces were effaced as lines are effaced from paper, became the homes of owls and raven. In places, women leapt into open flames to avoid capture.

The vanquished presented gold and prisoners. Flawless gems. Indian elephants. Tipuchaq horses. The emperor's harem swelled with new wives and slave girls. And still more artists arrived, filling the Khwaja's kitabkhana to bursting point.

Agra surpassed all. What was once a resting place for garrisons, a cluster of tents for marauding armies, a ramshackle fort, was now the centre of the Mughal empire – the greatest city to the east of Samarkand, and infinitely richer. Not simply now a stone encampment for soldiers and their general, but a hive of merchants, artisans, labourers, fakirs, poets, artists and musicians, whores, and hopefuls. They arrived from as far as Turkey and Persia, some even travelled from China and the cold mountains beyond. It was only a matter of time before Agra's bazaar rivalled the souks of Constantinople, its mosques the glorious minarets of Arabia. Under the Mughals, Agra became the world – its streets bustling with men and women of all faiths, all colours, ringing with the sound of many tongues.

Perhaps its arrogance was its downfall. At its gates stood a new enemy. A new city beside a lake, an upstart, built by force on land sliced off the top of a ridge, bordered by treacherous ravines. Fatehpur Sikri, The City of Victory, born of the emperor's whims. Old Agra moaned her loss. The kitabkhana was set to move too, to a new home in the new capital. Like a good general, the Khwaja strove to assemble his troops, readying them to follow the soldiers, prisoners, stonecutters and masons.

*

'Man rose from the sea, and like the sea is in constant churning.' Returning from Satan's Palace, Salim Amiri consoled the Khwaja. His days at the kitabkhana were soon to be over, the Khwaja had been informed by senior courtiers. The emperor had his eye on him. Anyone who could complete the massive *Hamzanama* fables – fourteen hundred paintings in fourteen volumes – in such a short time, deserved a higher honour. Master of the mint, perhaps. Chief of the armoury. The Royal Paymaster.

The Khwaja spread out both palms and gazed at them. 'Useless!' he sighed. The emperor's father had offered a thousand gold pieces for these fingers, he reminded Salim Amiri for the hundredth time.

'But you'll still be an artist.'

'An artist herding men like sheep?'

'You'll still be his favourite.'

'Yes … but favourite for what?' The Khwaja sat down on the steps of a stone fountain at the door of his haveli. 'There was a time when he'd wait anxiously for me to finish his portrait. Then, I was his favourite. He had no eyes for anybody else. He examined each portrait carefully, praised every stroke of my brush, he could spot my painting even if it was hidden under a thousand. And now ...'

Salim Amiri lay a hand on his friend's shoulder in consolation.

'Now he has even forgotten my name! Sweet Pen, he called me! Now, he wants nothing but my sweet mouth to coax others. Do you know what my teachers in Persia would say if they could see me now?' The Khwaja sighed deeply. 'A pimp ... Worse than a whore.'

Salim Amiri tried again to console the Khwaja. 'You will be the first to draw up the new city in the heart of the empire. And then ...' Salim Amiri paused. The Khwaja waited.

'And then your son will be the master of the royal workshop. Surely, he'll ask his father to lend him a hand from time to time.'

The Khwaja frowned. 'But he is still young. Too young ...'

Salim Amiri was quick to remind him of the imperial custom. The emperor wanted the best, nothing less. If an artist was indisputably superior to all others, but still too young to lead them as the master of the royal workshop, then the emperor would wait. A caretaker would be appointed to arrange the day-to-day affairs of the kitabkhana, while the child grew up and assumed his noble duties as the rightful leader of all imperial artists.

'What if someone else is appointed the master?'

Salim Amiri misunderstood. He thought the Khwaja was worrying about the old teacher, Mir Sayyid Ali.

'A man who has said no before can't say yes later. Plus, his eyes are now as weak as his ears. The young emperor will surely want a younger master ...'

'Not him ...'

Salim Amiri misunderstood again. 'Dust Mohammad!' He thought the Khwaja was thinking about Dust-i-Divana, Dust the Mad, who had escaped to Hindustan to avoid the Persian Shah's fatwa against wine drinkers. 'If the emperor was looking for a singer, why would he choose a poor artist with a sweet voice!'

'Perhaps the next Khwaja won't be a Persian.'

'Not a Persian?' Then Salim Amiri understood. The Afghan named Adili. He had impressed the emperor with a chameleon. The creature was painted with utmost care, its skin painstakingly dotted all over with green spots and its spine, saw-toothed from neck to tail, in perfect points.

'The chameleon! He drew himself!'

'In just three years in Agra, he has married more than four wives.' The Khwaja sounded sour. Adili the Afghan. His eunuchs were known to be tyrannical. Among artists, he was a laughing stock. He painted flattering and sumptuous portraits, but frequently mistook the scene. He would depict, for instance, the emperor bidding farewell to his milk-brother before he went into battle, *smiling*, when the noble face should have been darkened instead by the sorrow of parting.

On a painting, his signature appeared always on the steps on which the emperor would place his foot to ascend the throne.

'Let him design carpets,' Salim Amiri laughed. 'Fit for the emperor's feet, not his eyes!'

As he helped the Khwaja to his feet, Salim Amiri turned serious. 'You must start now. Prepare Bihzad to take your place.'

The Khwaja's face clouded again. He knew his boy. He was fleet of hand: what took most artists a month, Bihzad finished in a week. In delicacy and firmness, none matched his talent. His drawings were remarkably mature, his methods as fluent as his mind. He could fool everyone with his faultless imitations – Mirak to Muzaffar, even the Great One came alive in his young fingers. His teacher marvelled at his restraint, the Darogha, forever complaining, fell silent before his rapturous compositions. But above all, he showed the clear sign of a genius – mastering a difficult subject with the casual flair of a child.

The Khwaja knew his boy. From the moment of his birth, he knew the spirit of the Persian masters had travelled with him to Hindustan. It was in his young eyes, his innocent words, even before Bihzad could manage to hold a pen in his hand. The Khwaja knew he hadn't named his son in vain after the Great One, Kamal-al-Din Bihzad, the jewel of Herat and Tabriz, the great Persian eagle who had flown from this world when he himself was but a child.

From the beginning, he had treated the boy with caution, avoiding punishment. He had forbidden the teaching of the Koran. *The rare ones must be left alone,* the Khwaja had remembered his own teachers saying. *They are still unaware of who they are, in which world they have appeared.* The boy must live in his own dreams, not in the dreams of others. He had kept Bihzad illiterate, so that he would discover his own secrets before he discovered the secrets in books, before words and numbers spoilt his love for glowing images.

And he had refrained from drawing in Bihzad's presence, lest the boy tried to follow him by example. He had forbidden him from entering the kitabkhana, taking him instead to see the acrobats and jugglers, the sword-plays and cockfights in the bazaar. On nights of the new moon, they went to the banks of the Jamuna for the fireworks. A giant paper elephant stuffed with crackers bursting all at once at the command of the emperor watching from his jharoka, the window of the royal palace. At dawn, they waited at the fort's edge to catch the mischief of the sun.

As much as Zuleikha complained, he had held his son prisoner in his haveli, barred contact with the slovenly lot of their neighbours, fearing the infection of impure thoughts and worthless desires.

He knew Bihzad wouldn't follow the normal course: sketching scenes from a story, then finishing the most promising one with details, adding colours and gentle touches to the faces. Just as with his other mischief, the boy might start wherever he wished – colouring a pair of lips even before he had drawn the face, perhaps – disregarding the usual maxim of teachers… *follow the right path! Patterns to Shape, Shape to Portraits!* Even when he suspected that something was going wrong, he had kept his mouth shut.

'Wrong? What is going wrong?'

Still holding on to Salim Amiri's hand, the Khwaja groped for words. 'What's going wrong is…. the boy is being misled, shown the wrong way, his mistakes glossed over.'

'By Mir Sayyid Ali?'

'Yes.' The Khwaja nodded gravely.

Out of the corner of an eye, he had watched Bihzad draw every morning, seated on the floor before an open window. The fragrance of rose would fill the air. The boy drew from stories. Occasionally, he would spring up and dart into Zuleikha's room to check on a vital detail, then return in a whirlwind of laughter. He had seen him draw the likeness of Majnun, the lovesick Majnun, pausing briefly at the bridge of the nose, then rather than the narrow slit for eyes, he had watched him draw a full lotus petal – just one, not two – in full profile, rather than the customary three quarter face revealed below a lofty turban.

The boy had seated the lover in a garden, then surrounded him with trees. Instead of the lean cypress or the chinar of Kashmir, he had drawn the overgrown pipal, obscenely fecund, like a dancing whore with arms raised towards the sky.

'But...'

The Khwaja grew agitated.

The figures that he drew were unusually large. They bore the burden of the whole scene, stood isolated in the foreground, clinging to the earth, refusing to recede. In painting after painting, Bihzad drew them as if to challenge the viewer.

'He signs his name, not in the lower margin of the page, but in unusual places. On a ewer, a gilded vase, or the knotty branch of a large tree. And he returns without the mark of a whip. Or cheeks reddened by slaps!'

'But it's his teacher's duty to correct him.' Salim Amiri looked confused. 'Surely a man of Mir Sayyid Ali's stature can tell right from wrong, help him to perfect his skills.'

The Khwaja shook his head. Perhaps Mir Sayyid Ali was the kind of teacher who doesn't wish to part with all his secrets. Saves some from his students, leaves them flawed, so that he alone would shine as the master.

Even Salim Amiri looked worried.

*

At fourteen Bihzad refused to go for his lessons. It had started a few months earlier, with a few arguments. First, he had refused to draw the shamsa, the ornamental sunburst that was the frontispiece to all important manuscripts.

Mir Sayyid Ali, normally severe, had ignored his defiance. The word was spreading of a child wonder. Wealthy patrons of Agra were keen to have their portraits drawn by his young fingers. A touch of youth to soften the blows of time. The courtiers' servants would stop Mir Sayyid Ali frequently, on his way to the kitabkhana, whisper their requests into his good ear. The boy had an exceptional hand, it was time now to share its fruits.

The emperor's physician – the Royal Hakim – was his first commission. 'Draw him,' Mir Sayyid Ali said, then he left the room.

Bihzad looked in silence, gazing straight into the hakim's eyes, as if *he* were the physician and his subject the patient. The Royal Hakim frowned.

When Mir Sayyid Ali returned, he found a portrait in black and white. Wrinkled fingers, worn knuckles, veins rising up the neck like a pair of snakes, cross-legged and cross-eyed.

The elderly artist had made excuses, showed the Royal Hakim out of the room, inviting him to return soon for another sitting. Then, he turned to Bihzad. Holding out a brush in one hand, the other raised to strike, he ordered his pupil to begin again.

'But you asked me to draw his likeness.'

'Not of *him*! Of his *true* self.' The blow struck Bihzad's face. 'Who do you think you are? A clerk? A convict under oath, speaking the truth and nothing but the truth?'

Then, the boy refused to illustrate the memoirs of the emperor's grandfather, Babur, the first Great Mughal himself.

'Who are you to refuse? If the great Kamal-al-Din Bihzad, your namesake, could illustrate the warrior Timur's life, why should you refuse to do Babur's?'

'Why should an artist only draw razm o bazm?'

'Razm o bazm?'

The words seemed too big for his sweet face. 'War and love. Love! War! Love! War! Love! War!'

For once, Mir Sayyid Ali looked at him kindly. The artist was awakening. It was time perhaps, for the child to become a man. He laid his hand on Bihzad's shoulder.

'Neither war nor love. You haven't understood, Bihzad.'

With a great effort, he reached inside an old box, recovered three miniatures from it and laid them out in front of Bihzad, dusting the first lightly with a brush.

'The most magnificent painting in all of Persia.'

It was the Night of the Chosen One. Mounted on the mythical horse Buraq and preceded by the Archangel Gabriel, the Prophet, from whose head streamed a fiery radiance, emerged from the clouds into the profound blue of the night sown with stars. The black sky became a garden. The earth swam far below him. Winged angels rushed to his company, as he passed beyond the realm of this world.

The two sat silently.

Then, turning to the second, the Death of Majnun at Laila's Grave, Mir Sayyid Ali started to recite Nizami's poems.

Bihzad saw the child-lovers. One dead, the other dying. The throbbing passion muted, then returning with an ever-deepening note. Eyes like black narcissi shedding tears upon a rose. A dazzling gold from the glare of the desert under a sky of pure lapis into which drifted curling wisps of white cloud.

'*The likes of which the eye of time never beheld,*' quoted Mir Sayyid Ali.

In the last painting, a bare-headed dervish knelt, a woollen soof thrown over his shoulders. A stark chamber matching his sombre face. Fingers counting beads. Eyes penetrating.

'Not *war*, but triumph. Surrender, not *love*. And prayer.'

Mir Sayyid Ali continued as if in a trance, 'He was the first artist who revealed the power of light, adorned an album with leaves of the universe, without colour or brush set life to radiant faces. It is He, Bihzad, who has sprinkled the sky with silver specks, bordered the lusty sun within a red horizon.'

Bihzad listened.

'You must see what He sees. Not the view of the mortal, but a glorious world washed clean in magical light and dazzling with colour. You must copy in miniature the world He has drawn. One where everything is carefully chosen, the profusion of nature simplified, men and women incomparably beautiful, everything as precious and perfect as He willed them to be.'

Mir Sayyid Ali sighed. His hard face softened. 'Remember, Bihzad, the artist is closest of all to the Creator.'

*

At fourteen he stopped going for his lessons. Sent word through Nikisa to his teacher. 'Tell him,' he said in a voice just breaking, 'Bihzad is now an artist.'

Qamargah. The imperial hunt began. Soldiers accompanying the emperor surrounded the forest, laying siege to its inhabitants. Starting just before dawn, they took up drums, lit torches, and moved slowly inward, closing the circle until only a narrow opening remained. Forced into a tight enclosure, the animals could be spotted and killed easily, unable to escape. Following hours of preparation, the emperor would arrive at blazing noon, riding into the circle, killing the frightened beasts with arrows, a sword, or firearms. His courtiers would join the hunt, generals and respected guests, and then the soldiers. When they had had their fill, the dervishes would be summoned, to pray for mercy for the surviving beasts.

Every year, the emperor rewarded his soldiers and his loyal courtiers by leading them to hunt in his favourite forest between the gorge of the Jamuna and the gentle slopes of the western hills. The forest was known for its riches. The lion, reserved only for the emperor, although trappers were sent in beforehand to capture the newborns to save for future hunts. The rhino, so rare that its sighting called for a special reward. The blue-bull, standing as high as a horse. And the plump doe. The chikara antelope, tame ones trained to trap the wild, locking them with their horns. The hog deer and the white deer. Goats, asses, monkeys.

The courtiers arrived on royal elephants, and stood behind the cordon of soldiers observing the proceedings. The carrier elephants were specially chosen to stay calm if a wild herd rushed out through the opening. Hawks and falcons sat on the arms of noblemen. Hunting leopards, the cheetahs, trained to stalk and kill, and return with prey to their master, sat blindfolded on majestic carpets, their coats studded with jewels.

High up in the trees, in giant nests built over many months, perched the royal artists. Brush in hand, they waited for the hunt to begin. Some, distracted by their chirping neighbours, had started to draw a nearby colony of parrots, or the fearless peacock dancing among the soldiers.

Smoke rose from the burning torches, hanging like a low cloud over the forest. Shrieks of the trapped animals, running madly inside the circle, whetted the soldiers' appetites. They too became restless. Clanging armour and the trumpeting elephants made it impossible to hear the general's command, cautioning his men to protect the cordon against an accidental breach. With every passing hour, the noise became more deafening.

At noon, the drums' beat grew louder. A cheer rose from the circle, and at the same time a volley of musket.

The emperor arrived on his horse, sword raised, ready for the qamargah. He entered the circle.

Akbar.

Spirit entered form.

'Three kinds of blood flow in his veins. Turki, Mongol, Persian. He doesn't have a drop of Hindustan.'

Perched on a tree with Salim Amiri, Bihzad watched Emperor Jalaluddin Muhammad Akbar – Akbar to his subjects. Recently inducted into the royal workshop, he had come for his first commission – depicting the emperor in the qamargah. The other artists around them drew rapidly.

But the paintseller kept distracting him with jokes about everybody. 'Watch, Bihzad! Here comes the Royal Paymaster. Akbar will certainly take him for a bear and kill him! Watch him fall from the elephant's back!' He made fun of the courtiers, forced to rise early and accompany the emperor, pretending to enjoy the excitement while secretly scared of the animals.

They watched Akbar galloping after a wild ass, shooting one arrow into it, then another. The animal did not die, but kept running, slowed by its wounds. Akbar spurred his horse on, and getting close, chopped it on the nape of its neck behind the ears.

'Allahu Akbar ...!' God is Great – a roar went up among the soldiers.

Salim Amiri gulped down another piece of mufarrih, his favourite sweetmeat laced with opium. His voice slurred as he imitated a courtier's flattering words, '*Insan-i-Kamil*. The Most Perfect Man. *Zil-i-Ullah*. The Shadow of God.' He laughed. 'Never mind that he is surrounded by *The Most Imperfect Men!*'

Akbar rode back from the circle, a slain antelope draped over his shoulder. Another roar went up.

Bihzad saw the large head. The broad forehead. Thin eyebrows and firm features, nostrils dilated. A man of moderate stature, a narrow waist, long arms. With his closely trimmed moustache, he resembled his Tartar horsemen. His eyes sparkled. A fleshy mole sat above his lips – a sign of good fortune.

*

Later, sitting in the paintseller's haveli and showing him his sketches of the qamargah, Bihzad recalled the exact count of dead animals. A hundred and fifty-five. A few young ones had been spared and returned to the forest. 'Why?' he asked Salim Amiri.

'You mean why he kills animals for pleasure?'

Bihzad nodded his head.

'Maybe he wishes to scare somebody.'

'Who?'

'His enemies. Showing them what he'd do if they dared to challenge him. Trap and kill them like animals!' Salim Amiri's eyes twinkled. 'But the emperor's knife won't cut a vein until God wills it!'

Bihzad had taken to visiting the paintseller, just like his father, on his way back from the kitabkhana. The Khwaja had left Agra for Sikri, to join the emperor and his court. He had gone to prepare the new workshop for the arrival of the artists, who would follow him soon. But only the very best would go, it was rumoured, the ones he'd select himself. The failed ones would remain in Agra, making copies of the emperor's face for the bazaar, in their thousands.

Before leaving, the Khwaja had introduced Bihzad to the kitabkhana. Although he was the son of the master, he too would have to prove his merit, and please the Darogha. Climbing up the stairs of the building, tall and narrow, the Khwaja had pointed out each room, describing the inhabitants and their work to Bihzad. The two had started at the foot of the staircase, looking in through the open windows. 'The kitabkhana has few artists, *real* artists, mostly workers and servants,' the Khwaja had whispered. 'A painting is like a palace. To build it you need more muscles than brains.' He had pointed out the team of lapis washers, the clerks buying supplies, and the young boys running from room to room carrying stacks of paper under their arms or jars of paint balanced on their heads. Voices fell silent as they climbed up the stairs to the higher balconies, peering into the large halls filled with men kneeling on the floor, busy colouring the sketches drawn by the senior artists, or adding borders to the completed paintings. The Darogha's assistants kept an eye on the colourists and border painters, rebuking them sharply if a mistake had been made.

The Darogha sat halfway up the kitabkhana, his room adjacent to the Khwaja's. He sat at the confluence of two streams – the drawings flowing down from the senior artists who had their rooms above, and the finished paintings that came up from the lower halls. Bihzad had seen the Darogha examine each painting carefully through a monocle, spelling out the defects. Then, depending on its merit, he would guess the reward it was likely to receive from the emperor – the number of gold coins – dividing it among the artists who had worked on the painting. An attendant recorded the rewards faithfully in a giant ledger.

From time to time, the Darogha would stop to receive a visitor, usually a senior courtier come to commission a painting, or leave his room and climb up the stairs to convey an imperial request to a senior artist.

Short of breath, the Khwaja had stopped at the top of the stairs, then pointed at the row of small chambers. Inside sat the senior artists, invisible from the corridor. Tugging on the Khwaja's tunic, Bihzad had started to go down the stairs to the hall of the colourists and the junior artists, expecting to be seated among them. But the Khwaja had stopped him, leading him to an empty room on the top floor.

'Here,' he had told his son. 'The Darogha will come to meet you here.'

*

Unlike other new entrants, Bihzad sat in his own room. He

didn't hear around him, the murmur of the colouring hall, or the playful shrieks of young boys carrying supplies on their heads. Even the Darogha's voice seemed remote. He heard the silence of the rooms, an occasional cough, a low whistle. Unlike his attic in their haveli, he sensed a strange solitude. Unable to dash out to the roof and fly his kites, or peer down at his neighbours, he felt trapped by the silence. He'd imagine a voice calling him, and step out of his room to stare down the staircase. But the others were hidden from view. He saw nothing, except a blue stream of water flowing into the kitabkhana's courtyard from the lapis washers grinding the stones. He would spit on the blue stream, setting off ripples, then return to his room.

Occasionally, he saw his teacher entering or leaving the kitabkhana. A severe Mir Sayyid Ali, his tunic pulled tightly over his chest, counting his rosary. They avoided meeting each other. From his room, Bihzad strained his ears to catch his voice arguing with the Darogha.

Just as in his teacher's studio, the Darogha came to hand him a book with pages marked. But he didn't offer to read the stories to Bihzad. Just as before, he left with the book. Later at home, while Zuleikha read to him, he composed the scene in his mind. The Darogha returned each week with his reward – gold coins wrapped in a silk purse – and praise from the emperor.

Unlike the other senior artists, Bihzad worked alone on his paintings, from beginning to end – drew, coloured, burnished and bordered all by himself. He wasn't asked to assist or be assisted – a rare honour usually reserved for the master of the kitabkhana. Before leaving, the Khwaja had warned him not to teach or learn from others. He had warned Bihzad not to gossip with the other artists, or quarrel. 'They know who you are,' he had said, then added, 'Here, *you* will discover who you are.'

*

Alone at the kitabkhana and alone at the Khwaja's haveli, he grew up suddenly – from a mischievous boy to a brooding young man, eyes lowered as if perpetually contemplating a painting. Used to hiding behind his father's door listening to him chat with his visitors, he'd lift his face to meet the Darogha when he visited him in his kitabkhana room. He expected to hear more than the requests. But the chief clerk was a man of few words. 'The emperor has praised you, Bihzad ...' he'd begin. 'The emperor wishes ...' 'The emperor ...'

Only with Salim Amiri, he'd resume acting his years – behaving like the boy of fifteen that he was, who had only recently applied a razor to his face. He'd ask the paintseller about the emperor.

'Akbar? He doesn't cut his hair! He's like a boy, keeps twenty thousand pigeons!'

\*

'Akbar! He's illiterate, just like you!'

Zuleikha sat on her bed, watching Nikisa thread a garland. 'Of course, he has learned everything directly from Allah, not from the mouth of a foolish teacher!' Between reading the stories, she'd tell Bihzad her own stories that she heard at the harem.

A race was on. To become the mother of Akbar's son. The emperor had more than a hundred begums, each a rival to each. They spent all day bathing and perfuming, braiding their hair, dressing up in robes and jewellery – only to be disappointed at night. The first to catch Akbar's eye, when he entered the harem, could be the lucky one. He'd go to her private chamber, spend an evening with songs and stories, but then he might leave with her slave girl! The next morning, the begum would call for the whip, each stroke to the slave's back would lash the emperor. Akbar! The whole harem would be suspicious. What if the wretch carried the next emperor, their future guardian, in her wretched belly? It would be the hour for potions, Zuleikha's hour; the women would get busy trying to spoil her womb, make her smell the acrid smoke of rare herbs.

Her maid looked on with slow, humid eyes as Zuleikha sat on her bed talking. Bihzad listened, drawing absent-mindedly.

Then she'd rise, take off her taq and dance like a slave girl. Dancing and talking, she'd tell one story after another, bringing the harem inside her haveli. She'd drop her veil. Bihzad would look up from his drawings.

'Akbar! He's a master of two harems – his women and his artists. He pampers them both!' She winked at Nikisa. 'That's why your father has gone to Sikri. He is the chief wife in Akbar's other harem! The harem of artists.'

Bihzad frowned, unable to follow.

'Just imagine! One emperor, two harems! In their new home, the artists will fight to show him their albums. They'll be jealous of each other, bribe spies to find out what he fancies most. Each night, Akbar will select one, examine his work.' She laughed, imagining a contest among the parading 'beauties' – the artists holding up their paintings. 'Just think, Bihzad, he'll bring pearls and garland the winner, he'll select one among the many to be his…'

Her maid offered her a cup of wine.

'And you, Bihzad. You'll be his newest bride. Soon!' Still dancing, with the empty cup in her hand, she laughed again. 'Shall we colour your lips, mark your palms with henna?'

'Why…'

'Because you *are* the best, aren't you? You're the Khwaja's favourite. Aren't you the Little Master? The spirit of the Great One? Aren't you, Bihzad?'

Through the window, he heard the lovebird calling – lamenting the long monsoon.

His stepmother blew him a kiss. 'Remember, Bihzad, the singing bird lives in a cage. The owl roams free.'

*

When Bihzad first arrived at Salim Amiri's haveli, he had been quarrelling with his grandmother. She was a hundred and eleven years old. Her father had come to Hindustan, a Persian wanderer, a poet banished by the Shah for penning blasphemy. She could count up to two hundred descendants, grandchildren and great grandchildren, but her hair was as black as Salim Amiri's beard. Sitting on a balcony above the courtyard, she pronounced judgement on the errant paintseller's sins, like a divine messenger.

Beneath the balcony, Salim Amiri sat surrounded by his jars. Under his watchful eyes, a servant hammered a gold pellet between two sheets of vellum, then ground it with salt in a mortar. He watched closely as water was poured from a jug till the salt dissolved, leaving the fine grains sparkling over the stone. A handful of pigeons pecked at the heap of eggshells. The yolk had been extracted from them to be mixed with gum and stirred to form a yellow pigment. Rotting leaves drew flies. The servant poured a cup of resin, then started to beat the mushy leaves with a spoon till they turned a lush green. Empty jars stood ready to be filled with fresh paint.

Wearing a soiled nadiri – a long robe, slit in the front and wrapped on the sides – Salim Amiri stroked his beard, looking carefully in a hand-mirror, then plucked out the single strain of white.

'The messenger of death!' He smiled at Bihzad, blowing it away. Then he raised his voice towards his grandmother. 'I have two lips. One for wine, the other to beg your forgiveness!'

'Forgiveness! Not even if you lament for a thousand nights! Fire shall fill your belly, floods drown…' Her verdicts grew harsher as his servant poured the first of the many cups of wine that he drank every day.

'How can you cure the drunk except with wine? I am drinking my medicine, don't you see!'

To Bihzad, the paintseller was a different man when they met at his ramshackle haveli from the cunning merchant he saw frequently at the kitabkhana, chatting up the artists, pretending to be everyone's 'best friend,' including the Darogha's. Sitting under his grandmother and offering Bihzad his first cup of wine, he seemed like a friendly uncle, but mysterious, speaking often in words that confused him. Listening to Salim Amiri, Bihzad recalled the gossip heard outside his father's door at the haveli. The paintseller had married thrice, each time to become a widower. Poetry was his consolation, and wine. His *real* friends weren't the artists who fell for his gossip and paid through their noses, but wandering mystics, the Sufis, frowned upon by both the immigrants and the natives of Hindustan.

'A real Sufi,' he told Bihzad, 'neither fears hell, nor dreams of paradise. He craves nothing for himself, willing to change depending on where he goes. If he goes to a country where nakedness is the rule, he becomes naked. Just like an artist – ready to draw, whatever his commission. The artist is like a Sufi – a dead man, alive only to truth.'

'Then why must he lie?'

'Lie?'

'Making an ugly face look beautiful. That *is* a lie, isn't it?' Bihzad spoke with his eyes lowered over his lap.

Salim Amiri replied quickly. 'Because he must follow the rules that others follow. But the artist only *pretends* to be a slave.'

'Pretend or not, he isn't free to draw whatever he likes.'

'Tell me, Bihzad, does it really matter what or whom you draw? A king or a slave, a warrior or a saint? As long as it gives pleasure to the emperor? Even if you mixed up Khosru's face with Majnun's, Laila's with Shirin's, you'd still receive your reward if you can fool the barbarian Darogha!'

'Then an artist would be no better than a liar!'

'No. But it doesn't matter, as long as in your heart you paint no one but Him.' Salim Amiri raised his sight towards the sky.

'The jar in your belly is too large for your heart!' came a voice from above.

They argued often. Rehearsing his arguments all day at the kitabkhana, Bihzad would show few signs of giving up, despite Salim Amiri's clever words. He'd voice his anger with the Darogha to the paintseller. Why must the artist follow orders, serve the whims of the emperor? Why must he draw nothing but stories? Why should he be praised for imitating others? Why?

'Because we are born to serve our ruler. Artist to executioner, judge to poet. Isn't it better to serve one man's whims than those of thousands?'

Before Bihzad could go any further, Salim Amiri would bring the argument to a close, confusing him once again with his lofty words. 'But remember, your ruler is different from your Master. Akbar and Allah. One wants pictures, the other wants you!'

*

On his way to the kitabkhana, Bihzad would remember his arguments with Salim Amiri. In the middle of drawing Khosru's face or Shirin's, he'd be distracted by the voice of his father's friend. *Does it matter… even if you mixed up Khosru's face with Majnun's, Laila's with Shirin's… as long as you can fool the barbarian Darogha!* Out of curiosity, he started to exchange them – drawing Majnun's lovesick face on brave Khosru's shoulders as he charged into battle. From one painting to another, it became a game, mixing up the faces. Like his earlier mischief – painting the kites – he'd laugh to himself, drawing whatever came to his head without regard to the prescribed scene, even the story.

At first, the Darogha was confused, blaming his failing sight and memory for his inability to recognise a face. He'd look at a delectable scene, and sigh. There were too many stories. Too many kings, too many lovers. Who was to say which one ruled in which story, who was the lover and who the unloved?

Then he became suspicious. The boy was illiterate. He knew that the stories had to be read to him. Perhaps it was his reader who was behind the mischief. He asked Bihzad to describe the scene he was to paint. The boy recited perfectly, telling the story in the very words of the scribe.

Maybe a different ploy would solve the mystery, the Darogha thought. As he handed over his weekly reward, he asked Bihzad to draw the imperial court.

'In Sikri? But I haven't even been there.'

'No, you haven't. Draw it from your mind, Bihzad. Copy it from other paintings, if you want.'

Bihzad saw the trick, of course. Even a junior artist could draw the court scene, without ever having set foot there. It was the same everywhere – in Sikri as in Agra. The emperor presiding over a pyramid of nobles arranged below him in two balanced groups facing each other. Each group divided in turn to express degrees in rank. The higher a noble's rank, the closer he stood to the emperor. Khans, sultans, mirs, and mirzas on the first row, alongside exalted courtiers, ambassadors, learned men, skilled physicians. In the second row, merchants and landowners. At the bottom, standing together to form a half-circle, swordsmen, quiver-bearers, musketeers, mace-bearers, keepers of horses and elephants. The emperor's face would appear at the apex of the pyramid, under a canopy bearing the imperial sign – a lion lying next to a lamb.

How could he not know the faces? Every citizen of the empire knew who they were, who would stand next to whom, who was above and who below.

This time, Bihzad drew the scene without fault, recalling numerous paintings of the court scene by senior artists of the kitabkhana. He drew solemn faces, arms resting on ceremonial staffs, seals of silence on their lips, ears and minds strung in unison towards the apex of the pyramid.

But Akbar himself was invisible in the scene. Awash in a shaft of light, illuminated from heaven.

'Where is the emperor?' the Darogha asked.

'He surpasses all beings in lustre, like the sun.' Just as he had quoted the stories back to the Darogha, Bihzad recited from the imperial salutations.

'He is the invisible among the visible!'

The Darogha sensed mockery in his voice.

*

He grew tired of his mischief. By instinct, he had adopted the Khwaja's habits, waking late when the sun was almost in mid-heaven. Then a solitary walk to the kitabkhana, where he spent the afternoon in his room, by himself. There were infrequent conversations with the Darogha, and silent greetings exchanged with fellow artists. When not visiting Salim Amiri, he would walk home along the Jamuna, sometimes visiting the ruins left over from earlier invasions, the dynasties who had ruled Agra before the Mughals. He found a deserted palace, still standing, still bearing the marks of its dead inhabitants. From the arches and domes, the ornately carved balconies, he tried to decipher their pleasures. Passing quickly through the public halls, he entered the private courtyard and through it the sultana's room, full of delicate carvings and an array of mirrors. There was an antechamber as well, for her maid. He stood silently before the empty baths, his mind conjuring faces and laughter. Peeling walls showed a cascading fountain. Fading. Then he entered the harem, behind a crumbling balustrade. Robbers had stolen the latticed screens, the marble beds lay in gaping invitation. Passing between them, tracing a line on the dusty stone with his finger, he imagined the tumble of robes, jewelled armbands and belts released from their clasps, the fragrance of rare flowers.

Long after sunset, Bihzad would sit at the foot of the palace's tower, once lit up at night to guide travellers on their way.

He would think, not of the Darogha's requests, the stories, or of the absent Khwaja. But of Akbar. Incessantly. The invisible among the visible, the shadow of God. He would think of him as he had seen him at the qamargah, chasing his prey. His arm raised to strike, face glistening. His delight at the sight of blood. Akbar! Shutting his eyes, he saw him. *A hundred thousand adore his face!*

In his dreams, it was different. He saw the emperor everywhere, replacing the heroes in the stories. Akbar as the wandering prince Nushirwan, alone amidst haunting ruins. As Alexander, setting off on his great conquest. As an angry Rustom, the legendary warrior, searching for his missing horse. As the pious Jamshed, conversing with demons.

*Tell me, if there exists another as I am?*

*Thou art alone. Mightiest. There is none such as thee!*

At first, he resisted drawing Akbar's face. Then when he tried, his pen ran over the page in mysterious ways. Eyes became rosy, like apricots with a pair of subhani – dark kernels. The broad forehead turned itself into a rare khusrawi melon. The mole bloomed as a full kishmishi grape. Anxious, he hid his drawings.

Sitting in his kitabkhana room, he worked on his own paintings of Akbar, neglecting the Darogha's requests. But he avoided the usual scenes drawn by other artists featuring the emperor – battle scenes, court scenes, even scenes of private audience – the emperor receiving an ambassador, or listening to a dervish. As his passion grew, he always drew Akbar alone. Always.

He drew his face in three-quarter view, as the early Persian masters like his father and Mir Sayyid Ali would do. He drew him in profile. But the full face was his own preference. A full face, staring back at the viewer, a smile on his lips, eyes gleaming like a boy's.

The Darogha worried at his slow pace. As he grew more obsessed with his secret paintings of Akbar, his kitabkhana commissions took longer to complete. What used to take him a week to finish now took a month. He seemed more and more uninterested in his work, listening absent-mindedly to the praise he received each week. Even the rewards didn't seem to matter to him. He rarely counted the gold pieces, dropping the small silken purse unchecked into the pocket of his tunic. One week, the Darogha reduced the amount, just to test him. Bihzad didn't notice, and greeted the next request with similar indifference. The Darogha was embarrassed by his own trick.

Perhaps the boy was missing his father. The Darogha wrote to the Khwaja at Sikri about the sudden change in Bihzad. Next time he met Bihzad, he tried to raise his spirits by speaking about the wonders of Fatehpur Sikri that was soon to be their home.

'What used to be a village of wild beasts is now a garden of gardens.' He spoke of the four gates, the halls, the homes of courtiers, the baths, the mosque, the tower. A maze for the emperor and his women to play hide and seek. A small marble tank was being built out of a single mass of rock, to be filled with wine when finished. There was much to be done still, the Darogha said, then allowed a rare slip of exuberance. 'When finished, it'll be a city of dreams.'

'When?' Bihzad asked impatiently. 'When will it be finished finally? Everyone has left Agra, except the artists. Does he really want us there?'

The Darogha tried to reassure Bihzad. The emperor had started with the essentials – palaces for his wives, barracks for his soldiers, stables for their horses, the mint, the mosque... The kitabkhana would come up soon. At their future home, the artists would start on a new album of paintings, the Darogha told Bihzad. They would begin work on the story of the emperor's life. The *Akbarnama*. Like his Mughal ancestors, the emperor too would have his own biography – the chroniclers had already started to record his life in precise detail. What he wore, what he deemed for his empire, whom he promoted and whom exiled, his words on warfare and weaponry, his views on the religions. Even his nights would be recorded. Which wife he visited, and for how long.

Bihzad looked up. The Darogha spoke with glowing eyes. 'Soon!' he said. Soon, he'd be asking Bihzad to begin the first page of that glorious album.

Still the pace remained slow. Between the commissions, he drew Akbar. He hid the portraits meticulously among the sheaves of blank paper. Although the Darogha rarely entered his room without asking, he began to keep his door shut. Inside, he heard even less, became even more cut off from the life of the kitabkhana. The heat of Jumada and Rajab, the dry summer months, made him boil.

*

His pale Persian face took on the shade of mourning. When neighbours or fellow artists at the kitabkhana caught sight of him, they said he looked as if he was suffering from lack of blood. They were used to his unusual features. His eyes, unlike the eyes of Hindustan, were like the desert grass. His pale skin, unlike others in Agra, was tinged with the pomegranate. Now, like a young antelope, hungry for days, he took on a withered intensity.

The Darogha sighed as he stopped to knock on Bihzad's door. This, he hoped, holding the letter in his hand, would bring cheer to the boy. The Khwaja would arrive soon in Agra, he told Bihzad, to take them all back with him to Sikri. Bihzad too. The emperor, the Darogha announced, had shown a fondness for his paintings.

*

A long corridor separated the Khwaja's wife and son in the empty haveli. It seemed like a recently abandoned palace, its walls seeping with Zuleikha's fragrances. The neighbours watched in vain for a flicker of life, waited to hear voices during the day or night. Why hadn't she left for Sikri with her husband? There were those who believed that the Khwaja had left his wife for another, that it was only a matter of time before she started her lonely trek back to her parents. Others disagreed. She was too tempting to be spurned. She has left *him*, neighbours whispered. Zuleikha has refused to join the Khwaja in Sikri, when wives of other courtiers are falling over each other in their haste. The pomp of the court means less to her than her perfumes, perhaps she has a secret lover in Agra…

On most evenings, Bihzad visited Zuleikha in her room, sat on her bed and smelled the brewing perfumes. He no longer needed the excuse of her reading to him, starting to visit her without the books. The silence of the kitabkhana would follow him to his stepmother's room. He would sit, eyes lowered, while his fingers – free from the stories – sketched aimlessly from his mind as he listened to Zuleikha. She missed her visits to the harem, she told him. The emperor's women had all left Agra. The courtiers had departed for Sikri with their wives, to fill their posts in Akbar's court. She felt sad for Agra. 'A city for the dying,' she would moan, sipping from her cup, or drawing a wisp of smoke through her delicate lips. She didn't speak any more of the harem's secrets, rarely mentioned the Khwaja, except mumbling to herself when she was almost asleep.

She'd flick back a strand of hair from Bihzad's forehead. 'But it's not your age to be sad, Bihzad. Your age is meant for pleasures. For adventures! Touching a flame with your fingers!' She pointed at her maid. 'Look! Wouldn't you barter an empire for that lovely mole on her cheek!'

He nibbled on a piece of mufarrih. Majun and mufarrih, the two intoxicants – sweetmeats with opium. Zuleikha broke a piece, then fed Bihzad, sitting on her bed, drawing absentmindedly.

'Her clothes hide much of her beauty!' Nikisa dropped her eyes. 'Why don't you take her into your service?'

She asked her maid to come close, turned her face towards Bihzad. 'Would you like to see how these jewels look on her?'

47

She held a necklace around Nikisa's neck. A sapphire coronet crowning her locks. A silver breastplate. The plain Nikisa became an alluring begum.

'Even the emperor must please her to receive her favours!'

Bihzad turned his face away. Zuleikha laughed. 'And how will *you* please your begum?'

Out of habit, she started to recite for him from *The Tales of the Parrot*, imitating the parrot, describing the ten qualities of an ideal lover.

'*O Nakshabi, there's a trap in every wish, a lurking danger in every woman. She's poisonous from head to tail!*'

He spoke only to correct her story, to ask for a sip of her wine.

She pointed at the dried flowers around her bed, started telling Bihzad her secrets. 'Unless the flower decides,' she said, 'none can force her to release her fragrance. Just like the lotus.' She gave Nikisa a knowing look, she smiled and left the room.

'The lotus is the queen of flowers, and the black bee is her ideal lover. He alights on her and goes inside to suck her nectar. She closes her petals, traps him. He doesn't struggle, for a whole night lies quietly inside her. In the morning, she sets her lover free, then releases her fragrance.'

In one hand she raised Bihzad's face. He sat slumped at her feet, his eyes tinged with her wine.

'How will you please her, Bihzad?'

With the other hand, she drew him towards her, releasing his pen. Then she led his hand past her anklets to her slightly bent knee, moving quietly under the jaguli gown till she laid it to rest on her lotus. Eyes closed, head tilted to one side, she tempted the bee to sting.

The wax was melting, he felt. Awake. A drop on the tip of the brush ready to leave its mark.

'What are you hiding from me, Bihzad? Whatever it is, remember, love and musk never stay hidden!'

Salim Amiri wiped his fingers on his gown. 'And, sadly, neither does wine.' Before his grandmother could start, he fired his first defence. 'The wines of Shiraz prevail over the laws of the Prophet!'

'And the urine of Hindustan that you drink every day?'

Salim Amiri stuck out his tongue in embarrassment. 'See how she speaks!' He gave Bihzad a close look, frowning at his strained face.

'Your inside is hurting your outside. Who is she?' Bihzad kept silent.

Salim Amiri waved his hand dismissively. 'Whoever she is, there are others just as fair. There's much in this world beside love. It's nothing but an addiction.'

'Better be addicted to wine than love!' the voice came from above.

'It's a peculiar condition, Bihzad. A man in love feels even the touch of an ant's foot. If a stone moves under water, he knows it. He can touch the body of a worm. But, he is unable to see himself in the mirror!'

Like a friendly uncle, he tried to probe cautiously – why did Bihzad seem miserable, quieter than usual, not willing to jump into arguments. Then he gave up, trying instead to revive him with news from Sikri.

'Your father is coming to choose the best of artists. They'll begin the *Akbarnama* soon. The greatest album. It'll make the world remember Akbar for ever. No, remember Hindustan!'

'The greatest?' Bihzad seemed unimpressed. 'You mean the artists will begin yet another long and boring story – another *nama*. After the *Hamzanama*, the *Akbarnama*.'

'No, Bihzad, it'll be different this time. Jalaluddin Muhammad Akbar's life story is different from his ancestors'.' Salim Amiri wasn't prepared to give up. He started to imitate a flattering courtier. 'If a hundred books were written on him, it would be as though not a single word had been written! If a thousand volumes were composed, it would be as though the pen had not touched the paper!'

Unable to interest Bihzad sufficiently, the paintseller decided to surprise him with the secret that even the Darogha didn't know, confided in him by his friend the Khwaja.

'Your father will leave the kitabkhana...he won't be the master at Sikri.'

Bihzad raised his eyes. 'Leave...?'

'Yes. He'll become even more important than he is now. A senior courtier. But he has convinced Akbar to have you lead the *Akbarnama* artists instead. Imagine, Bihzad...'

Bihzad interrupted him. 'And how did he convince the emperor?'

Sensing his audience's excitement, Salim Amiri decided to give him the full story.

'The Khwaja was present when Akbar sat viewing your paintings. He spent a long time over the court scene, went over every face, pronounced each of their names. "They are all different!" he exclaimed, then asked your father, "Why do you draw the faces all alike when they are so different?"'

Bihzad smiled. 'You mean he didn't mind...'

'No!' Salim Amiri knew what Bihzad was referring to. 'He didn't mind that he himself was invisible!' Then, with a look of triumph, the paintseller said, 'Do you know what he asked your father? He asked him to erase your signature in the margin, and replace it with another. Instead of *al-abd Bihzad* – the Slave Bihzad – it was to read *hazrat-i ustad Bihzad* – the Exalted Master Bihzad!'

'He *is* different then, isn't he?' Bihzad mused. 'Not like a child hankering only after stories, as the Darogha makes him out to be.'

'It was then that your father made his request to Akbar, and he accepted readily. He likes your energy. Unlike his courtiers, he isn't impressed just by opulent scenes and elegant designs.' Salim Amiri paused. 'He is a true Mughal – a warrior. In him, the wines of Shiraz prevail over the laws of the Prophet.'

Bihzad told him about the unusual reward the Darogha had brought back to him recently, after showing his paintings to the emperor – a jewelled inkstand, a stool inlaid with mother-of-pearl, and a short robe worn by Akbar.

'See, he has fallen for you, Bihzad! But...' Salim Amiri frowned. 'There is still a small problem...'

'He still wants his stories, doesn't he?' Bihzad made a face, preparing to relapse into his sullen mood.

'No... not that. Now the chameleon has started its mischief. Adili, the Afghan artist.'

Adili had started spreading rumours. How could Bihzad lead the *Akbarnama* artists? How could he become the kitabkhana's master? The boy was unweaned, hadn't even applied a razor to his face yet. The paintings were really done by the Khwaja himself. He had started to court the courtiers. The Mughal empire was superior to that of Persia. Why then must it behave as if it was inferior? Borrowing everything from Persia – poets to artists, and now even sons of Persians? From the Hindukush to the Jamuna, couldn't the emperor find a single native of his own empire to exalt his likeness? The Afghan had raised the question of merit, appealed to the emperor to consider his own order. Merit over blood.

'The chameleon has changed Akbar's mind. He wants you still to lead the *Akbarnama* artists, but now he wants a contest. The one that pleases him the most with a portrait of himself at the inauguration of Fatehpur Sikri will become the future master of the kitabkhana.' Salim Amiri smiled. 'A contest! As if artists were wrestlers. Archers!'

'And who will enter the contest?' Bihzad asked.

That's why the Khwaja was coming soon to Agra, Salim

Amiri said. Surely not every artist of the kitabkhana, not one hundred of them. It was his own view that the *real* patrons of Agra should decide on a handful who would have the privilege to enter the competition.

Bihzad had seen the real patrons at the kitabkhana. Men who knew. Those who had had their portraits drawn, purchased rare manuscripts from merchants. Those who knew the difference between the early masters, could tell a Mirak from a Muzaffar, could spot the Great One even in a dark room. Men of taste, who spent their leisure in refined company, among poets and philosophers, not among horses and elephants.

There was to be a garden party by the Jamuna, Salim Amiri said, with colourful tents hosting the very best of Agra and Sikri. The Khwaja would introduce his son there – present the future master of the kitabkhana.

'The wolf-cub is born to be a wolf!'

'Even if it is raised among asses!' came a voice from above.

'Ah! The Little Master! Sick with love! If I don't cheer him up, who will?' Salim Amiri dropped his voice. 'But the real contest, Bihzad, will not be between you and the chameleon, but between you and your teacher.'

*

At sixteen, he refused to accept the Darogha's commissions. Violating the custom of the kitabkhana, he drew from his own mind, followed his own wish. The Darogha kept on knocking on his door, but Bihzad refused to open it.

'There's just a dozen of the stories of Hamza left to do,' the Darogha pleaded.

'Then do them yourself.'

'Just this one …' In despair, the Darogha broke the Khwaja's express rule, and begged Bihzad to draw the faces – the most delicate part of a painting – while others drew the patterns, coloured and bordered.

'That is against my father's wish.'

'But he wished too that you should draw and paint, not simply lock yourself in.'

'I *am* drawing.'

'Yes…?' The Darogha was hopeful. Perhaps the boy has memorised the remaining stories of the *Hamzanama*. When he came with his imperial reward, Bihzad opened the door.

Each week, he presented the Darogha with his paintings, sending the ageing man into a series of nervous fits. 'Take them to the emperor,' he said, in a grave voice far exceeding his age. 'He'll reward you more for these than the silly Hamzas.'

In one of them, he had drawn the Simurgh. The mythical bird in flight against a blazing sky. Dreamlike, as if born of a mysterious vision. In another, he painted the imperial hunt. A noble blue buck standing alone in the circle, and the arrow of an invisible hunter streaking along its path. An animal unaware of danger. The Darogha lowered his eyes, as if struck by tragedy.

Unlike the *Hamzanama*, these paintings didn't illustrate a story. They didn't demand either a beginning or an end. His figures seemed chiselled from stone rather than drawn. He loved the twilight, nocturnal scenes, bold and unexpected turns, unearthly colours. Against all custom, he drew children, playing among jugglers and acrobats at the bazaar. When he did draw portraits, flowers in the background disappeared in favour of a stark sky.

The Darogha gazed in disbelief at scenes of young men and women enjoying themselves in gardens, floating like clouds above the ground, like jinns. A priest roasting a demon over an open spit. In one painting, he depicted the Jamuna, seen from the top of the fort. The first ray lighting up the rows of poplar and cypress. The stonecutters' mosque reflected on the river. A fine rain. Not a trace of an animal or even a bird. Not a living soul. Just the lapis sky, the turquoise river, the crimson fort, and the golden sun.

'The painting is dead,' the Darogha said with a grim face.

The only story he drew was of the two physicians, a large painting with several scenes, flowing from one to the other. The two physicians were locked in a contest. Each was set to prove his might by creating the deadliest poison. One made a pill from rare herbs and challenged the other to swallow it. With great

foresight, the second physician mixed the pill with its exact anti-
dote, and chewed it up like a lump of harmless sugar. Then, he
went about his own trick, plucking a rose from a garden and
breathing an evil spell on its petals. Smell the rose, he challenged
the first. What could be easier, more pleasant? Death struck with
the first breath of fragrance.

Buza! The boy had been drinking the local brew, the Darogha
was certain. A clear case of dementia!

*

The real album he kept hidden. His own *Akbarnama*. The
emperor as a young man with dangling earrings and long
unkempt hair seated by a rivulet and playing the stringed ektar,
a barren blue landscape matching his solitude. Then Akbar as a
cup-bearer, a posy tucked in his buttonhole – holding a tray,
offering a cup, pining for an absent lover. Almond eyes, ivory
skin, a slim waist. In some paintings, he appeared in the
embrace of another, gazing fondly at a boy who was hiding his
shy face in Akbar's bosom. Akbar caressing his young lover,
dressed voluptuously as a maid, a loosely fitted turban down his
back, holding a half-eaten apple, a foot raised coyly. Lips joining
lips. He dressed the emperor in jewels, in the languor of silk, an
undulating hem. In one he drew the rites of a secret betrothal –
Akbar showing his bare arms, sleeves rolled back to receive the
burns being inflicted by his lover.

Hidden among the other paintings in the album was a double
portrait. A pair of young men drinking from the same cup
under the wings of angels, and a sky filled with birds. He drew
them, not as emperor and artist, but as Akbar and Bihzad.
Lovers.

*

Sitting alone in Mir Sayyid Ali's studio, Bihzad wondered where
the students had gone. The room appeared just as before. The
four ink-stands in a half-circle, empty oyster shells and jars full
of colours. A window left open as if to allow the sun's rays to
illuminate the ivory-toned sheets propped up over raised knees.

He wondered why his teacher had summoned him. He remembered his first day, and Mir Sayyid Ali's astonishment at his blank page. In four years, the studio had become more familiar to Bihzad than the many rooms in the Khwaja's haveli. Unlike its empty stone passages, winding around like a sinister puzzle, here he felt a certain comfort, the comfort of a bare room where the same scene enacted itself every morning. He sensed a familiar stirring as he smelled the fresh resin and the pungent gum oil. He sat for a long while staring out of the window at the road that led to Sikri. It was empty now, just a few riders bearing the emperor's summons down to Agra. He imagined Sikri glowing at a distance. The garden of gardens. He felt a rush of blood in his temples as he remembered the Darogha's words.

A slim volume lay on the floor before his seat, opened on a page with a single line. He picked it up, tried fruitlessly to read. Perhaps his teacher had left him a book, as had been his custom in the old days, to have read and illustrated.

Later, even Salim Amiri sat frowning over the line. He looked at Bihzad a few times. It wasn't a story. No. Just a line of verse from a Sufi. The greatest one. A line from Jalaluddin Rumi's epitaph.

*When we are dead, seek not a tomb in the earth, find it among a million hearts.*

'Can you tell how many crows there are in Agra at this very moment? Not elephants or horses, but crows.'

The Khwaja's guests laughed. No one ventured an answer to Salim Amiri's question.

'The elephants and horses, we know, are in Sikri, left with the emperor. Agra has none. Simple!' Salim Amiri continued. 'Only crows and artists remain – too many to count!'

'And how many artists would you say there are in Agra at this very moment?' Naubat Khan, the veena player, seemed interested in the puzzle. His eyes danced. Even at seventy-five, he was an active employer of singing girls. He was cunning, friends said, had tasted the water from several hands, but still as afraid of his mother as a five-year-old boy.

'Certainly more than the number of crows! A man can't stretch his leg without kicking an artist's backside!' Everyone laughed at Salim Amiri's wit. He raised his voice to attract the Royal Paymaster.

'The emperor has opened his treasury, it seems. His emissaries are going around villages to lure painters. Anyone with five fingers qualifies to join Akbar's artists!'

The Paymaster beamed, but he was engrossed with Murtaza Beg, the philosopher and chess player.

Servants filed by, spraying rosewater, offering wine and sweetmeats on giant trays carried over their shoulders. The men had gathered by the Jamuna on a pleasant spring afternoon, under a coloured tent. The Khwaja had invited the senior courtiers from Sikri, coming down to Agra with them, joining a few old friends who had stayed back in the old capital. The wives of the courtiers had been invited as well, with a special tent set up for them close by, although few could come to join their husbands, busy arranging their new havelis close to the emperor's new palace. The party had got off to a good start – everyone seemed happy to have returned to old Agra, if only for a day.

'Take Murtaza Beg.' Naubat Khan drew everyone's attention to the man reputed to know from five to ten thousand chess moves by heart. 'He has had everyone's likeness drawn in his house. Including his four wives!'

Abdullah and Hassan, both renowned poets in the Turki language, shook their heads. 'What lies you spread! Artists entering the harem?'

'No, no … It's a matter of translation, just as the emperor has ordered the books of Hindustan to be translated into Persian.' When Naubat Khan went on to explain the devout Murtaza Beg's novel 'move', everyone applauded. He had made his eldest daughter, blessed as she was with a fine eye and nimble fingers, draw the likenesses of his four wives. Then he had employed a kitabkhana artist to copy from the drawings, and make them up to be really beautiful.

'The emperor has infected us! Now we want to have our own paintings too. Whatever Akbar wants, we want. Stories, portraits – some mirs and mirzas are even asking to have their pets drawn. Cats, horses, parrots, caged spiders. No wonder there are more artists here than crows!' Naubat Khan was most emphatic. 'Just imagine what will happen when the kitabkhana moves to Sikri. There will be even more demand then.'

'Then we'll have more crows in Agra than artists,' Salim Amiri laughed.

Abdullah, known to be a heavy drinker, leaned towards the paintseller. 'If only the emperor could read! Then, there'd be more poets than artists. More poets than crows!'

The Paymaster turned at last to the small group sitting around Naubat Khan. Bowing respectfully at the veena player, he teased Salim Amiri in his pious and elegant voice.

57

'The treasury is being robbed by a certain paintseller. He claims not a line may be drawn before his dues are paid. As if the Almighty needed the luxury of colours to draw the universe!'

Standing close by, the physician Ismael Safawi was discussing the relative merits of gems with Shaibaq, his brother-in-law, the inspector of the imperial kitchen. There were rubies of three colours, he was saying, and all emeralds were not the same. He was a gifted man, had composed a commentary on the *al-Qanun* – the Canon on Medicine. His knowledge was reputed to be greater than his skill. For years he had served every courtier of Agra.

'An emerald can resemble a soap. Or the seeds of wild saffron. It could be the colour of a scorpion, or that of raw meat. The ones from Syria are more precious than those from Spain.'

Shaibaq glanced quickly at his own fingers, at his emerald ring.

Overhearing the two, the Royal Paymaster joined them. He was an expert, being one of the very few with the privilege of inspecting the imperial gem collection. Normally, he would have drawn at least half of the party, describing the royal gifts and the exquisite ransom from sieged cities. The story of the diamond Koh-i-noor, of course, was his favourite, pledged as it was as the price of a defeated queen's honour.

A different kind of gossip occupied the Khwaja's guests after the meal, among the Chief Justice, the Paymaster, the Inspector of the imperial kitchen, and the court musicians.

Shaikh Murad, the flautist, the most respected among the musicians, started mumbling soon after the servants had removed the dinner cloth. Twirling his fingers in the hot water bowl, he tapped his neighbour Ismael Safawi on the shoulder, and with a conspirator's wink blurted it out for all to hear.

'He won't stop just with translations. He's going to make us read the books of Hindustan every day in place of namaz prayers.'

'He'll make us memorise the names of thirty million gods!' The physician added his own comment.

From his post in Sikri's imperial kitchen, Shaibaq the

Inspector had seen the emperor at the jharokha window, eyes raised towards the sun, his lips moving. A Hindu monk had hypnotised Akbar, he said.

'Infidels. Flatterers!' Naubat Khan spat out.

The Paymaster reminded everyone of the emperor's famous leniency. 'At twenty he abolished the tax on unbelievers. He even married their daughters. Lit lamps, paid homage with fire. Whether in jest or not, he grew his hair past his shoulders, marked his forehead just like...' The Paymaster choked, unable to hide the disgust under his pious and elegant voice.

Murtaza Beg frowned, but he kept silent. His head resting on Hassan's lap, Abdullah opened his eyes for a moment. 'He has been seen kissing the holy book of Christians, the one presented to him by the Portuguese.'

'No!' The Paymaster shut his eyes.

'No!' The muscles on the physician's face twitched.

'I swear,' the poet Abdullah started a round in perfect verse, 'by the tail of the dove, by the hood of the falcon, by the melody of the wren, by the feathers of the raven, by the lovesick nightingale...'

The Chief Justice entered the discussion for the first time. He had heard the emperor pronounce on religious matters at the court on more than one occasion.

'He says,' he repeated in an impartial voice, 'that all faiths hold the same measure of truth and untruth. Dough is dough, and one is no better than the other.'

'The day the same as the night?' Ismael Safawi sounded sarcastic.

'The dove the same as the owl?' – The flautist.

'The widow the same as the virgin?' – Naubat Khan.

'He's a child with a lamp in his hand,' the philosopher Murtaza Beg sighed.

*

Servants arrived to light the torches which surrounded the tents. The river became a sky of blinking stars.

*

Through the folds in the women's tent Bihzad saw Zuleikha. She was alone. Unnoticed at the party, he came in and stood before her, bending a knee out of respect as she was his honoured elder. She bent a knee too, out of courtesy. Both advanced, then repeated the ceremony. Bihzad felt her eye on his fingers. The thumb, from the ring to the blunted tip of the nail. He wondered if she was considering its secret adventure. A silent shiver passed between them.

He had brought her a garland of narcissus. She turned her face away and drew her veil.

'Why?' he asked.

'The narcissi have eyes. I don't wish to be seen by others.'

*

From a wine party it became a majun party. Sweets from the finest sweet sellers of Agra, mixed with opium, wrapped in rose petals and sprinkled with water. Fresh from a nap, the Khwaja had resumed entertaining his guests. From Abdulla to Ismael Safawi, everyone begged Naubat Khan to play his veena. Even Shaikh Murad, normally the first among musicians, joined in the chorus. Seated in a circle, the guests seemed ready for the final hours of the gathering.

Then Salim Amiri re-entered the tent. Like a comet, with his long turban trailing behind. Returning from a quick visit to his haveli, he brought news to silence the veena player, and everyone else. Rarely at a loss for words, he seemed struck by the abruptness of his own entrance.

'The Nadir-ul-Mulk has decided to stop.'

'Who?' Naubat Khan seemed cross at the interruption.

'Mir Sayyid Ali. He has decided to give up painting, give up his students. He has decided to stop.'

'Stop?' The Khwaja brought his face close to Salim Amiri's.

The paintseller nodded his head. 'Yes, he has announced his desire to lay down his brush and return.' He himself hadn't believed his ears, thought the elderly artist's student who he had met on his way to the haveli was pulling his leg. 'I went off to his studio at once,' Salim Amiri continued. 'He said an artist must know when to stop, otherwise he'd start painting like a child.'

Hiding behind the partition, in the enclosure reserved for servants, Bihzad froze, a piece of majun in his hand.

'Go back to Persia?' the Khwaja whispered.

The others started to murmur to each other.

'Return to Tabriz?' Murtaza Beg frowned. Then his smile returned. 'Of course. When an artist no longer cares about his subject, then his paintings die.'

'To cross the Hindukush at his age?' The physician seemed not to approve. The Paymaster agreed with him. Surely, the emperor would honour him with a suitable residence in Sikri.

'Tabriz!' The poet Abdullah was awake. 'Where else? He must return, mustn't he, to gaze at the blue lake of his childhood and wait for the supreme artist Allah to add the last touch to his life?'

'But here, it's the first touch that'll count the most. The one to add the first touch to the *Akbarnama* will be Akbar's chief artist.' A sufficiently-recovered Salim Amiri seemed eager to leap into the matter of succession at the kitabkhana.

All eyes turned towards the Khwaja. He looked upwards.

'What if someone has started to paint the emperor's album already, without his permission?' Salim Amiri's eyes gleamed. 'What if the painter of strange animals thinks it's his turn now to draw the mightiest?'

'What if, what if…' the physician muttered, irritated, unable to decipher Salim Amiri's puzzle. 'Who? Who is that painter?'

The guests exchanged glances. Then, Naubat Khan blurted out. 'He is what in Hindustan one calls a Banmanush. A monkey! A di li!' He spat out the Afghan artist's name.

Both Abdullah and Hassan were about to employ suitable curses when the Khwaja interrupted them.

'The emperor will choose his artist. Wisely. For he is wise.' Then he ordered his servants to bring in an easel and set it down at the centre of the tent, asking his guests to rise and assemble before it. A small painting stood on the easel, covered in a velvet cloth. The Khwaja hushed his departing servants, then raised his voice to the ladies in the other tent, telling them that their turn would come next to view the painting. Tired at the end of the evening, his tunic showing marks of spilt wine, his buttons perilously close to bursting, he addressed his audience – the real patrons of Agra and Sikri.

'Bihzad,' he pronounced the boy's name lovingly, 'is offering you a painting, to wish you all a night of tranquillity after our merriment.'

The boy was shy. Dragging him out of the servants' enclosure, the Khwaja nudged him forward, then, taking his hand, made him pull the silk cord to part the curtain over the easel.

The guests strained to look over each other's shoulders.

It was a scene from a story. The story of Zuleikha and Yousouf. The most shameful tale in all of Persia. Most dishonourable. Yet the most arousing. The painting told the story of Princess Zuleikha's lust for her handsome slave Yousouf. Bihzad had drawn her in a garden among violets and bees and over a golden ground. She had been waiting anxiously for the young man, bare to his chest, weeding the grass. As they meet, she rests her head on his shoulder, touches him between the folds of his dress. The princess sighs, her lips parted in pleasure.

The audience fell silent save for the rustling as each shifted from one leg to the other, and a few nervous coughs. The real patrons of Agra and Sikri looked on in disbelief. None had expected a story, but a tribute to the emperor. His portrait perhaps, or the emperor among his courtiers inspecting his new capital, the emperor praying. They were hoping to see the victorious entry in Akbar's contest, the triumph of the child prodigy. The Khwaja looked confused. Frowning, he glanced around him, as if expecting another painting, the 'right' painting, to be unveiled next.

Then Naubat Khan stepped forward. 'What fine blooms! I am tempted to pick one and fix it on my turban!'

The Paymaster spoke over his shoulder. 'I felt so too! But I was afraid if I did, the birds would fly off the branches!'

Everyone spoke glowingly of the setting – a perfect garden – without mentioning the story. After the initial shock, there were murmurs all around, loosened tongues spoke words of praise for the Little Master.

'Let the Banmanush beat this, if he can!' Salim Amiri let out a laugh.

Then the poet Abdullah spoke. 'Shh…Mustn't disturb the lovers!'

＊

The Khwaja's eyes glowed. Yousouf and Zuleikha! They were there for all to see. The princess had the eyes of his wife. The slave, those of his son.

＊

'Akbar.' Back at the haveli, father and son sat facing each other in the Khwaja's room, lit by a powerful lamp.

'Show me a portrait of the emperor.' He avoided looking at Bihzad's face – pale and drifting after the long party.

'Where is it?' He glanced up impatiently, turning the paintings over and over, looking for the single most important one. With each one he passed, his face became more grim.

'Stories! Do you draw nothing but stories? Didn't the Darogha say it's enough? Forget the parrot, the kings. This isn't Persia. We are in Hindustan, Bihzad. The stories here are different. Akbar. He's our story.'

'These aren't stories.'

The Khwaja feigned surprise. 'Not stories! Do you mean Yousouf and Zuleikha aren't really who they are? Don't be a fool, Bihzad. If it isn't a story, then why does the Persian chinar bloom over Hindustan's rotten soil?'

'It's not Yousouf and Zuleikha.'

The Khwaja looked genuinely surprised. 'Then who?'

'Surrender.' He spoke with his eyes lowered.

'And this?' The Khwaja threw down the mythical bird Simurgh.

'Triumph.' He spoke in the voice of Mir Sayyid Ali, as if describing The Night Of The Chosen One.

'And this?' The Khwaja pointed at the empty landscape seen from the fort at the hour of dawn.

63

'Prayer.'

'Prayer?'

'The earth's prayer to the sun.'

The Khwaja fell silent. Then, changing his tone, he tried again. 'Stories would be enough in Persia. The Great One never drew a shah or a sheikh. Artists and poets were alike, their pens obeyed no one's command. But here ...' The Khwaja's voice seemed weak and distant. 'In Hindustan, there's but one spirit. Akbar's. It's his triumph, Bihzad, that commands the prayer of thousands.'

The contest, the Khwaja said, trying to reason with Bihzad, was almost over before it had started. Without Mir Sayyid Ali in the fray, the real patrons of Agra and Sikri would most certainly suggest that the emperor choose Bihzad as the rightful inheritor of the new kitabkhana. He was both a Mughal and a Persian. The only one worthy of being considered among the hundred artists of the kitabkhana. He was young, like the emperor, and already a master like the Great One himself. But he'd still have to please Akbar by drawing his portrait.

Bihzad pushed the album of paintings back to the Khwaja, opened it at the scene of the royal court. He pointed towards the apex of the pyramid.

The Khwaja shook his head. 'No, Bihzad. The emperor is invisible. There is just his throne.'

Bihzad turned over the pages till he arrived at the picture of the imperial hunt. The blue buck awaiting her death by the emperor's arrow.

'He is *still* invisible.' The Khwaja grimaced. Then he swallowed his frustration, and in a teacher's voice, started to describe the many scenes an artist could draw to exalt the emperor.

'Battles. Think of him approaching an enemy's column, on the saddle of a tipuchaq horse, a spear raised in his right arm.'

'Battles? How strange ...' Bihzad spoke with his eyes closed. 'Didn't his father pay you a thousand gold pieces to heal the wounds of war?'

The Khwaja was startled. 'What wounds?'

'Didn't he ask you to erase bloodshed with beauty?'

The Khwaja raised his hand. He tried describing a different scene. 'How about Akbar accepting the surrender of a rebel prince? No bloodshed. Just the grace of pardon from a mighty one.'

'Pardon? Should the artist draw the shameful ransom too? The plates full of gold, the jewels, the palanquins full of captured women...'

The Khwaja looked aghast. 'Who? Who taught you all this?' Instinctively, he turned towards Salim Amiri's haveli, as if it was his friend's voice he was hearing, not his son's.

'And if the artist himself was the rebel? What riches would the emperor demand for his pardon?' Bihzad went on.

For a moment, the Khwaja agreed with Adili the Afghan. *A boy yet unweaned! Hasn't yet put a razor to his face!* An illiterate pretending to know the secrets of a mighty ruler.

'The emperor's spirit lies in his conquests. Where does the artist's spirit lie?' the boy asked.

'Beware!' The Khwaja made as if to rise from his seat in his anger. 'Beware of those who speak ill of everyone. Recite poetry and seek pleasure. Pray not, keep no fasts, live like the heathen. An artist,' he thundered, 'should see with his eyes, not jabber with his tongue.'

'An artist must show what the eye cannot see.' There was a steely resolve in Bihzad's voice.

Once more, the Khwaja controlled himself. It was almost dawn. Once more, he offered a scene in which the emperor appeared, not among beasts or enemies, but with his courtesans.

'Holi! The festival of Hindustan! Think of Akbar among his begums, spraying water, blowing a cloud of coloured powder towards his favourite one. Judge him, if you must, but admire too his infinite charms!'

The boy sat with his eyes on the floor. Eyes like desert grass, tinged with majun. He seemed not to hear the Khwaja.

Slamming down an ivory toned sheet before Bihzad, the Khwaja thrust his pen towards him.

'Draw!'

It was Akbar's most awesome portrait. The emperor's head and neck taut as a drawn bow. One hand clenched, the other in the gesture of pardon. Fingers like weapons. His gaze icy. Lips firmly pressed. The mole like a half-ripe cherry. The image of a king with the heart of a brute.

The Khwaja smiled. Raising himself from the floor, he grasped Bihzad's head in both hands and kissed it.

'The Little Master!'

Then, taking the pen from Bihzad's hand, he signed the name of his illiterate son in the margin.

Sikri. A new capital for the triumphant emperor. From the age of fourteen when Akbar ascended the throne, till twenty-six when he was still childless, Hindustan waited anxiously for the birth of the next emperor. There were fears every time he went into battle. What if the unthinkable happened? Who would take his place? In the event of his death, succession to his throne would be open to question. Rivalries could then plague the great Mughal Empire, tearing apart the delicate union crafted over decades of war and truce.

Early in his reign, there had been the excuse of war. The emperor was hardly present in Agra. His seat rested firmly on the back of a horse, not on the soft beds of his harem. Unlike the decadence of his enemies, his was the motto of conquest, of a vigorous expansion, till Hindustan's mosaic of kingdoms became one. Before every battle, his subjects prayed – for Akbar's victory, and for an heir to fill the throne should the unthinkable happen.

But the one with an ample supply of wives and concubines managed to remain barren as an old tree. There were rumours about a jealous harem. Perhaps the begums were conspiring against each other – robbing a womb with bitter herbs before it could bear fruit. Better for him to remain childless than father a son with a rival wife. His mother and aunt despaired – if he waited any longer, he'd be an old man robbed of the pleasure of raising his son on his knee, even if he did manage to have one in the end.

The emperor prayed daily for a son. He started an annual

67

pilgrimage to shrines of dead saints. Prayed and gifted alms, kissed the prayer cloth repeatedly in his private mosque. Then word had come of a living saint – Salim Chistie of Sikri. Akbar had visited him and repeated his prayer. Salim Chistie had promised that Akbar would succeed – not once, but thrice. Soon his Hindu wife complained of sickness. She was sent away from Agra to rest under the eyes of the saint in Sikri. The harem rued its misfortune. Then the heir arrived. Akbar's heir – the future master of Hindustan. Almost immediately, a second wife fell pregnant. Another son was born. Then, a third, just as the saint had promised. The emperor was triumphant.

The empire raised its hands in gratitude. But Akbar had resolved to do more – he would turn the village of wild beasts into a garden of gardens and make it his capital, the City of Victory.

There were those among the elderly courtiers of Agra who had disapproved. Of all the conquerors who had set foot in Hindustan, none had ventured away from a river. Sikri was but a village on a barren rock. Even the water needed to make the emperor's perfumes would have to travel to the new city on the backs of mules. No king had ever built a palace in Hindustan without surrounding it first with a fort. And, no one had built a fort without the safety of steep ridges on its flanks. Sikri, some said, was an act of foolish impulse. Many suspected the Hindu wife – it might have been her idea. Maybe she had swayed Akbar by presenting him with a son.

Akbar commanded that the rock be blasted to make a lake. He spared neither the mint nor his army. Soldiers worked alongside craftsmen and builders, the whole of Hindustan was ransacked for precious stones, silk and gold to decorate the buildings. Palaces were begun and finished with lightning speed, as if they had been conceived in a dream and needed to come alive before that dream faded.

Then there were those who applauded the emperor. After all, Agra had been the dream of other invaders, who had come before the Mughals. At twenty-six, Akbar was dreaming his own dream. He, the mightiest, mightier than Persia's Shah or the

Caliph of Baghdad, his empire richer than either of theirs and more securely at peace. He had already rebuilt Agra, tearing down the old brick walls, replacing them with sandstone, from the top of which he could gaze across the Jamuna. Like Babur, his Mughal ancestor, he slept under the dome of Agra's fort dreaming of a land that was no longer the prize of invasion, but his very own. The man without a drop of Hindustan in his veins had made her the envy of the world. It was time for him to build his own capital.

The artists were eager to move to the new kitabkhana. Sikri would belong to them, not traders and journeymen, kite-sellers and whores. Musicians and poets too fancied its aloof grandeur. It wouldn't be like any other capital. Its artistry not limited to mosques and gigantic gates. In all its glory, it would provide a glimpse of the most precious – the heart of the emperor.

*

In the city's second year, the saint died. Akbar had a tomb built for him, a womb of white marble where men and women could enter to pray for a son.

*

Arriving in Sikri on a mule-cart with Salim Amiri, Bihzad was woken by the clamour of the bazaar. They had started from Agra before dawn to avoid travelling under the hot sun. He had slept, curled up in the cart, till the fruitsellers yelled into his ears. Fruitsellers, cornsellers, butchers and dressmakers – traders of every kind squatting at the village's centre, near the imperial walls. Salim Amiri had kept up a constant chatter with the cart-driver, nudging Bihzad from time to time to share his caustic views about the new capital.

'*This* is Sikri the village, and *that* is Fatehpur Sikri – the imperial city,' he said, pointing to the not too distant walls. 'The poor of Sikri have always lived here, and will live here for ever. Akbar won't let them into his palaces. It's a pity one must pass through the village to reach the city, rather than the open fields that lie on its other sides – more suitable for noblemen and women.'

They travelled on narrow and winding roads full of rocks, the cart swaying from side to side. The villagers, used to seeing courtiers, didn't give them a second look. Passing the last cluster of huts, they started to climb up a mild slope that would take them to the main entrance of the fortified city. As they left the bazaar, Bihzad started to doze again, ignoring Salim Amiri's constant stream of comments.

Arriving at the archway of the tallest of the six gates of Fatehpur Sikri, Bihzad heard the call of elephants and the thunder of drums. Yet he didn't raise his head as the mule-cart passed the royal mint and treasury, the stables for visitors, not even the entry to the royal court where petitioners waited in a long queue. He passed the Chief Executioner's quarters, but didn't look up to see the manacles, handcuffs, chains and irons hanging from the gateway. Salim Amiri nudged him awake, pointing at a party of soldiers leading a prisoner to a stone platform on which an elephant stood swishing its trunk. Bihzad saw a slightly ill-shaped man, eyes with small pupils, a prominent chin and a flowing beard, walking between the soldiers with his turban in his hand, eyes downcast.

'The book of his life shall end soon.' Salim Amiri said, staring grimly at the prisoner. 'Unless, of course, the elephant decides to spare his life. Then not even its keeper can make it change its mind, make it lift its foot to squash the man's head. Justice comes twice. Once from a man's tongue, and once from an animal's foot!'

'And if the elephant spares him?'

'Then he'll be set free. To roam and repeat his crime.'

The two sat in the mule-cart, waiting for the crowd to thin. For Salim Amiri, it was his usual visit, coming up from Agra with his supply of paints. He had offered to bring Bihzad along, the last of the artists to arrive in Sikri, owing to a bout of sickness that had kept him in Agra for a whole month after the kitabkhana had moved. Now there were no more artists left in the old capital, except the few rejected by the Khwaja and condemned to roam from haveli to haveli drawing for a pittance. Those with a broken thumb, or a jar of wine in their bellies, unable to hold a steady brush. Only Salim Amiri had had the heart to plead for them.

'Take them too,' he had called aloud to the Khwaja. 'Better kill an artist than treat him as worthless!'

Salim Amiri too had stayed behind, to care for his hundred and eleven year old grandmother. He had offered another reason as well. 'Remember, the colour you see on paper is born in a gutter!' Only an ugly old Agra, full of rotting plants and a dustbowl of rocks, held the ingredients for his paints. Sikri, he'd complain, was pure. Agra was vital for its bazaar, attracting merchants from the East and the West. The merchants brought precious items – turquoise from China and mother-of-pearl from the southern seas to decorate the leather-bound albums.

'Sikri enjoys, while Agra toils!' Salim Amiri had chosen to toil, coming up to Sikri's new kitabkhana from Agra every week with a mule-cart full of fresh paper and pots of colour.

A roar went up as the prisoner was made to kneel and rest his head on the platform. Chin up on the rock, he raised his eyes to the elephant, as if pleading in the last court of justice.

'Do you know why Akbar has escaped from Agra?' Seeing the intense look on Bihzad's face, Salim Amiri tried diverting his attention from the execution scene. 'Because he can't stand the nodding and frowning elders. The old and retired courtiers. Here, he'll be the master of the soul of his Hindustan, not just of her soil. He'll be supreme, choosing only those he wishes to spend his days and nights with. You'll be closer here to Akbar than anywhere else.'

The elephant brought down its foot on the convict's head.

Bihzad's face turned red, and started to twitch. His body, erect in the excitement of the execution, slumped back inside the mule-cart, and he lay with eyelids fluttering. Fearing a return of his boyhood fits, Salim Amiri spoke urgently into the ear of the cart-driver, who raised his whip. They went through the crowd at a gallop, distracting those who had drawn closer to the block to have a look at the crushed head. Holding Bihzad up by the shoulder, Salim Amiri wiped his own forehead with his turban, and glanced nervously at the row of guards lining the road. At the new kitabkhana, he jumped off and called aloud for the Khwaja. The driver helped him lift Bihzad from the seat and carry him inside, where they laid him down on the floor. He started shutting the windows one by one, darkening the room.

The Khwaja stood at the doorway and saw his Bihzad lying on the dark floor of the kitabkhana. Turning to Salim Amiri, he frowned, then opened a single window to cast a beam of light on Bihzad's pale face. Picking up an earthen pot, he knelt beside him and splashed the water on his head, patting it gently with the back of his palm. He called his boy.

'Bihzad.'

Bihzad opened his eyes. In a flash, he saw Akbar's face close to his. He shut his eyes, then opened them again. The worried face of his father appeared before him. The Khwaja, dressed in the robes of a courtier. He glanced sideways to the open window. Sikri glowed under the sun. Palaces of red stone, as if drenched in the blood of slaughter.

*

Gradually, he met the Khwaja's friends, the courtiers who had built their houses around the walls of Sikri in humble imitation of the emperor's palaces. He knew them as regular visitors to the kitabkhana. They came with their requests, to fill their personal albums, and even sometimes to inquire if the Darogha would secretly sell them a painting commissioned by Akbar himself.

Naubat Khan, the veena player, came to the workshop every week. He had a flatterer's tongue, full of talk. Conferring alone with the Darogha, he would try to pry into the recent imperial commissions. Then he'd offer to pay to have these paintings in advance of the emperor, in order to present them to him, and so solicit his favours. 'He gives paper and gets elephants back!' the artists joked.

The physician Ismael Safawi came too. He was ill-tempered and mean, talented, it was said, but congenitally mad. Some said his real skill lay in the forbidden art of curing his patients by speaking with the dead. Like the Paymaster General and the Chief Executioner, he too was willing to pay for a copy of the

*Akbarnama.* Among the courtiers, a race was on to be the first to possess it. 'Then,' the Darogha winked, 'The lucky one will boast that Akbar himself presented it to him as his most trusted man.'

Murtaza Beg, the philosopher, was the only one who went past the Darogha's chamber and sat with the artists. A man of universal curiosity, he was reputed to be a brilliant inventor. Murtaza Beg came, not to order his paintings, but to observe the artists at work.

The poet Abdullah came to quarrel with the Darogha, demanding that his lines be set in colour and offered to Akbar.

From his quarters next door to the new kitabkhana, Bihzad heard the visitors clearly. He met them too in his room near the Darogha's at the centre of the workshop. Although smaller in size than Agra's kitabkhana, the Sikri workshop was built to be more open, with multiple windows allowing one's sight to wander among the various rooms. Bihzad sat in the room designated for the master of the kitabkhana, but he wasn't the 'Khwaja' yet. The emperor had decided that the Khwaja would retain his title, although henceforth he would have little to do with the kitabkhana. Instead, Bihzad would lead the artists in the *Akbarnama* project. It was also Akbar's wish to hold the matter of succession in abeyance till Bihzad was old enough. The Khwaja now came to the kitabkhana as one of many visitors, sat with the Darogha and exchanged pleasantries. Bihzad took his place, selecting scenes from the emperor's chronicles to depict in the miniatures. He assigned tasks to junior artists, sketched scenes to be coloured by the colourists and examined the finished paintings. But, he was excused from attending all imperial events. The Darogha stood in for him, providing for the needs of the artists, calculating their rewards, presenting their works to the court. The Darogha has become the Khwaja, the junior artists whispered.

Although he was free to mix with the others, unlike his days in Agra, Bihzad still kept to himself – sitting alone in his room, arriving and returning late from the kitabkhana. But, he no longer felt trapped by his solitude. In its place, a wondrous anticipation kept him awake at all hours of the day and night.

Akbar! *You'll be closer here to Akbar than anywhere else...* he recalled Salim Amiri saying. Unlike some of his fellow artists, he hadn't suffered at the move from Agra to Sikri, shared none of their contempt for the emperor's whims. In the last few months before leaving Agra, he'd quarrel frequently with the paintseller. 'He's squandering his fortunes,' Salim Amiri would complain. 'Akbar has gone mad.' Agra is eternal, he'd say. 'What's not here, isn't anywhere.'

From his loneliness in Agra's kitabkhana and his loneliness in their haveli, he had dreamt of Akbar's Sikri. What could be more pleasurable than to sit before him – face to face? To draw his portrait, wait while he issued an order to his servant, then resume drawing. What could be more exciting than to be invited back to receive the emperor's praise in person?

'Agra, Agra, Agra...!' he had quarrelled with Salim Amiri. 'What's Agra without Akbar?'

*

For a whole year Bihzad admired Akbar's dream, from the window of his room at the kitabkhana. 'This,' he remembered the excited voice of the philosopher Murtaza Beg, 'is the dream of an artist born with a sword in his hand!' He would stare at the intricate marble lattice surrounding the House of Dreams, the emperor's living quarters, hoping to catch sight of a pair of eyes peering out. His gaze fleeted from palaces to towers, from court-yards to elaborate baths. Everywhere, he saw the care of thousands of artists and builders. Unlike Agra, where all was in profusion, here he saw a measured brilliance, the awe of the empire frozen within carved walls. This is what it feels like to live in a painting, he said to himself. He started to imagine himself as a figure in a classical miniature – a chess-player, a prince, a visiting emissary. He felt the harmony of lines surrounding him, the subtle intoxication of colours, the comfort of a story within a story. He felt strangely relaxed peering out of his window, yet every time his eye returned to the blank sheet propped up on his knees, a thousand questions entered his mind.

'You are alone,' Salim Amiri tried to explain when Bihzad confided in him during one of his visits. 'It is not like Agra. There you had your father and Zuleikha. Even in your room you were surrounded by others, by their breathing. Now, you must listen to your own breathing.' He hesitated, then added an afterthought. 'You must forget your old love and wait for the new.'

The Khwaja was also in Sikri, but he spent his time now at the mint where he was the master, not in the artists' kitabkhana. He was respected still among the artists, still the *Shirin Qalam* – the Sweet Pen – father of their future master, Bihzad.

'Your father is busy ...' Salim Amiri frowned. Everyone knew the Khwaja was busy, running under the emperor's order to build three new mints across his far-flung empire. Busy, half of Sikri whispered, with his new concubine, a dancer from his own Persia.

'Agra is more beautiful now. Like a forsaken lover.' Salim Amiri sighed. 'The rose has left the garden. Now the thorns must comfort each other.'

Strolling in the courtyard that separated the kitabkhana from the royal enclosure, Bihzad admired the five-storeyed pagoda where Akbar's Muslim wives came to see the new moon, and his Hindu wives waited for the full moon. Even before arriving in Sikri, he had known the landmarks, each tinged with a special story concerning the emperor. He had heard the fables that followed Akbar wherever he went, like his love for riding elephants when they were at their frightening best – in heat. Downing a few cups of wine, he'd call for Hawai, his favourite elephant, then set it to race against another. His courtiers worried over his strange passion, his ministers forbade the keepers to parade the elephants before Akbar during the mating season, ordered a daily feed of opium. The harem rushed to the latticed windows and started to wail as soon as Akbar took off his turban in preparation for mounting, and court astrologers were hastily summoned to predict the event's outcome. The beasts would charge at each other, blowing a sandstorm, shaking the pillars of Sikri's giant gates. Even their keepers would cower at their fury.

Occasionally, a spectator or two would be killed under the elephants' feet, and sometimes the beasts killed each other, dying from the impact of their collision, or the wounds from their tusks. Fable had Akbar always victorious. Sitting upright on his Hawai, appearing drunk yet unharmed.

From the window of his kitabkhana room, Bihzad could catch a glimpse of Akbar's private courtyard where he was said to play chess on a red sandstone court, using gaily dressed slave girls as live pieces. Going to meet his father at the mint, he'd stop before the walled maze, hoping to hear the squeals of women playing hide and seek with Akbar inside. He knew the precise reason why the emperor had built each building and for whom, including his favourite Deer Tower, whose winding staircase led onto a battlement where the emperor could aim his gun at the deer grazing below over the open fields. But Akbar was invisible.

For a whole year, Bihzad searched for Akbar among his courtiers, in the city of his dream. He woke early, waiting under the jharokha window with scores of subjects, for a glimpse. He went regularly past the Chamber of Dreams and the heavily guarded entrance to the royal court, peered through his window at the chess courtyard. When not in his living quarters or the kitabkhana room, he'd prowl the many enclosures, climb up the stairs of the imperial offices, walk around the fortified city from one end to the other, visiting each of the six gates. He went to the farthest edge of the boundary wall, hoping to catch the emperor in his favourite sport, waiting in vain to see Akbar's elephant fight.

But the *Akbarnama* kept him busy. The emperor's biographer worked at a hectic pace, flooding the kitabkhana with page after page of minute detail. Akbar at war. Akbar in his court listening to edicts read out in his name. Akbar measuring the size of a giant cannon ball. Akbar at the imperial stable. Akbar visiting a holy man. The colourists complained of sore thumbs, new artists stood in files before the kitabkhana like prisoners of war. Salim Amiri rode his mule-cart from Agra to Sikri so often that the guards did not know whether he was leaving or arriving.

'What's wrong with painting pictures by the hundred, like

casting cannon balls for the armoury?' Salim Amiri smiled at Bihzad's glum face. 'And what's wrong with a hundred artists following one master, as if each painting flowed from the same brush?'

Bihzad knew Salim Amiri was teasing him. He recalled his elderly teacher. 'Even Mir Sayyid Ali would encourage his students to draw as if the miniature belonged to them, not to their master.'

'Yes... That's why Mir Sayyid Ali has left, Bihzad. Akbar doesn't want artists. He wants a thousand cannon balls. More. A thousand paintings bearing his face. What do you think he'll do with the *Akbarnama* when it's finished? He'll make the artists copy it, over and over, then send it out to his vassals. He wants his edicts to reach every part of his empire. He wants his subjects to recognise his face.'

'But he values the extraordinary,' Bihzad protested. 'He rewards the best, tosses aside the flawed ones.'

'Yes, Bihzad. That's why he has chosen you. You are his best. But he doesn't need more Bihzads. Just one to teach the others.' Salim Amiri paused. 'Tell me, is every brick of Sikri different?'

Bihzad sat brooding. Then he spoke with a serious face. 'If he truly wants what you say, then he'll have to convince his artists. He'll have to convince the master of the kitabkhana to stop being an artist and become a clerk.'

'Yes, Bihzad. Maybe that's why Akbar hasn't chosen him yet. He is waiting.' Then he advised Bihzad to be cautious on the matter of succession. It was far from certain, despite what was said. 'Beware of the chameleon. The Afghan. As long as he is within Akbar's sight, he can do mischief. You *will* be the new Khwaja, but first you may have to suffer his sting!'

Bihzad recalled seeing Adili, hurrying across the vast palace courtyard of Sikri towards Akbar's personal quarters. The emperor had summoned Adili, the Darogha said later, to draw the likeness of a beautiful falcon recently presented to him. 'He drew quickly,' the Darogha reported, 'the falcon staring angrily at the fast moving brush.'

'The Little Master!' Adili would tease Bihzad when he came to visit the Darogha, his friend. He was the only artist in Sikri who had received the emperor's permission to work apart from the kitabkhana, claiming a rare affliction that prevented him from following the workshop's heavy routine. He lived beyond the city walls in his own house with four wives and zealous eunuchs.

'It's a lie, of course – this sickness of his,' Salim Amiri told Bihzad. 'Because of him, your father is anxious, I have heard. He is eager for you to take your rightful place among the courtiers.'

Why did he need a private artist to draw his falcon? Bihzad brooded over the Darogha's description of Adili's meeting with Akbar. No wonder he drew so swiftly, he must have drawn a portrait of the emperor too, secretly, without his knowledge.

'It isn't enough to be a great artist, one must be clever enough to become known as one,' Salim Amiri spoke in his usual way, confusing Bihzad.

He protested instantly. 'No. Either you *are* one or you aren't. It's a pity the Darogha can't judge properly, or he wouldn't have wasted a moment looking at Adili's paintings.'

Salim Amiri laughed. 'You are still a child, Bihzad. Paintings are for the human eye, aren't they? Eyes that frequently err, that are full of envy, drunk with power. The world can live without a great artist, but it can't live without hate. Even your father had to please many a fool to become what he is.'

'Akbar isn't a fool. He can tell ...'

'Yes ...' Salim Amiri smiled kindly. 'But he is less interested in the kitabkhana now. The ibadatkhana is more important to him.'

'You mean The House of Worship?'

Salim Amiri nodded yes. Bihzad already knew about the Ibadatkhana. He had heard the peculiar story about how it had started. In the middle of an imperial hunt, the emperor supposedly saw a vision and fell to the ground. He was paralysed, unable to move or speak. Wild animals surrounded him, he was in grave danger. Then, when he regained his senses, he ordered the killing to stop. 'Enough!' he said. 'A man shouldn't make his stomach the grave of animals.' At his courtiers' urgings, he had agreed to hunt in the future, but only on special occasions, banning the massive qamargahs.

Salim Amiri continued, 'These days he spends his time listening to the Koran from those who have learnt it by heart. He has started to meditate. Even counts beads like a Sufi, I'm told. But ...'

'But?'

'But now he wishes to know more. He has brought men of faith, of *all* faiths to his House of Worship. Sunni and Shia, Brahmins, Sufis, Jains, Jews, Parsees, even the Nazarene sages from Goa.'

Bihzad had heard that gossip too, at the kitabkhana. 'These men are putting the world to flames, turning everything upside down. Making a day of night and a night of day. These men are playing with our faiths ...'

A smile crossed Salim Amiri's face. 'He chooses the colour of his robes according to the position of the sun and the planets. Purple and violet for Jupiter, blue for Saturn ...'

'Better a Shia than a Sunni, a Parsee than a Jew, a Jew than a Christian, a dog than a worshipper of cows' – Bihzad recalled the physician Ismael Safawi's angry outburst when someone had mentioned the Ibadatkhana in his presence. He remembered too what the Chief Executioner had said when he heard that Akbar had decided to release his slaves, and delay all executions for a day till the court had time to reconsider the condemned prisoners' sentences. The man, normally reticent, had bubbled up before the Darogha and the inquisitive artists. 'Better for him to abandon all this,' he had pointed at the ibadatkhana, 'and go to war. The wrath of the emperor is good for his subjects.'

*

For a whole year and more, Bihzad drew just as the Khwaja would have wished. For the first new moon of the twentieth regnal year, he painted the emperor in a handsome robe of honour, a gold-embroidered tunic, a jewelled dagger, two superb steeds with gilt saddles, and a splendid elephant accompanied by its mate.

'A portrait that speaks!' The Darogha could barely conceal his excitement.

Whenever the Khwaja came to visit the kitabkhana, he'd ask to see Bihzad's work. 'Show me your mischief!' he would call aloud, then he would sit on the floor, the paintings propped up across his bent knees, the buttons of his tunic on the verge of bursting as usual. Bihzad watched him in silence. The Persian artist, among the very first to have arrived over the Hindukush, charming the warrior Mughals with his brush. He wished to ask if it was true – if indeed he had drawn for Akbar's father a whole army on a grain of rice. Despite the growing distance between them, he wanted to ask if the Khwaja missed their haveli in Agra, if he would ever return. Despite the rift he sensed between his father and Salim Amiri, and despite the rumours in Sikri, the man he saw was not the emperor's favourite courtier, but the master who'd rise early with him and wait by the fort's tower to catch the mischief of the sun.

He decided to ask his father about Akbar. If the emperor would appear in person to sit for his portrait. The Khwaja seemed surprised.

'But you have already drawn his likeness. He is happy.'

'But he is different now.' Bihzad reminded him that his portrait of Akbar was only a copy of the Khwaja's own, drawn more than a year ago. The Khwaja frowned as if trying to remember.

'He shows no sign of ageing. The empire's troubles have added no lines to his face. His hair is as black as ever, his skin ...'

'It is important for an artist to see his subject.'

The Khwaja stopped. 'But he doesn't grant personal audience ...'

'Except for Adili, you mean.'

'Adili?'

'When he painted the emperor's new falcon.'

'But that's different, Bihzad. The emperor has a good reason to record everything that looks unusual. Unusual or strikingly beautiful.'

'And his artists have good reason to see him in unusual settings. How he fights, how he pardons his enemy, how he prays, how he dresses in disguise and enters his harem ...'

The Khwaja laughed. He turned to the Darogha, who had been sitting silently in the corner. 'Maybe you should take him to the court, make him stand for hours for a glimpse of the royal feet!'

'It is unlawful to enter his sight without his permission,' the Darogha said grimly.

'Then tell him,' Bihzad cast an angry look, 'that the master of the kitabkhana begs the favour of entering his sight.'

'The master?' The Darogha raised an eyebrow.

'He will himself ask to see you.' The Khwaja calmed his son. 'When you've completed the *Akbarnama*, he'll praise you in public, offer gifts. You must wait for the time to come.'

\*

*You'll be closer here to Akbar than anywhere else.* Salim Amiri had lied to him. As months went by, he painted not one but two separate albums. The *Akbarnama* by day, and his own *Akbarnama* by night. Drew and painted furiously. Akbar and himself, riding on the same horse – a pair of arms wrapped around the emperor's waist. The two admiring a rare parrot, laughing at its words. Akbar lying on the banks of the Jamuna, blood gushing from his head after a fall from his favourite Hawai. Lying still as if he were dead, and a sobbing Bihzad kneeling beside him, touching his closed eyes with his fingers. He drew Akbar in his bath, naked to his waist, pulling off the last shred of cloth covering the modesty of his artist friend.

He hid his special paintings carefully under blank sheaves, away from prying eyes. Hid them carefully to avoid losing them, as he had lost the previous ones, when the kitabkhana had moved from its old home to the new.

\*

For a whole year and more, Bihzad kept up his vigil. Then he thought he had seen him at last, at dusk, a man sweeping dust off the marble tomb of the dead saint like a lowly servant. Akbar? Just as he had seen him at the imperial hunt, he saw the same stature – narrow waist, long arms, the broad forehead. Climbing up the Deer Tower secretly, he hoped to surprise the emperor, but found it empty. The hunters had gathered below, their torches fleeting across the darkness, glowing like the eyes of the deer.

ikri to Shaitanpura. Shaitanpura – Satan's Palace – the infamous brothel of Agra. At first, Bihzad asked Shaibaq Khan, the inspector of Sikri's imperial kitchen, a regular visitor, to take him along hidden under a pile of empty baskets in his mule-cart. After they passed the heavily guarded gateway, Shaibaq, elegantly dressed for the evening, would glance back and flick the baskets lightly with his whip. Then Bihzad would come out, brushing off the kitchen scraps from his tunic, and sit next to him. Shaibaq hid a coarse laugh under his breath. 'She'll smell rotten eggs on your precious parts!'

Then Bihzad became bolder. He started to go every evening on the mule-carts which went back from Sikri to Agra with the returning labourers or the poor who had come with their petitions to the court. He would show his face proudly to the sentries, pretend he had urgent business. The future master of the kitabkhana visiting a patron in the old capital, the guards whispered, before they grew accustomed to seeing him return, drunk, sprawled in the back of a mule-cart or held up by its frightened driver.

The first time in Shaitanpura, he had surprised his hostess, the elderly Madam of the brothel dressed piously in white muslin, as she led Bihzad into a room full of young and elderly men waiting for a contest between two poets to begin. The room was full, a candle placed before each of the contestants. The Madam whispered the rules into Bihzad's ear. Each poet would blow out his own candle after he had finished reciting his verse. The next would then light his and make his reply. Out of the corner of his eye, Bihzad saw Salim Amiri. After a round of excuses and coaxing from the audience, the first words were spoken by one of the poets.

> This candle leaves no shadow
> Touch it, dear friend, with the tip of your tongue
> And watch the flame glow

Shouts of approval rose from the crowd. Cups were raised, the poet made as if to kiss the flaming candle, then blew it out. His rival wetted his tongue, made a defiant gesture with his arms.

> Which flame do you speak of, dear friend
> Kiss now the wick
> Of your flaming soul

Vah! Vah! Vah! the men applauded, removing their caps.

> Kiss now your dead lover, for she is the bee
> Kiss her now
> Before her wax turns to stone

Then again, the other poet.

> Kiss now...

The room filled with voices taking up the refrain. Kiss now! Kiss now! Kiss now! Kiss now! Candles were lit and blown out in rapid succession. Cups rattled to the rhythm of stamping feet.

Bihzad stood up and left the room. Stopping the Madam as she was ushering in new visitors, he abruptly demanded to know where the whores were.

'Oh, the dancers. The singing girls, you mean...'

'The whores.' He demanded to know where in the whorehouse the whores were hiding.

It was against the custom, the elderly hostess protested, too early for a young man to visit a lady privately. He must listen to the poets first, then join a majlis – a musical soirée. He must taste the wine in many rooms before tasting it from his own consort for the night.

Bihzad started climbing up the stairs towards the private

chambers, the Madam in pursuit. 'Stop!' she called out behind him. Perhaps he would like to visit the courtesan who entertained her 'friends' with naughty stories of the wedding night. She clung to his robe as she made a final offer: a glimpse into a private chamber through a secret window.

Bihzad turned and blew a cloud of wine on to her face. 'Kiss now!'

He entered a room, its floor covered in a spotless white sheet, shining mirrors lining its walls, and silk hanging from the ceiling like a canopy. He thought he heard laughter, and expected to find a lady and her visitor. But the room was empty. He stood looking at his reflections in the mirrors, forgetting where he was, till the loud bang of the door behind him brought him back, the click of the key and the laughter of the Madam.

*

On later occasions, he'd sit listening to the poets quietly, drinking one cup of wine after another. Like father, like son, those who recognised him said. He sat with his chin on his chest, as if meditating, appearing to follow the poets, even cheering them with his eyes closed. But the other regulars came to expect the unexpected from him. In the middle of a contest, he'd suddenly sit up and accuse a poet of stealing a line from another. He'd argue cogently, as if completely sober. Why should one enjoy the praise due to another? Bihzad would keep on interrupting until the Madam took him out of the room to listen to a courtesan's secrets.

He would walk in the labyrinth of streets surrounding Satan's Palace, mumbling to himself. Those who saw him mistook him for a luckless trader, or a peasant robbed in the bazaar. Sometimes, even Shaibaq refused to take him back to Sikri on his mule-cart. 'The soldiers at the gate will take you for a robber!'

Yet there were other times when he dressed like an elegant courtier himself, overcoming the Madam's suspicions and gaining entry into the special chambers reserved for private visits. He sat on the floor before a lady listening to her singing, tasting the sweets from her hand, and as the evening advanced, lay down with her under the canopy, becoming one with the reflections in the mirrors.

He puzzled the courtesans of Shaitanpura. At once the lotus and her bee, they said of Bihzad.

*

Back at the kitabkhana, there was not much to trouble the Darogha. The Little Master kept him busy counting the imperial rewards. What took others a month, Bihzad finished in a week. The race for the *Akbarnama* was on, between the biographer and the artist. But the kitabkhana seemed more than equal to the challenge, with the artists well settled into their new home. One saw less of Salim Amiri, though, than before. He blamed his grandmother's health, but the artists knew the truth. The friendship between the Khwaja and his paintseller, two Persians together among the Mughals in Hindustan, was now the story of parting streams. One had remained in his crumbling haveli in Agra, the other had become Akbar's favourite, as trusted as his courtiers and generals. The Khwaja was a new man in his new mint, distrustful, it was said, of those who had known him simply as an artist. It was unseemly for him to be seen in the company of a poor paintseller. He was troubled too, by men like Salim Amiri who spoke so openly about everything, often questioning the wisdom of the emperor, and wished no part of the gossip that came up from Agra in his mule-cart. The Khwaja had distanced himself from his friend, everyone knew.

The Darogha had sensed the change and moved quickly, inviting other paintsellers to bring up their mule-carts to Sikri.

To Bihzad, Salim Amiri was still the one with the entire wisdom of the world from creation till today on the tip of his tongue. He'd still confuse Bihzad with his lofty words whenever he came to meet him in his kitabkhana room after his business with the Darogha. 'Fools burn candles. These poets stealing words from each other to keep their flames alive. They should've learned from Rumi... *Ah! The dying light, free at last from pride and shame...*'

They made no mention of having seen each other at Satan's Palace.

Bihzad asked Salim Amiri about the House of Worship. 'Is it true Akbar has stopped being a Muslim?'

Salim Amiri smiled. 'What makes you think he's no longer a Muslim?'

'What if his subjects believe so?'

'Tell me, Bihzad, will you bury a man alive if fifty men tell you he's dead?'

Bihzad didn't ask Salim Amiri if he could help him to meet Akbar. If his father wouldn't help him, how could a mere paintseller? Instead he asked Salim Amiri what he thought about the Darogha. He seemed to Bihzad to be the only friend of Adili, didn't seem to mind that he held private meetings with Akbar. And he was the only one who seemed reluctant to treat Bihzad as the future master. Did the elderly man with his straight moustache and neatly cropped white hair not wish Bihzad to succeed his father?

'He still brings up the contest every now and then. As if *I*, the chief *Akbarnama* artist, must still prove that I am better than others.'

'The barbarian! He should've retired and left for Mecca.'

'The Darogha won't let me see Akbar,' Bihzad blurted out.

After a moment or two of silence, Salim Amiri turned his twinkling eyes on Bihzad. 'Then why don't you ask Adili to help you?'

The paintseller's words took Bihzad by surprise. 'Adili? But why…'

'You possess that which nobody can destroy. Not even Akbar. But you must enter his sight for him to know and honour you properly, even if it means asking help from an enemy. You mustn't allow a cloud to shield the sun.'

'But the Afghan has vowed to be second to none. He thinks that *he*, over all others at Sikri, should be Akbar's artist.'

'Then you mustn't allow the emperor to err,' Salim Amiri winked.

*

There were days when he went back to Agra to visit Zuleikha. Finding his way around the old haveli, he'd enter her room and sit on her bed. She'd rise immediately and go over to the window, her face turned away from him. Bihzad smelt the breeze passing through her hair. She'd speak to him, eyes still averted, scolding him for his long absence, or pretending it was she who had called him to her door.

Gradually, he had come to understand the reason for her strange behaviour. Why she had refused to join the Khwaja in Sikri, choosing to remain alone with her maid in the deserted haveli. Why she had stayed on in Agra, in the face of vicious gossip that had found free rein after the Khwaja's departure. Why she had courted ruin, kept on stirring the vats of perfume even after the harem had left. Bit by bit, he had remembered her words, some spoken in jest, others after their bouts with wine and majun.

She had married an artist, Zuleikha had told him. 'Do you know what an artist is, Bihzad? The purest of the pure. The only one who dares to do what Allah has done – give life to form. It isn't wine that sullies an artist, not even the lovebites of a whore, but his greed. When he sacrifices his gift – his dreams – for the clever craft of his fingers.' Your Khwaja, she'd tell Bihzad, had stopped being an artist soon after their marriage, 'when he had married Akbar's kitabkhana.' He was on his way now to becoming a courtier – a man destined for much wealth, many wives, but few loves. She wouldn't sigh at her misfortune, but his. 'Can you imagine, he could once soothe the pangs of war with the mere stroke of a brush!'

Bihzad would point at the perfume jars, lined up beside her bed. 'For whom?' he'd ask her. 'For what?' His stepmother would snap back angrily. 'Use? A fragrance doesn't need anyone. They are not like your Khwaja's paintings – dead without Akbar's blessings.'

She'd chide him. 'Now it's your turn. To follow your father, to please the emperor, become what you are not.'

'No.' He'd try to shut her mouth.

'No? Then prove it to me, Bihzad. Prove it …'

Visiting her from Sikri, he sat facing her on her bed. She spoke with laughter in her voice. 'I have sent my scent your way to bring you here.'

87

Bihzad smiled. 'And I've come, like the blind fish of spring, unable to escape.'

'And how far is your ocean? Does it have clouds and rain too, like our poor Agra?'

They paused after each had spoken, just long enough to blow out a candle. She didn't wear mourning garb, as was often the custom among those whose husbands were alive but with someone else. Only rarely did she speak about how it was living alone with her maid in the haveli. Still surrounded by the wreaths for her perfumes, she'd tell stories to Bihzad, reading them not out of a book but from the open sky through her window.

'There was once a woman among artists. She was born Nadira, but she called herself Makhfi – the one concealed. Those who saw her work claimed there was no artist like her in this age. But she was ugly, her eyes were small and red-rimmed, she had a beard on her chin, a withered neck. Dazzling rings couldn't disguise her gnarled fingers.'

Zuleikha turned to face Bihzad. 'Do you know what she was most fond of drawing?'

He kept silent.

'Herself. Yes, her ugly face. She painted like no one else could. Viewers were puzzled at first, then some grew angry, thinking she was fooling them. But eventually they too became fond of her ugly face, spent hours gazing at it, begged her to draw more. She made her viewers happy, when they compared themselves to the ugly artist. When she grew old, the angels arrived at her door at the hour of death to record her sins and good deeds. Do you know what she said, Bihzad? She said "my sin was not to show them their ugliness." "And your good deed?" the angels asked. "To make them feel happy despite their ugliness." '

Bihzad sat on Zuleikha's bed, drawing from his mind the face of the one concealed.

'You, Bihzad, must make the ugly look beautiful, mustn't you?'

He growled at her.

Then there were days when he arrived at her door drunk from Satan's Palace, his tunic ripped through the front showing marks on his fair skin. He remembered the gossip he heard about the Khwaja's wife at Sikri. 'You could banish her to a desert on the back of a camel, she'd still seduce a hundred men!' He could hear a toothless Naubat Khan. 'She can cure a dying leper with a glance! The Bilkis of our age, a rose from the garden of Rum!'

He looked at her as a lion looks at a gazelle. She shut his eyes with her palm, started removing a thorn from his foot with a fine needle.

'What if I was carrying your child...'

With the murderous look still in his eyes, he asked if she would come to Sikri with him, to his own quarters next to the new kitabkhana.

'Sikri? You mean the emperor's playground. But it's different, Bihzad. It's the pleasure of the bee not of the lotus. A woman's pleasure is different from the pleasure of kings.'

He tried to argue with her. Sikri was no different from Agra. If she could live so close to the emperor here, why not...

'No, it's *not* the same. In Sikri, everyone will become his prisoner. He'll love them till they're reduced to a mere shadow – Akbar's shadow.'

When he persisted, she shut his mouth again. 'What would you do with me in Sikri? The Little Master with his stepmother! Should I be in Akbar's harem then, become his courtesan? Plotting with the begums behind each other's backs? Do you want the lotus to turn into a shameless rose, too eager to share her fragrance? Or do you want me at Satan's Palace...'

There'd be times when he'd ask her for her ring, or for a bracelet to pay for the wine he drank at Satan's Palace. He'd point to her jewels – her glimmering ears, forehead, arms, waist. She'd feign alarm... 'I can't be naked in your presence!' Then, he'd start to cast off his Persian turban, the ripped tunic. Her laughter would lift her veil. She'd remind the Khwaja's son of the day she had first entered the haveli – the very day of his circumcision.

'We shed blood together!' she whispered into his ears, as they tumbled on her bed.

*

Returning on the mule-cart, he'd start to dream, begin tossing and turning, wailing like a young camel. The driver would be alarmed. He'd stop, peer into Bihzad's face, then shrink back at the stink of wine and vomit.

He dreamt of unions – at once pleasurable and searing, inflicting a thousand wounds. He saw Zuleikha with Akbar, Zuleikha with Bihzad, Bihzad and the emperor. Three pairs of arms clasped at his ripped tunic, three pairs of eyes, he tasted three pairs of lips.

'Akbar!' he'd scream, clutching on to Zuleikha in his dreams. He'd weep uncontrollably for his stepmother. Wasn't it enough to have left the Khwaja…why did she have to leave him too… he'd plead with her.

*

At twenty-five, the khanazad – the one born on the steps of the artists' workshop – he was just the courtier in waiting, as he was expected to be. Other than a clipped beard, he looked no different than on the day he had entered Sikri, still a Persian face, even rarer now among the men of the empire. Praise for his miniatures came from those familiar with the likes of Mirak and Muzaffar; his father, it was said, hadn't named him in vain. Just like the Exalted Master, he too – the Little Master – marked each of his paintings with a rare gift, turning simple form into pure spirit.

Even his visits to Shaitanpura didn't raise more than an eyebrow in Sikri. It was common for a boy of his age. Hadn't wine existed before the creation of grapes? All that was expected, even his rashness that troubled the Madam, just as it was expected that Akbar should tame a wild elephant. How else would he become a man, if not in the company of whores? When Akbar proclaimed him master, he wouldn't need Satan's Palace any more. He'd have his own palace. Then he'd be like his father and the other courtiers. Just a few moons in waiting.

On the twenty-second of Shahrivar, corresponding to the seventeenth of Rajab, the solar weighing ceremony was held in Sikri. The astrologers had marked the day as auspicious by both the Persian and Mughal calendars, and it was decided to weigh the emperor twelve times, each time against a different item: gold, quicksilver, bags full of precious stones, bolts of silk, sandalwood, cotton, rare spices, flour, sugar, fragrant mangoes, Kashmiri melons, and opium. It was customary to thank Allah for the emperor's health, by weighing Akbar each year and distributing the items among the poor. His sons and a few favourite courtiers were invited to present the items as gifts, with the emperor returning the favours at the end of the ceremony. In addition to the weighing, one sheep, one goat and one chicken were gifted to an orphan child for every year of the emperor's life.

Akbar sat in a small room with open doorways on all four sides. To his east was the audience hall, to the west his mother's private chamber in the harem, north the oratory, and south a giant courtyard with an octagonal platform in the middle. He wore the colours of Jupiter – a purple-hued turban, a yellow cummerbund, a pendant set with sapphires – and sat on a black touchstone pedestal. His arms bearer sat on a carpet just below him, and facing him three princes knelt with their servants standing behind bearing gifts. The ladies, seated on silk carpets with the emperor's mother, watched the proceedings through a latticed screen.

The eldest prince, barely in his teens, stepped forward, placed the palm of his right hand over his head and bowed. The emperor embraced his son and kissed his forehead. Then he rose and went over to the giant weighing scales, sitting down on one of the brocaded pans. The prince started pouring a jar of gold coins into the pan, whispering the number of each jar to his servant. At the count of ten, Akbar sat in perfect balance with the gold.

The courtiers, sitting on carpets in the audience hall, cheered. A horn sounded from the Herald Tower.

Then the emperor's second son stepped forward with a tray full of silver.

Between weighings, the emperor returned to his pedestal, eunuchs standing behind, flapping away flies, agitating the air with peacock-tailed fans. Priests of various religious orders filed by praying for his good health. Then, for the sixth weighing, the emperor invited a senior courtier, Birbal, to step forward and present his gift. The Hindu rajah was famous for his wit; Akbar was known to be fond of his stories, and had built a palace for him in Sikri close to his own. The two men embraced. Birbal sat at Akbar's feet and stacked the pan with reams of milk-white cotton. As he placed each offering, he glanced at the other pan, to check if it was about to rise. With each ream, the emperor rose an inch. When the last of Birbal's offerings fell short of levelling the pans, the emperor kept on smiling. A servant was despatched to fetch more, but he returned unsuccessful. Sikri was empty of cotton. The rajah called a eunuch and whispering into his ear, asked for rose water to be sprinkled over the cotton. But Akbar raised his hand; it would be unfair he said, casting a challenging look at Birbal. Then the rajah took off his white turban and placed it in the pan. A round of applause went up, and the two men embraced again.

'It would've been easier if he'd asked his wife to send a lock of her hair!' Naubat Khan whispered to the Paymaster General standing next to him. In the audience hall, the courtiers were becoming impatient. It was the time for giving and receiving gifts. Servants flitted in and out of the room bearing trays of rose syrup and sweets.

'What would he have offered next if it hadn't been enough? Taken off the rest?' The poet Abdullah was more caustic. He was tired of waiting his turn to congratulate the emperor. But before the remaining courtiers could come up one by one from the audience hall to the emperor's chamber and present their gifts, Birbal escorted the Persian emissary to Akbar to read aloud the Shah's gifts, which were too numerous to display. With a hand over his heart, the emissary started, 'Praise God. The sapling of yearning has borne the fruit of destiny. May the breeze of prayer that causes the rosebud to bloom and perfume the divine nostrils, the flash of lightning that casts away the darkness from the celestial mind, bind us as brothers like our mighty fathers and forefathers. Praise God, may our faces turn towards his magnificence, may his blessed land be held safe from the blight of evil eyes. Praise God, may...' At the end of the long salutation, the list of gifts – fine horses, mules, camels, and rare black foxes – was read out, which kept the imperial chronicler busy.

'What if Akbar had killed the poor animals on their way to Hindustan!' Naubat Khan could hardly contain his laughter at Ismael Safawi's comment.

'The Lords of Persia and Hindustan exchanging animals like shepherds!'

The Paymaster General presented a small crystal chest of European manufacture. Its sides were transparent, so that anything that was put inside could be seen clearly. The inspector of the imperial kitchen offered a tray of fruits, some real, some made from precious stones: a Kabuli cherry made from amethyst, a polished sandstone disguised as a Kashmiri apple. The Khwaja had brought a fur shawl, the physician a jewelled saddle, Murtaza Beg a rare and priceless manuscript.

Then it was Akbar's turn to return the favours.

'They give only so they can take away!' The poet Abdullah spat out the words. He was angry at Birbal, at the courtiers, at the eunuchs for making him wait so long to deliver his own gift – his poems, which had been specially composed for the occasion.

Akbar called one of his servants to approach him. The poor

man had almost died last year saving the emperor's life, tasting the poison slipped into his drinking water by a secret palace enemy. Akbar presented him with a rare rose-coloured horse. Then he asked the eunuchs to carry around trays of gold coins. Take as much as you wish, he announced to his courtiers. As much as their palms could hold, and as much as their consciences allowed. There was a murmur in the audience hall as the courtiers hesitated, torn between reaching out for the trays and holding back.

'He's up to his old tricks,' Naubat Khan grimaced at the Paymaster General.

After the weighing, servants carried the items out of the emperor's chamber, to be distributed among the poor who had gathered outside the imperial walls. A fair had started there, with acrobats and jugglers, and tight-rope walkers who had stretched their rope high above the ground, performing breathtaking feats. Below them, craftsmen had set up stalls, ready to delight the villagers who had come from afar for the occasion.

Inside the palace walls, the court musicians took their seats on the octagonal platform at the centre of the courtyard, facing the emperor in his chamber, the courtiers assembled in the audience hall, and the ladies watching through the screen. Suddenly, to everyone's surprise, water began to flow in through secret channels until the vast courtyard, except for the octagonal island, was submerged. At Akbar's command, the musicians began the Garland of Melody – a string of ragas chosen from the very best of Hindustan.

Bihzad rose from his seat in the audience hall. Around him, the courtiers were dozing, the music soothing their nerves and tired feet. The sound of snoring floated above them. Naubat Khan slept with his mouth open, as if in the middle of a sentence; Ismael Safawi grasped a pillow in both hands as if examining a patient; the Khwaja, overcome with wine, sat with his head on one side, crushing a rose between his enormous turban and a stone pillar.

Walking steadily, Bihzad sidestepped the courtiers in the audience hall. The servants guarding the presents didn't think to look up as he passed them. Dressed as a courtier himself, he didn't arouse suspicion, except when he paused at the western doorway, and then quickened his pace. The musicians had finished the last raga in the Garland of Melodies, and amidst the dying strains, the courtiers were waking to the final hour of the ceremony. Rubbing his eyes, the Khwaja reached for a plate of grapes, then started. He saw Bihzad – upright among the reclining figures – walking resolutely towards Akbar. The Khwaja's mouth fell open, a single grape dangling on the slope of his tongue. At that moment, the eunuchs saw Bihzad too and rose in alarm, clambering after him with their peacock-tailed fans.

At the door to the inner chamber, Bihzad brushed aside the startled arms bearer and entered. All at once he found himself face to face with Akbar. The emperor, also suddenly awake, cast his bright eyes at Bihzad, as if to ask who he was. Bihzad bowed, then in one sweep held out a miniature mounted on a simple board. Akbar looked down at it without a word.

It was a strange painting. Most unusual. As if the whole scene was drawn upside down. Two elephants were fighting each other on the banks of the Jamuna – rushing in at full charge, trunks raised, baring mighty tusks, ears flapping, about to head into the river. Boatmen cowered under the awnings of their boats as the imperial servants struggled unsuccessfully to control the beasts. Some of them had already jumped into the river and were swimming upstream. From the walls of the fort, courtiers could be seen wailing, holy men in various poses of prayer. And Akbar? He was suspended in mid air, thrown from the back of his favourite elephant, head pointing straight down. But like an angel, he seemed not to be falling, but to be in flight.

The emperor looked. The audience hall, the oratory, the harem quarters, waited in silence. Then Akbar started laughing in his rich and throbbing voice, filling Sikri with his laughter.

Letting out a sigh, the Khwaja slumped back, the solitary grape popping out of his mouth and rolling along the floor of the audience hall.

Sitting before Adili, Bihzad was reminded of how the Afghan had behaved during the weighing ceremony. When his turn came to present his gift, he had offered a falcon made of solid gold, then laid his head on the ground before the emperor. The courtiers were surprised. As he returned to his seat, Adili had smiled in triumph. 'How can you pay your respects properly with hands and tongue?'

Bihzad watched the enormous Afghan, sparse-bearded, uneven teeth showing through his broad mouth. As he sat smoking an elaborate pipe, he seemed perfectly at ease before the future master of the kitabkhana. Bihzad had been warned of his zealous guards, but he seemed open and relaxed at his own house, within sight of Sikri's walls. Also, he showed no signs of the 'sickness' that had earned him his independence from the kitabkhana.

As planned, he decided to open the conversation by speaking about Salim Amiri – about the Darogha's sudden order forbidding the paintseller to bring up his mule-cart from Agra to Sikri.

'It isn't just the Darogha who's angry with him, but others too.' Adili spoke confidently. 'Now he must face his punishment. It is a matter of one man winning and the other losing.'

'And who is the winning man?' Bihzad probed cautiously.

'Anyone who supports the emperor.' Blowing a cloud of smoke, Adili dropped his voice. 'You know about Salim Amiri, do you? Selling lies in the name of paint and paper. Blaming the courtiers for pampering the emperor. Blaming Akbar for lavishing Sikri at the expense of the empire.'

'That's gossip.'

'Gossip?'

'Half of Agra is blaming Sikri for its neglect. Would you punish them all?'

'You know about him, don't you? He dresses like an infidel, acts like an unbeliever – praying to the sun, plunging into water…'

'Like Akbar, you mean.'

Adili smiled. 'Subjects shouldn't imitate the emperor.' Seated on his own pedestal in his own haveli, he seemed like a senior courtier, a master among artists, treating Bihzad like a naïve recruit.

As planned, Bihzad decided to ask Adili next about why he had chosen not to join arms with the other artists at the kitabkhana.

'You mean to paint the *Akbarnama*? But that is between you and the Darogha. What does it have to do with me?' The Afghan brushed aside Bihzad's complaint.

Bihzad reminded him that all artists of Sikri belonged to the kitabkhana. The kitabkhana's work was their work. The biographer had set a lightning pace, every hand was needed now to complete the story of the emperor's life quickly.

Adili seemed not to be concerned. 'But it's different from my work. The *Akbarnama* that you speak of is just a routine. Like working in the imperial kitchen.'

'Imperial kitchen?'

The Afghan smiled. 'Yes. Think about it. Five thousand meals a day! Enough to keep two hundred cooks busy. But where does the emperor go when he wants something special? To the harem. To his favourite wife's cooking pot.'

'I don't see…'

Adili moved the pipe from his mouth. 'A hundred artists must toil over the *Akbarnama*. And you, Bihzad, may indeed become their master, the master of the kitabkhana, but *I* shall be his artist.'

Bihzad had heard rumours – Adili was boasting that Akbar was soon to name him *Zarin Qalam*. Even better than the

97

Khwaja – the Sweet Pen – he'd be called the Golden Pen, nothing less.

As planned, Bihzad decided to make his request to Adili, just as Salim Amiri had advised. He asked if Adili could arrange a meeting between him and the emperor.

'Akbar?' the Afghan paused, then said with a serious face, 'Akbar has already asked to meet the Little Master. Didn't you know?'

*

'It's impolite to visit the emperor without a summons.' The Khwaja sat with Bihzad and the Darogha at the kitabkhana discussing the weighing ceremony.

'It's a crime,' the Darogha said with a glum face.

'But it has ended well.' The Khwaja glanced at Bihzad, then turned to the chief clerk. 'You have the emperor's order, don't you?'

The Darogha passed a scroll to Bihzad. He frowned. His father took it from him and read aloud. The emperor, the Khwaja said, was asking his artists to prepare for a grand event. He was asking a select few, including the Little Master, to accompany him and record every detail of the event.

'Didn't I say he'd ask for you?' The Khwaja seemed genuinely pleased. 'This is your chance, Bihzad. Once you present him with the paintings of the event, he'll proclaim you the new master. Then, you'll be known as the Khwaja, and I will be simply Abdus Samad Shirazi!'

'The event?'

The Khwaja glanced quickly at the Darogha before replying. 'The war.' The Khwaja cleared his throat. 'Akbar is going to war.'

*

Sitting under the balcony of Salim Amiri's haveli in Agra, Bihzad waited for the paintseller to return from his daily visit upstairs to his grandmother. At last his friend appeared.

'She's blessed with the herb of longevity, destined to live longer than emperors and artists charging off to war!'

Bihzad decided not to ask him about winners and losers. Despite the empty courtyard which normally bustled with servants filling up paint jars, he seemed as interested in Bihzad's questions as before.

'Why must an artist be forced to depict slaughter?'

'Both good and evil were created by God. Your task is simply to record them – like night and day.'

Bihzad protested. 'Is it right to ban the slaughter of animals but enjoy the slaughter of men?'

'Much in you is a man, Bihzad. And much still a dreamer. Emperors need men not dreamers. What right do you have to question his ways?'

Bihzad made a face. 'You speak as if he was God. As if it was a sin to question Akbar's whims.'

Salim Amiri laughed. 'Why not pretend they are one and the same – your ruler and your Master!' He poured two cups of wine. His grandmother coughed from above. 'She can see with her eyes closed!'

'The blind laugh as the drunk sleep!' came a voice from the balcony.

Bihzad wondered what would be the paintseller's fate. What would he do now? Push his mule-cart back over the Hindukush and return to Persia like the aged Mir Sayyid Ali? How would he live without the gossip of the court, the intrigues?

Salim Amiri started talking about the artists who travelled with their lords to battle, even died on the battlefield. Then he fell silent, suddenly looking older than his usual self. He seemed to be searching for words, trying to pass on a secret.

'Do you know what your teacher had told me about you?'

Bihzad looked surprised. 'No ...'

He started telling Bihzad of his conversation with the elderly Mir Sayyid Ali. 'Your father was worried about you. Your peculiar style of painting, when you were young. Your disregard for the norms. He felt your teacher was ignoring your mistakes. He asked me to talk to him.' He placed his right hand over his chest like the pious Mir Sayyid Ali, and spoke in a faltering voice.

' "An artist makes mistakes, but a master doesn't. He sees and shows us what Allah wants us to see, so that we may change this rotten world armed with His perfect vision." He said, your vision, Bihzad, is *His* vision. Different from all others, but divine.'

Bihzad sat upright.

Salim Amiri spoke slowly. 'Perhaps that is why he has left Hindustan and returned to Persia. Seeing you, he may have realised his mistakes and stopped painting. The old man must've felt that the way that he taught his students was in fact wrong, that it had simply been the dream of his forefathers. Not God's will, just the dream of mortals.'

Salim Amiri looked into Bizhzad's eyes. 'But he has left you a warning. Remember the line from Rumi's epitaph that you found in his empty studio? *When we are dead, seek not a tomb in the earth, find it among a million hearts.* Perhaps it was his way of warning you against powerful men who raise palaces and magnificent tombs. He knew your genius was too great to be ...'

'But you told me to obey the most powerful man, do as he commands me to do. What right do I have to question his ways?'

Salim Amiri sighed. 'No, Bihzad. I was wrong. It *does* matter what you draw and how. What a painting shows becomes the truth. For us, for *all* of us. It becomes eternal. You may not wish to draw Allah's truth, or the emperor's. It may be the truth of dying soldiers, of racing elephants and burning forts ... But it must be the truth of our times. How else would we be remembered – long after the Mughals are gone? The rotten leaves and rocks that I pound will become the truth when touched by the artist's brush.' He paused to catch his breath, a pleading note entering his voice. 'Whether in a battlefield or in a palace, you must see, then show us.'

The two sat quietly for a moment. Then Bihzad asked a final question. 'What if Akbar dies on the battlefield? What will happen to his artists then?'

Before Salim Amiri could answer, the voice came from above. 'Then you'll get what is there for you.'

He stood on the fort's ramparts overlooking the vast courtyard. Holding back from his usual visit to Satan's Palace, he walked along the arched corridors instead, viewing the full moon's glare on the sandstone. Not a single shadow marred its whiteness, it seemed like a lake without a ripple.

Akbar! he thought. Had his ruler become his Master?

First a white flag was raised outside the besieged fort, as a sign of peace, inviting surrender. Then, after a suitable length of time, a red flag was hoisted, threatening the rajah with imminent death. Akbar's army waited at the foot of the hill, torches lighting up the tents of the invaders. No one slept. Gunners and infantrymen, cavalry, elephant keepers, carpenters ready to cut down trees for gallows. At dawn, a black flag flew, the sign for the enemy's burial.

The rajah was the only one within Akbar's sight, his kingdom barely a few hundred miles downstream by the Jamuna, who hadn't paid his respects to the Mughal throne, refusing to send gifts and his daughter to Sikri's harem. His might had grown at the expense of his corrupt neighbour, who was Akbar's vassal. The rajah had become popular among his peasants by waiving their taxes after a year of drought. The popular rajah might challenge the emperor, it was feared; spies had returned with alarming news of his powerful army.

Two hundred mounted musketeers and five hundred artillery were despatched over the rocky slope leading up to the foot of the fort's walls. As planned, the sappers charged forward under the cover of guns, dug burrows and packed them with gunpowder, then withdrew. Down below, the assault troops waited for the explosions before they advanced.

Then the enemy responded. A flood of glowing embers tumbled down the walls to meet the charge of rushing soldiers, a swarm of poisonous arrows flew. A well-aimed spear pinned down the leader of the advancing men.

The emperor received the news calmly. His army was twice as large and ten times as powerful – the cannons, specially forged in his armoury, were unrivalled, his generals the very best. He ordered a dozen elephants to be brought before him, then ordered gallons of wine to be emptied into their tills, mixing it with their drinking water. The drunken elephants led the charge, three abreast, towards the giant door of the fort.

A cry went up as the first elephant fell under a hail of bullets, his rider trampled beneath his feet. But the beasts charged on. A burning log fell from the fort's wall in their path, then another, but the elephants smashed them, flying over the leaping flames. Few expected them to survive the mighty collisions against the fort's iron doors, hoping they would breach a passage for Akbar's men to enter.

From his seat in the camp below, the emperor watched as the dark column charged up the rocky slope, almost to the entrance of the fort. Then, pairs of arms appeared above the giant doors, holding out a string of cauldrons, almost in a gesture of welcome to the beasts. A flood of oil, burning oil, descended like a sudden waterfall, dousing the elephants. A glint of fire appeared, like a sparkler, thrown over the gate. It landed on the charging beasts, setting them aflame.

Akbar watched the fireworks, as if he was sitting at the jharokha window of his own fort in Sikri. The elephants, among them his favourite, Hawai, leaping up on their hind legs, twisting around, smashing their trunks against their flaming bellies, smashing their heads against each other, rolling over on their sides. As more burning oil poured down from the fort, raging streaks danced over the dark mounds of flesh, like a flurry of rockets. The beasts ran around in circles – an orange coloured ball spinning madly like a pinwheel, crackers exploding as the tusks snapped, trunks resembling the charred remains of spent sparklers. Akbar watched the elephants burn, transfixed, listened to their ghastly calls as the rest of the camp shut its ears and gazed on in disbelief.

'Sabat!' the emperor shouted. Sabat – a covered way, spacious enough for ten soldiers to pass abreast, built of rubble and stones and held together by a wooden roof – was the most potent weapon in the Mughal arsenal. Like a snake, it would wind up a hill, hiding the builders and soldiers in its womb. Turrets along the side walls would allow musketeers to provide cover as the front end saw rapid advancement. More than a hundred would die each day – the builders working to advance the tunnel inch by inch towards the enemy's gate. The surrounding forest would be flattened for the beams, animals slaughtered to provide curtains of leather to cover the mouth of the sabat, to repel the bullets and poisonous arrows. The dead could be carried back through the tunnel to the camp below, more builders sent up to take their places. The whole process could take months, depending upon the nerve of the defendant, until finally Akbar would arrive at the fort's gate through the sabat.

With infinite slowness, the snake started to slither up the rocks, to latch its fangs on to the enemy's wall. Word went to Agra to delay the celebrations that would accompany the emperor's return.

Then, within days, something amazing happened to raise the invaders' spirits. As he inspected the sabat at dawn, chatting with the soldiers at the mouth of the tunnel, Akbar saw a solitary head appear above the fort's wall. The head wore a saffron turban, and looked down at the soldiers. He seemed peaceful, simply gazing down, unconcerned about the siege. With one shot, Akbar felled the man in the saffron turban, then resumed chatting with the soldiers.

Within an hour, they saw fire rise behind the fort's wall, and heard the cries of wailing women. The soldiers gazed at each other in disbelief. Jauhar! The final defiance. An act of war not surrender – an act of death, inflicted by the defeated on their women, to protect their honour, lest they fall into the hands of the enemy. From the camp below, the emperor smelt the burning flesh and the rosewood pyres. He raised an eyebrow as if to imagine the rows of women – wives, sisters, daughters – of the slain rajah weeping around his body, clutching the saffron turban. As if he could see the naked flames and the plunging women.

In a fleeting moment, Akbar arrived at the enemy's fort.

*

'Bihzad…'

The Chief Executioner called Bihzad over to the row of prisoners. He had already seen the smouldering pyres, when he entered the rajah's fort with the soldiers. After a while he was unable to stand the stench.

The Chief Executioner, usually reticent, seemed full of energy after the days of waiting at the camp. 'What's the use of killing them? From every drop of a demon's blood a new one is born.' He eyed an exceptionally handsome man, bare-headed, the red mark of a martyr on his forehead. The last of the elephants was brought for him. The man kneeled, expecting to die swiftly under its foot, but the elephant caught him in its trunk, squeezing him, flinging him from one side of a shallow pit dug by the soldiers to the other. Without a clear sign from his master, the elephant went on playing with the prisoner. The soldiers surrounding the pit cheered.

Bihzad stood up to leave, but the Chief Executioner stopped him. 'Wait, Little Master! Won't you draw the brave feats of the soldiers?' He ordered a young prisoner, almost a boy, to be brought over to him. 'Blind him!'

The soldiers discussed the various methods that could be used. Should they stitch up his eyelids, to be reopened later as a reward for good conduct? Should a hot iron be held before his eyes, as was the custom in Persia? A drop of poisonous herbs? Or should a wire be inserted, causing a pain beyond all comparison?

Where is Akbar, Bihzad wondered. He recalled the words of Salim Amiri… *Remember, he is from the seed of the Mongols – barbarians!*

Akbar had banned the Victory Tower, he knew – the building of a small minaret with the severed heads of prisoners. But Bihzad had seen the fate of the rajah's spies, who had entered Akbar's camp in disguise hoping to pry out his battle secrets. They were impaled along the road to the fort, each headless torso marked with its name and rank.

'Come!' The soldiers called Bihzad over. The blinded boy stood dressed in ox hide, mounted backward on an ass. He'd be paraded down to Sikri, punished for hurling abuse at the emperor when he had entered the courtyard of jauhar. 'Barbarian!' the boy had screamed, accusing Akbar of starting a war for no reason.

'He's fortunate,' one of the soldiers said. 'Now he'll live long enough to set foot in Sikri!'

A courtier stood at the Herald Tower and read out Akbar's commands. 'Beware! The soldiers mustn't rob the treasury. They mustn't poison the well. No one should destroy the temple or desecrate the idol. No widow should be forced to burn against her will.'

*He hits hard till victory has been achieved, feels no scruples in starting a war, then shows his better side* – Bihzad remembered Salim Amiri's words. All around him, he saw the once proud fortress in disarray.

'A princess has become a widow!' He heard the jubilant Chief Executioner say, laughing at the burning palace.

\*

The roads were unsafe, leading from the battlefields to Sikri and Agra. Bandits, it was rumoured, were waiting to pounce on thieves who had looted the rajah's treasury and were trying to escape. Distressed by the scenes of torture, Bihzad fled the camp and joined a caravan of merchants on their way to Agra, following secret trails that led through a forest, travelling by day and hiding by night. They took him for a merchant too, a jeweller perhaps, travelling without servants or belongings, hiding his wares in his large turban wound in many folds. Walking as if in sleep, and lying awake at night, he reached Agra just as the old capital was beginning to celebrate Akbar's victory.

Sick after the journey, and still anguished by recurring visions of death and torture, he seemed unable to find his way, wandering along aimlessly, till a neighbour from their old haveli recognised him and brought him back. He went straight to Zuleikha's room. She didn't seem surprised to see him, as if expecting his visit. As he rested with his eyes closed on her bed, she asked him about the war.

'Did Akbar kill the young prince too?'

'No, there was no need to …' Bihzad remembered the boy being led to the emperor, to kneel before him and beg to be pardoned.

'And prisoners? How many prisoners has he taken?' She seemed to know already, told him how the prisoners had started arriving in Agra. 'The ones he'll need for his future wars, and for his pleasure now.' Soldiers, virgins, young boys with sweet faces. 'They'll become the courtiers' attendants. The wrath of the emperor is good for his subjects!'

She seemed just as before, although the haveli was even quieter now – quieter for the absence of Nikisa, her maid of many years, who had left to join the harem of a rich merchant in Agra.

'And the rajah's artists? Did the soldiers steal them too? You'll be their master now, won't you?'

He ignored the soft moaning of doves outside her window. Ignored Zuleikha's stories, his mind returning, every moment he was awake, to soldiers cheering the emperor: '*Allahu Akbar* … God is Great!'

Then he thought he heard a different chant … *Akbar is Allah! Akbar is Allah! Akbar!*

The words rang in his ears till he was able to sleep. When he did, he dreamt of strange things. A god punishing his enemy, lighting rosewood pyres by his own hand. A god embracing the flaming women, dragging them out of the fire. A god riding on the back of his Hawai.

What if Akbar had fallen into a trance in the middle of the siege, as he had during the imperial hunt, and said, *Enough!* Try as he might, he couldn't erase from his mind the vivid delight of the Chief Executioner.

'And you were sent to record the event, weren't you?' Zuleikha tried to bring him back from the restless tossing and turning. 'Did you record every detail?'

He gave her an angry look.

'But it's your duty.' Bihzad made as if to rise from her bed, unable to free himself from the trance of mufarrih and majun. She held up his chin and brought her face close to his. 'Are you ready now for his harem? An artist is like a lover, Bihzad. If you lie, he'll blind you. If you're foolish, he'll leave you for another.'

In all the years he had known her, she appeared for the first time as the Khwaja's wife, comforting him like a real mother. She made him rest his head on her lap, soothing his forehead with a damp cloth.

'Akbar! It's *he*, isn't it? It's Akbar you love.'

Bihzad turned his face away. There was a look of pain in Zuleikha's eyes. Then she spoke to him softly, as if consoling a spurned lover. 'Does your father know?'

He shook his head.

'So it's better for you, after all, to be in Sikri.' She remained silent for a moment. 'At least you can see him there. Feel him close to you. You can visit Akbar and gaze upon his face.'

Bihzad shook his head. A tear rolled down his cheek.

'No? There's nothing more painful, is there, than to see your lover but to know you'll never even be able to touch him?' She sighed, a sadness entering her voice. 'Then go in a blindfold, Bihzad, if you can't bear to see his face.'

She kept on speaking to him, rocking him in her arms like a child.

*

'It's impolite to leave the emperor's camp without his permission.' The Khwaja sat facing Bihzad at the kitabkhana. He had worried over his son's sudden disappearance.

'It's a crime,' the Darogha repeated grimly.

The Khwaja observed Bihzad's pale face, downcast eyes, and drooping mouth. Then, he cleared his throat.

'The event, as we all know, has ended with success. Allahu Akbar! The emperor has returned to Sikri in triumph. It'll soon be time for rewards and promotions. He is waiting for your paintings, Bihzad. Waiting to see how you have drawn him in battle. We are all waiting.' He paused, expecting Bihzad to reach under the sheaves and take out his album of paintings. The Khwaja waited. Bihzad sat silently.

'We shall be happy to view your new paintings. I could inform the emperor...' He stopped abruptly as Bihzad looked up, reading an uncertain look in his eyes.

'No?'

The Darogha started to fidget with the edge of his turban.

'That's why you went back to Agra so suddenly, wasn't it? To finish your work without interruptions?' Then his voice hardened. 'As I am still the Khwaja, I have a right, Bihzad, to inspect your miniatures.'

Bihzad looked up at his father. The Khwaja looked away. Then he asked the Darogha to leave the room.

'They will still be *your* paintings. I only want to ...' The Khwaja edged closer to his son.

'There are no paintings.'

The Khwaja stopped. His expression changed rapidly from disbelief to anger. 'No paintings? Why?'

Bihzad gestured with his hands, offering no explanation.

'What were you doing all this time then? Forging cannon balls for the emperor? Building the sabat?'

He paused for a moment, then spoke firmly. 'Do you know what you're saying? That you have returned from the war without even a single sketch. Not one of the emperor inspecting the rajah's fort, ordering the siege. Not one of him felling the infidel with a single shot! Not one of him pardoning the young prince who is now his vassal.' The Khwaja stopped again to catch his breath.

'But the court is waiting. The poet Abdullah has already composed the verse that'll adorn the Victory Album. The calligraphers are waiting. Your enemies are waiting. If you fail there will be no more Persians in the Mughal court.'

Then he knelt on the floor, knees raised, plucked a blank sheet from the stack beside him and held up his pen. 'Tell me what you saw.'

Bihzad kept silent. The Khwaja started to draw miniatures for the Victory Album. He sketched a charge of the infantry across the enemy's moat. He drew Akbar inspecting his troops seated on a royal elephant. He drew the sabat inching its way up the rocky cliff like a one-eyed snake. He drew the line of miserable prisoners, and the emperor, his right palm raised in the gesture of pardon.

'Take them, and return tomorrow when you've finished with the colours and borders,' he said, just as he would order a junior artist at the kitabkhana.

*

Bihzad sat awake all night, painting. Yet he painted, not the Khwaja's album, but his own. He drew a tormented landscape as if a great storm had just passed over, tearing the leaves from the trees, and leaving the clouds in tatters. Mutilated flowers withered over the branches. A rose tearing its petals, the jasmine turning yellow, the tulip's face drenched in blood. In the landscape of death, he placed a single human: the artist – Bihzad – contemplating his face in a small spring. As if it were a severed head on the tip of a lance.

*

The next day, he met the Khwaja again, sitting with the Darogha and Adili in the kitabkhana. The Darogha opened his safe and took out an album. With a quick glance at Adili, he proceeded to lay it open for all to see.

'This is Bihzad's album celebrating our emperor's victory over the rajah,' he announced in his usual grim voice, but touched by a strange irony.

Bihzad sat with his painting under his arm, the one he had finished just at the stroke of dawn. The Khwaja leaned over and turned the first page. He frowned, a look of confusion clouding his face. Then he turned more pages, looking up every now and then at the Darogha.

It wasn't the Victory Album. Not Akbar at war. Not even the album the Khwaja had sketched the night before. But the *Akbarnama* – Bihzad's own *Akbarnama*. The one he had drawn at Agra's kitabkhana and hidden from everyone under piles of blank paper, the one that had gone missing when the kitabkhana moved into its new home. 'When?' There was a look of utter bewilderment on the Khwaja's face. 'When did you do these things ...?' He glanced quickly at Bihzad, then stared at the portrait of Akbar as a young man with dangling earrings and unkempt hair. Akbar embracing a young man dressed as a maid, holding a half-eaten apple. Akbar caressing a boy with a face as delicate as a woman's – kissing him like a wife. Akbar showing the marks of his lover's bite.

There was a faint smile on Adili's face. The Darogha looked on impassively. Turning the pages, the Khwaja came to the double portrait, the one that showed Akbar and Bihzad sitting together on the royal bed, drinking from the same cup. And the verse underneath in fine calligraphy, copied from a book of poems.

> What is life without you
> And a world, without you

The Khwaja made as if to crumple the page.

A shock passed through Bihzad, as he saw his own paintings on his father's lap. In a flash, he realised that his secret album hadn't gone missing from Agra's kitabkhana by chance, but had been stolen. He knew now why the Darogha had refused to treat him as the master, why Adili had seemed so confident of his success, why the two frequently whispered together, as if planning a surprise attack. Through a dreamlike haze, Bihzad heard the Darogha muttering, 'A fort's gate can be kept locked, but not a man's mouth.' Word had already reached the emperor, he whispered to the Khwaja, of these strange paintings. The courtiers were awaiting his orders regarding Bihzad's fate. A severe punishment was feared for the scenes of unnatural and forbidden love. At first, it was thought an enemy had played a trick, trying to discredit the noble emperor, making him seem vile in the eyes of his subjects. Perhaps a mad artist ... But a search at the kitabkhana had failed to produce a single specimen that matched these horrible ones. No, the Darogha was certain. It wasn't the act of an enemy, but Bihzad's. 'Look ...' The

Darogha made as if to re-examine the paintings. Even without his monocle, he was sure. Such strokes couldn't have come from any other brush, such portraits, such vivid backgrounds. Such exquisite depravity.

The priests of the House of Worship had been consulted. None could find sanction for such deviance in their scriptures. There was talk even of the death sentence. 'Yes, even that is possible.' The Darogha averted his eyes. Then with a conspirator's glance at Adili, he rose to leave. The Afghan bowed to the Khwaja and left too. Father and son were left alone.

As the sun entered the kitabkhana, Bihzad opened his eyes. He placed his landscape before the Khwaja and nudged his arm. His father pushed it away.

'You are useless to me now.'

On the first day of the holy month of Muharram, he left Sikri in a mule-cart holding the emperor's order exiling him from his empire. *The One Who Is Without Need commands his servant to leave his blessed realm, to forego all claims within his celestial empire, to cease any trade with his subjects, and to desist from all acts of conspiracy or be punished with certain death.* Unlike earlier, guards didn't exchange smiles among themselves. As Ursa Minor – the constellation of harmony – started to fade on the horizon, the driver of the mule-cart raised his whip, then turned back with a questioning glance at Bihzad.

# Tarkh

shape

*

*Zaman, makan, ikhwan*
Right time, right place, right friend
SUFI SAYING

'Death. Nothing less.' Hilal Khan shook his head. 'Weren't you afraid of the death sentence?' He had the head of a boy – smooth chin and blubber lips – on the body of an old woman. Hilal Khan, once the head eunuch of the emperor's harem in Agra, the faithful keeper of the loveliest women in Hindustan. As the owner of a serai – a resthouse at the end of the desert – he seemed equally in charge, now as the head of a household of wandering men. Recognising Bihzad instantly, Hilal Khan lodged him in a room next to the stables, sending off the driver of the mule-cart. The two sat facing each other. Then the eunuch started whispering.

'Couldn't you see what was happening right before your eyes? Were you blind? Half of Sikri knew about your paintings before the Darogha showed them to Akbar. Even Hilal Khan knew about them, sitting out here in the desert, from the gossip of travelling men.'

Bihzad sat quietly, listening to the animals through the stone wall.

'Long before your exile, the courtiers were whispering. The artists too. The Darogha and that Afghan Adili had secretly shown them a few of your paintings. Those who cast their eyes on them shivered, it was said. They were vile and perverse, with the power to blind a healthy man, like the evils of the infidel.' Hilal Khan sighed. 'Did you know what they were saying about you?'

Bihzad kept silent, his chin on his chest.

'Why didn't you hide them, Bihzad? Hide them well. Why

didn't you drown them in the Jamuna, before anyone saw them?'

'They were stolen, they were not meant to be seen...'

'But they were yours, weren't they? Akbar embracing a man! The emperor in the act of forbidden love. A lowly artist pretending to be the consort of the mightiest!' Hilal Khan paused. 'Didn't you know what the price would be? Haven't you heard the story of the poet who professed his love for his king? He had imagined himself as his lover, written shamelessly. Banishment or death – he was given the choice. In the ancient land of Egypt, he would have been skinned alive, or turned into a eunuch.'

Hilal Khan sighed. 'Do you know what they were saying about you? They were saying the Khwaja had fathered a mad artist, for whom one could but wait for life to end.'

'So why wasn't he killed? There was no shortage of elephants in Sikri.' Bihzad threw his head back on the pillow.

'No...' Hilal Khan rose from his seat, came over to Bihzad and sat beside him on the bed. He laid his palm on Bihzad's forehead. 'Exile is better, Bihzad. For Akbar. He has shown that he can be kind to sinners. He has sent you to die away from his sight.' Hilal Khan pointed through the window at the horizon. 'Away from Hindustan.'

Bihzad gazed back at the desert.

*

Leaving Sikri, he had travelled first to the south then east, following the bends of the Jamuna. Passing villages, tracts of fertile and barren land, skirting the edges of dense forests, he went further and further from the Mughal capital, only to be reminded each day that he was still within the empire's reach. 'All this belongs to Akbar. Even the land beyond our sight,' villagers told him as they passed through. 'All belongs to Akbar, his empire covers the universe...'

He turned back to the very walls of Sikri, then travelled westward. Everywhere he went he heard the same words. How will I leave his realm, Bihzad wondered, clutching Akbar's order. Had the emperor played a cruel joke on him, condemning him to

118

roam the length and breadth of this world? He would lie awake at night worrying, confer with passing travellers during the day, starting to distrust his driver's motives. Perhaps the Darogha had bribed him to keep Bihzad within the empire, so that he might be executed for flouting Akbar's order.

From other travellers, he learned of the north – the fearsome north, the birthplace of the Mughals. He heard pitiful stories of how men lived like beasts in the inhospitable deserts and mountains that guarded the vast plains of Central Asia. Once crossed, they left a traveller with nightmares. That was why Akbar's grandfather had chosen Hindustan over Samarkand, hadn't dared return to confront the wild mountains and the even wilder men. In the land of Akbar's ancestors, he would be far from Akbar.

Along with the driver, he joined a caravan of merchants travelling north to Samarkand, marching through towns with fewer and fewer inhabitants, passing a graveyard of animals too weak to cross the desert and killed by their owners out of mercy. Soon, there'd be no birds in the sky, no trees, not the ripple of a stream. Nothing but horse-droppings and heaps of bones to guide them through the shifting sands, changing course at the whim of the howling wind. From fellow travellers, Bihzad learned the name of this immense wasteland: Ha Dervish. A caravan of dervishes had encountered a violent whirlwind in the desert, lost one another and kept on crying 'Ha dervish! Ha dervish!' till all of them had perished. It was summer every day and winter every night in the desert. The cold night air was capable of biting off hands and feet, and swelling up the ears like peach and apple.

Following the caravan's routine, Bihzad rose and slept with the others, listened to the same stories from the merchants over and over again, of the enemies that surrounded them in the desert at all times – heat, winds, and sand. He saw members of the caravan succumb to their enemies and fall swooning to the ground. A frightening moment was sure to come, he was told, when the sky would grow dark and the sun burst into a ball of fire. Through the howls and piercing whistles, the storm would break, lifting enormous masses of sand into the air and dropping them again with a crash. Wracked with a burning heat, he'd hear the scream of men and beasts, but above all, he'd hear the call of the spirit eagle that arrived precisely at that moment to relish the terror. It was the hour for the sane to turn mad, leaving their meagre shelters and rushing out into the desert, or loosening their hold on their horse's bridle and letting it gallop to its death.

As they crossed the desert, Bihzad waited for that moment, desiring it more than he had ever desired anything. In his mind, he drew and re-drew the same scene – of a tranquil desert at dawn, unperturbed by the sin of mortal crossings, with a lifeless caravan – like a dead serpent – at its centre. Unlike the merchants and their servants, he didn't wake to nightmares. He didn't dream of an army of robbers charging at him from the dark horizon, didn't imagine their bloodcurdling yells. During the day, his ever-present companion failed to distract him from his thoughts, the nervous driver of the mule-cart chattering on about the merits of their destination. Waking and sleeping with the others, his mind – just like the caravan – had started to lose one weak animal after another.

When the moment came, Bihzad saw the ball of fire, heard the terror of men and beasts. In that hour of madness, he lost the very last of the caravan that he had carried in his mind since he left Sikri.

*

Alone in his room at the serai, Bihzad tried to remember the last time he had met Hilal Khan. It was in Agra's kitabkhana. 'The head eunuch has come with a special request,' the Darogha had announced to the artists with a grim face. 'He wishes to have his wife's portrait drawn.'

*A eunuch's wife!* The artists had left their rooms to crowd behind the Darogha's door, and listen to him talk to Hilal Khan.

'A monster,' they called him at the kitabkhana. 'Half man, half beast.' The Darogha said he was a cheat, claiming to have a wife when he must beg others to satisfy her every night. 'Maybe that's why he has come.' A rare smile had passed over his face. 'Who's ready for the eunuch's wife?'

Bihzad had been struck by the eunuch. Although he was ill to the eye, he was good humoured, frequently flashing his golden teeth. He appeared weak and frail, but his power was immense, the only harem eunuch permitted to ask for an audience with the emperor. Skilled in flattery and intrigue, he was rumoured to take large bribes from visitors who desired a royal audience, and for helping Akbar's wives to receive more attention from Akbar. Unlike the other 'monsters' – the watchmen, chair-bearers, gardeners – ill-tempered and morose, petulant and fawning, he was respected almost as much as a courtier, a 'husband' and 'father' among his family of adopted wives and children.

'Hilal Khan?' Bihzad remembered Zuleikha's laughter, when he told her of the eunuch's visit to the kitabkhana. 'It is *he* who rules the harem, not Akbar!' He was both a servant and a master to the women, she had said, serving their innocent pleasures, entertaining them with music and dance, relieving them of their anxiety, escorting them wherever they went, plying them with wine then waking them from their dreams. 'He's a true master! He can tell if a slave girl is a virgin or not without laying a finger on her!'

'Hilal Khan?' Bihzad recalled Naubat Khan amusing artists during his numerous visits to the kitabkhana. 'Only he dares to lay a hand on what Akbar has caressed, taste what the emperor has savoured!'

The artists had pressed Naubat Khan to reveal the truth behind Hilal Khan's sudden departure from the harem, and Agra.

'Because he is imperfect,' Naubat Khan had said with a knowing smile.

'Imperfect?'

'Yes. You know! Not clean shaven. Not completely struck off with a knife, or burned with red-hot irons.'

The Darogha had held up his hands in horror.

'Or perhaps his organ has grown back over the years. He has escaped a second cut by escaping Agra.'

'It's a loss, then, for the harem ladies, isn't it!' commented a cheeky artist.

Naubat Khan smiled. 'Yes, if he was indeed imperfect. Capable of giving infinite pleasure without planting his seeds. Maybe he had grown too close to one of the ladies, and had to flee the jealousy of others.' Naubat Khan had given them a know-all look. 'The jealousy among artists is nothing compared to that among love-starved harem wives.'

While he was still in Agra, Hilal Khan's hair had already started to grey although his face had remained boyish. But he had left of his own free will, earlier than usual, before the ladies could start complaining about an ugly old eunuch spoiling the immaculate grace of the harem.

Why has he chosen the desert over the capital of Hindustan, Bihzad asked himself, his eyes wandering over to the open window. A distant city hung like a curtain beyond the dunes. He felt perplexed. Who could have fancied such a forsaken land? Chosen to breathe the air of the wastes, swim in the shallow oasis, brackish and bitter? Hazari, the city of a thousand wells, dug by the rich to capture the infrequent rain that was then drunk throughout the year. The swamps grew nothing but thorns, surrounding the city like a bed of nails. How could a good breeze blow through, he wondered.

Travellers had given it other names. Dustbowl. The City of Thorns. The Realm of the Devil. To Arabs it lay outside Arabia, among Persians the name was a curse, to the men of Hindustan it was beyond Akbar's realm – beyond civilisation.

Hazari – at the end of the desert – nestled at the foot of a looming Hindukush in the lap of Arabia, Persia and Hindustan, despised but rich, coveted for its busy market and the constant bustle of merchants.

Hazari – even in Agra Bihzad had heard of the caravan trains that ferried the world's treasures through that tiny desert city to the Mughal capital. Borax from the eastern mountains, saffron from Kashmir, gunpowder, musk from the abundant muskrats, vats of blue indigo, diamonds. He had heard of its slave market, a favourite of the eunuchs who went regularly to buy the best of the best for the emperor's harem. They went too to buy more of their own kind – young love-boys and evil-looking guards – men stolen from all over the world and castrated at nearby serais.

How, he wondered, had he ended up in a land where men spoke a dozen tongues, but where the artist was as unknown as the lotus.

*

'The mad man lives merrily,' Hilal Khan grimaced at Bihzad, after the last of Haji Uzbek's soldiers had left the serai at night. Flashing his golden teeth at them, he bolted the door, then went wearily to Bihzad's room.

The serai had fallen silent after the soldiers had left. The three-storeyed building had been made from slabs of rock carried on mules' backs from the mountains. It stuck out like a lonely watchtower at the edge of the oasis, halfway between the city and the palace of its ruler. Like a lone sentry, it kept watch over both, giving shelter to those who came to visit the city's bazaar, as well as to those visiting the palace's court. The tea hall at the centre was as dark as a crypt, lit up only when shutters were opened, letting in the desert sun at dawn. Stairs led to the upper floors, to a score of bare rooms in which the visitors lodged. Hilal Khan's own was nestled between the tea hall and the kitchen, near Bihzad's – a small room kept for new visitors. A courtyard and a stable surrounded the serai. Its large iron door faced away from both the city and its palace.

Settling on the floor beside Bihzad's bed, Hilal Khan continued. 'Haji Uzbek is our mad ruler. Mad and cruel. He killed his stepbrother and mounted the throne of Hazari. From Haji Abul Bey Uzbek became a Lord of Lords. Men high and low have become his disciples through fear.'

'He has enough gold to buy the world, I hear.' Within a few days of his arrival in Hazari, Bihzad had heard enough of Haji Uzbek.

'He's really our bridegroom!' Hilal Khan giggled. 'A bride-groom who demands a different woman every night. He's what you'd call love-crazed. Whenever he hears of a beautiful girl, he can't rest till he has married her. But his mind is in constant turmoil, now troubled, now cheerful, now dark and sullen. He kills men over trifles, yet laughs at his own misfortunes. Only his laziness prevents much bloodshed.'

'Happy are his eunuchs then,' Bihzad teased. 'Rewarded every night for leading a virgin to his bedchamber!'

'Punished too.' Hilal Khan's face grew dark. 'Once he ordered a eunuch to be buried in a snake-pit for kissing one of his concubines. Another one was rolled up in a carpet and trampled by elephants for a minor sin, as the Haji can't stand the sight of blood.'

'How will he face his enemy then?'

'His enemy? You mean his neighbour, the ruler of Kas? The Haji won't face him at all. He'll think of a clever ploy, perhaps invite his opponent to fight a tiger barehanded, offering his throne as a wager, then erect a monument over his dead enemy's grave.'

Bihzad asked Hilal Khan about the soldiers of Kas swarming around Hazari. Roving bands arrived at the serai every day, exchanging secrets among themselves. Spies entered and left through the back door by the stable. Assassins plotted over benches in the tea hall. Sometimes, servants were dispatched to the market to buy suitable weapons.

'Nothing unusual,' Hilal Khan assured Bihzad. 'As long as there are markets and merchants, there will be war.' Kas – a northern neighbour named after the mountain deer that roamed there freely – laid siege to Hazari's palace every year, hundreds of horsemen arriving at the city dressed as merchants. Burning and looting the oasis, the soldiers of Kas would plan the assault on Haji Uzbek's palace, as the real merchants waited behind doors for the crisis to end. Sometimes an entire season passed before the fighting was over.

'It's like a game,' Hilal Khan said, 'like a bout between wrestlers. Hazari sends out its soldiers too, to Kas, to besiege its palace.'

'Why doesn't he come himself and settle the game once and for all?'

'He?'

Bihzad pointed through the window to the eastern horizon. Hilal Khan shook his head. 'No. Akbar has conquered enough. He doesn't need Hazari, doesn't need to meddle in petty squabbles outside his empire. If he did, Sikri would be always empty. He'd have to become like Allah, present everywhere all at once. It's better this way.'

'But surely even these wastelands must belong to someone? Wouldn't an emperor be better than your bridegroom?'

Hilal Khan frowned. 'Hazari belongs neither to Mughals, nor Afghans, nor Persians. It belongs to he who threatens most harm today. Tomorrow there will be someone else.' Then he looked Bihzad in the eye. 'You must stay hidden until the soldiers leave. Otherwise they might take you for a spy – or worse, an assassin. Whoever wins this time, there will be a general massacre. When they've gone, you can visit Hazari's palace, teach the winner to draw and paint.'

Bihzad looked away towards the palace.

Hilal Khan's laughter returned. 'Perhaps you can teach his pet!' Within a few days of arriving, Bihzad had heard of the pet – Haji Uzbek's daughter, his only child, the jewel of his eyes. He gave his host a questioning look.

'A true Laila she is, if you can find a mad Majnun! She either eats you alive out of love or devours you in her rage. To know what she is really like, you must first know her victims. Haven't you heard him cry at night?' Hilal Khan pointed to the ceiling. Bihzad had seen the young soldier of fortune who occupied the room above his. At the serai, men talked about the sudden change that had come upon the soldier since his return from Hazari's palace. He had been known before as a joker, fearless in vice. Once settled down to drink, he'd finish twenty or thirty bowls of wine. Since arriving in Hazari a year ago, he had struck upon Haji Uzbek's real passion – a fondness for strange birds and animals. Hazari's palace was full of flying rodents, horse-like creatures – white with dark stripes – bought from foreign merchants, hairless cats reputed to be capable of giving birth as well as fathering a litter of kittens. The soldier of fortune had delighted Haji Uzbek with an albino leopard, with ugly black marks on its bluish white coat.

'The Haji loves trapping wild animals and having them mate in his presence,' Bihzad had heard at the serai.

For his gift, the soldier had become the Haji's favourite, captivating him with tales of strange beasts and their customs. He had left the serai to live in Hazari's palace. He was the strangest among all the animals there, the eunuchs had complained, capable even of distracting the 'bridegroom' from his many wives.

'Then the pet wanted the young soldier for herself,' Hilal Khan continued. 'The lioness chose him as her mate. The two disappeared; some said they had gone to live in the wilderness. Others said they were plotting together to poison the Haji.'

Bihzad heard a soft whimper coming from above, and a shuffling of feet.

'Within a month the soldier was back at the serai. No one knew why, or what had happened, except that he drank no more, spent his days and nights indoors. Now he sleeps no more than a watch and a half each night, as if constantly on guard.'

'What if it's a ploy, locking himself in?' Bihzad glanced up at Hilal Khan. 'Who's to say he isn't an assassin, sent from Kas, plotting behind his closed door?'

'No, Bihzad.' Hilal Khan seemed certain. 'Something must've happened over there,' he motioned with his eyes. 'Must've come across something frightening ... Maybe he has seen what none should ever see.' Then he returned once again to Bihzad's exile. 'Hindustan's emperor may have no need for you, but you must find another patron. Otherwise ...'

'Otherwise nothing.'

Hilal Khan smiled. Flicking the hair back from Bihzad's forehead, he patted him like a child. 'You mean you'll keep on painting just as before, even without a patron? Like the Little Master?'

Bihzad looked out of the window.

'But you'll need someone to show your work to those who'll pay. How can an old eunuch like me be your Darogha – carrying your albums to distant courts?'

Still gazing out of the window, Bihzad shook his head.

'No? Do you not want to be an artist any more? What would you be, Bihzad? A soldier of fortune? An assassin for Kas? A saint? Do you want to spend the rest of your life as a tea boy in Hilal Khan's serai?' He laughed, and made as if to rise.

'If Hilal Khan would kindly accept my services, then yes.'

'Come, Bihzad.' The elderly eunuch sounded a touch weary. 'A wolf-cub is born to be a wolf.'

'Not if the wolf has left it to die.'

'Bihzad!' Shutting the door behind him again, Hilal Khan returned to sit beside Bihzad on the bed. After a moment's silence, the shuffling resumed above them.

'You don't mean …'

'Yes.'

'You don't mean you'll never take up the pen again.'

'Yes.'

'That's foolish, Bihzad. Remember who you are …'

'An artist is nothing without his master.'

'You mean you and your father are nothing without Akbar?'

'A wolf is worthless, Hilal, without a hunter.'

Agitated, Hilal Khan rose from the bed, and started pacing the room. 'The world will see many emperors. Many soldiers, many merchants. There'll be many who boast of their harems, their palaces. But the world will see few artists.' Cupping Bihzad's face in his hands, he spoke in a quivering voice. 'I'd give up my manhood again, for just one thing. Think, Bihzad. I'd be you, even if I had to live again as a monster.'

Within days of arriving at the serai, Bihzad grew accustomed to the violent quarrels. The first of these started the morning after the band of Sufis left the resthouse, after a night of songs and dancing. Shirhindi, a grim mullah on his way to Mecca, left his room and came to sit in the middle of the tea hall, surrounded by empty cups and shards of broken glass. He called his servant and ordered him to wake up the culprit.

'But no one's here. They've left...' the poor boy muttered, pointing to the door through which the last of the billowing trail of robes and turbans had departed before the arrival of dawn.

'Not *them*. The eunuch.'

By the time Hilal Khan had risen and set the first of the many kettles of the day to boil, Shirhindi was seething under his indigo robe.

'How can one hope to reach Mecca, in the company of the impure!' With just the water bubbling in the kitchen, the silence spurred him on. 'They pray not, keep no fasts, in their blood flows wine. Pleasure seekers pretending to be saints!' he shouted at Hilal Khan. 'How dare you allow them through your door! How dare you serve them Satan's juices, let them keep everyone awake by their singing and dancing? I swear, Hilal, by all the prophets in heaven, that He'll hold your life in no greater account than the insects that we tread upon.'

At first Hilal Khan pretended not to hear him, managing to smile through his golden teeth, barely offering a mild protest. 'Why blame me? Not even Allah has the right to banish someone from his kingdom, let alone a poor serai owner.'

Having risen earlier than usual, Bihzad followed the conversation from his room by the kitchen.

'Banish! In the past our great rulers would execute a whole family for the sin of just one of its members.'

Hilal Khan tried to quieten the mullah in an even gentler way. 'Forgive them Shirhindi. Man is subject to error, they say ... the whole of mankind even.'

'The pure never err,' Shirhindi thundered.

By then, Sabi the fake mystic had risen. A long-term resident of the serai, he was known for making prophecies that rarely came true. Prophecies such as old men being reincarnated as ravishing beauties, or a meteor landing on the serai's roof, imparting magical powers to its residents. Despite repeated failures, he was tolerated, as his words were thought to bear no malice. Still nursing his sore limbs after a night of ecstatic dancing with the Sufis, Sabi entered the tea hall and pronounced the first of his prophecies of the day. 'He who is the gentlest of slaves will have the most miserable master on the face of the earth.' He winked at Shirhindi's servant and poured himself a cup of tea from the boiling pot.

Eyes glowing, Shirhindi recited his own prophecy, casting a mean look at Sabi. 'They who dress like unbelievers, sing like unbelievers, drink like unbelievers, they who dance and embrace like lovers will burn on the day of judgment.'

'Wait!' Sabi interrupted. 'Are not five sixths of all mankind unbelievers? Will you have enough wood to keep the fire going?'

'Enough for your friends.' Shirhindi angrily waved to his servant to bring him another cup of tea. 'Enough to roast your special friend, the one who was pouring wine from his bowl into your mouth.'

'He who devotes his life to God, *is* God.' Sabi blew a kiss at his departed friend.

The mullah raised his eyes upwards. 'Allah!'

By then the rest of the serai had awoken – the master stone-cutter on his way from Samakand to Sikri, the merchant and his son from Agra travelling to Persia with finely carved boxes and ivory chess sets. The wrestlers were awake too, unusually late for them. Voices came from the stable – the servants were readying the horses for a light gallop around the oasis, or a duck shoot, taking advantage of a lull in the fighting. The shuffling started behind the door of the soldier's room. The tea hall filled gradually, tall shutters letting in the sun running zigzag through the columns of rising smoke. Kanu, the orphan birdseller, sat with his eyes downcast next to Sabi. He had failed to sell a single bird in a whole month. Last evening, he had started releasing the birds, thinking it was better to set them free than have them die of hunger. But his birds had refused to fly away, returning to their cages after flapping awkwardly around the serai. A few had landed on the turbans of the dancing Sufis, adding to their joy.

Warmed by the tea, Shirhindi started again. 'Call them what you wish. Sufis or unbelievers! We have no need of friendship with unbelievers. I have sent my servant to strew sand across their footsteps to prevent the same soil touching my feet.'

'And who'll throw sand across your path from here to heaven?' Sabi observed. 'Perhaps the mullah will fly like a bird to Allah!' There was laughter among the tea drinkers at Sabi's comment.

Then Shirhindi rose from his seat, his short frame rigid, palms blue from constant rubbing against the indigo robe. Circling the fake mystic, he lunged at him as if about to stab his finger into his eyes. His voice rose above everyone else's.

'The world is made evil by the evil. Only He is unlike us all, unlike His own creation. Do you know the wisdom of the Lord in creating a fly? His purpose is to irritate the powerful, till they are moved to squash His enemies like flies.' He brought his fist down with a thud on the table, spilling tea over Sabi's already soiled tunic.

The door next to the kitchen opened, and a tall man dressed in white came out. Eyes turned from Sabi and Shirhindi to the newcomer's broad frame, blocking the sun through the tall window.

'Zinda Pir,' the birdseller Kanu whispered to Bihzad who had come out of his room and was sitting at the top of the stairs. The Living Saint. The wrestlers stood up and bowed. Before Hilal

Khan could step forward and offer a cup of tea to the newcomer, to Father Alvarez, Shirhindi screamed again.

'And here's another!' This time he charged at Hilal Khan. 'What have you built here? A house for god-fearing men, or a stable for wild beasts?'

'Haven't we had enough for one morning?' Hilal Khan said wearily. 'Enough punishment for just one evening of laughter?'

'You are truly cursed, Hilal,' Shirhindi raged, pointing at the tall figure in white, 'for allowing him a roof over his cursed head. If only you'd be satisfied with your dancing friends.' Like a wrestler tying his girdle before a bout, Shirhindi spat his words over the heads of the men seated in the tea hall. 'Mark my words. This one's the devil himself.' The mullah wagged his finger at Father Alvarez. 'A master of sorcery, casting spells on young men and tricking them into slavery. Shut your ears or you'll hear nothing but the hideous and heinous words of his gospel. Ask him why he is here, where he is going.' Shirhindi looked around at the quiet room, then resumed shouting with greater vigour. 'He has crossed the seas, not with goods of trade, but his book and his cross. A wooden cross to cross swords with our prophet of Mecca! He has come to upset our laws.'

Father Alvarez seated himself on a cushion on the floor, his bare head bobbing at the level of the men sitting on the wooden benches. 'If laws are enough, Shirhindi, why do we need prophets?'

Sensing the start of a duel, the onlookers sat up straight, neglecting even the steaming bowls before them.

'Prophet? You mean your Son of God, don't you? Then tell me, Father, by what miracle did your God father a child? Did he have a human wife? A favourite slave girl? Does your gospel describe what he did on his wedding night?' The mullah's rigid face remained impassive, but the muscles of his jaw twitched. 'Tell us, Father – did he sin too, like Adam?'

'Am I the unbeliever, or is it you, Shirhindi?' Father Alvarez replied calmly. 'Only an unbeliever refuses to treat reason as a servant to faith, accepts nothing as true which his feeble mind cannot fathom, subjects matters that transcend human laws to his own imperfect judgment.'

'Then help us, Father.' Shirhindi seemed jubilant at his success. 'How did he transcend our human law of flowering a womb? Perhaps it was indeed a miracle.' He turned to Sabi with a mischievous twinkle in his eyes.

The wrestlers had started to giggle, sensing an easy victory for the mullah. The merchant from Agra was fidgeting; it was time for him to be off to the bazaar in search of bargains. Hilal Khan sat quietly on his haunches, flicking away the flies with the loose end of his turban.

'Well, then.' Father Alvarez raised his voice. 'Does your God have ears and eyes?'

'No!' Shirhindi wagged his forefinger before his audience. 'He is not like the kafir's idol. Our God is entirely unlike His own creation.'

'Then how does he hear your prayers? Watch over his kingdom, tell the sinner from the pious?'

'He doesn't need eyes and ears,' Shirhindi glared at Father Alvarez.

'Likewise, without our mortal weapons, He kills, without lips speaks in the ear of the devout, flowers seeds without the need for union.'

In his corner, Sabi the fake mystic started twittering. The wrestlers fell silent, not knowing which way the argument was going.

'Prophets, Shirhindi, are human. They need wives. The Creator doesn't.'

*

From the top of the stairs, Bihzad watched Father Alvarez. Salim Amiri had told him about the religious man known as the Living Saint. From travellers of Hindustan, Persia and Arabia he had heard of the Christian Father – a Portuguese by birth, born into a family of ascetics and raised to wear the martyr's crown in defence of his faith. Bihzad had heard too from Salim Amiri of the emperor's interest in the Christian faith, of the letter he had written to the Archbishop of Goa and through him to the chief priests of the Order of St Paul, inviting a few learned Christians to Sikri's court. But he had written, Salim Amiri had told him, not as the emperor, but as a simple Muslim – Jalaluddin Muhammad Akbar – in quest of an unknown faith.

From Lisbon to Goa, Father Alvarez had come by sea, then joined a caravan travelling over an unsafe land, carrying Akbar's invitation and an order: *I command all to honour him, ensure he suffers neither in his person nor in his effects, allow him to pass free of all dues and conduct his passage safely to my presence, else face punishment even to the loss of their heads.* While he was at Sikri, Bihzad had heard of Akbar welcoming the Christian Father with gifts and large amounts of gold. Father Alvarez had refused everything, presenting Akbar instead with a Persian Bible. The emperor had kissed it fervently, then, removing his turban, placed the book on his head. From his kitabkhana room, Bihzad had heard rumours about the Portuguese priest preaching his gospel, converting men, and holding candlelight marches through the streets of Sikri.

'The emperor has abandoned the road to paradise for the road to hell,' Bihzad had heard them say at the kitabkhana.

'He eats nothing but a little dry bread, drinks only water, remains on his knees the whole day,' Hilal Khan had told Bihzad about the Christian Father, who had arrived the day before, on his way back to Sikri after a visit to a neighbouring kingdom. Interrupting his prayers, Hilal Khan had urged Father Alvarez to join the residents of the serai and the Sufis for the evening meal. But he had agreed only to bread and water, confusing Hilal Khan with words unknown among the twelve tongues of Hazari: *cum infirmor, tune fortior sum.* 'I am strongest when I am sick and infirm.'

'Is he returning to Sikri now?' Bihzad asked Hilal Khan.

He nodded his head. Hilal Khan told Bihzad the rumour he had heard from other travellers. 'He's returning to baptise Akbar. The emperor has decided to exchange the Koran for the Christians' book.' Even Hilal Khan looked worried. Sabi the fake mystic had asked Father Alvarez to perform a few miracles before they could convince themselves of the emperor's wisdom. Perhaps the Father could heal a sick child with the water used to wash his feet. Or cure a childless woman. As the rumour of Akbar's impending conversion had spread among the residents of the serai, Sabi had suggested an even more stringent test: Father Alvarez and Shirhindi were both to step at the same time into a fire, each clutching their sacred texts. Whoever emerged unhurt would be regarded as the teacher of the purer faith.

From the top of the stairs, Bihzad observed Father Alvarez closely. He tried to picture him at Sikri's House of Worship, surrounded by men of faith. And Jalaluddin Muhammad Akbar, his disciple, sitting at his feet with a wooden cross around his neck.

*

'Beware!' Shirhindi screamed at the squatting figure. 'Remember you're among Muslims! If you speak evil of our laws we'll thirst for your blood.' He reminded everyone of the plight of the Brahmin – that foolish one from Mathura – who had insulted the prophet.

'Not even Akbar could save him from the pleasure of the sword.'

Rangila – the pleasure seeker – he was called at the serai and in the market of Hazari only a few months after his arrival. Mixing among the soldiers and spies, he went regularly to inspect the stalls. The latest siege had impoverished the city. Most of the merchants and stallholders had downed their shutters and gone, leaving behind their meagre stocks to be pillaged by petty thieves. It was hard to believe that this had been, not long ago, the crossroads where the treasures of the world could be bought and sold. Without much left to interest him there, Bihzad went to the slave market, an open court reached through dark and dirty lanes at the back of the stalls. Gradually, it became his favourite.

The slaves and their owners sat in rows, row upon row stretching out to the courtyard's boundaries. In the outer rows, boys lay on woollen blankets, chatting among themselves. The girls sat bunched together around their owners in the inner rows. Visitors could pass from one row to the next, walking around the courtyard in several loops, till they arrived at the centre, where the head merchant sat with his servants before a strongbox, and a ledger with jars of coloured ink to record the sale of his varied items.

At first, the slave owners took Bihzad for a buyer – a wealthy man from a neighbouring kingdom, a courtier perhaps, looking for slave girls to give as gifts to a king. Some took him for a spy in the employment of a wealthy man, scouring the slave markets for a concubine who had stolen and fled from his harem.

He paced himself, like a seasoned buyer, looking into the

faces of young children lying on thick wool blankets, taking care not to stop before a sleeping child, as his master would then wake him with harsh words or a slap, force the child to bow and smile. He stood in the crowd around the singing boys, dressed in white like travelling minstrels. The merchants observed the crowd closely, ordered the boys to sing songs from different lands: a song from Turkey for a buyer who appeared to be a Turk, in Farsi for a Persian. From time to time, someone in the crowd would call the merchant aside, whisper an offer into his ear, inviting a smile or a frown.

Making his way to the inner row, Bihzad stuck his head through a maze of bodies to watch the girls. They sat on the stone ground, watching the crowd with equal interest. Some had covered their heads with a fine veil, others wore their hair in braids, or falling down to their shoulders like a horse's tail. Once in a while, their owner would poke them with his stick, make one of the girls stand and come before the crowd. Then he'd pull down her tunic, baring her to the waist, and look proudly at the buyers.

'Look! She's one of a kind!' He'd turn her face from side to side, commenting on the rise of her nose, her full lips, pull her hair to prove it was real. If someone should come forward and look closely, he'd draw out a tin of butter and pour it over her head, spreading it on her face and breasts with his hand.

'Look! The envy of Busra and Baghdad!'

The glistening stream running down, she'd walk up and down, visitors gauging the firmness of her breasts, the arch of her neck, the merchant whipping up a frenzy with his incessant chatter. 'You won't find another one like her in Hindustan! Not in Khurasan! Not one with such a pleasant voice, not one …'

If tempted, the buyer would step forward and push a finger into the girl's open mouth. 'Bite!' She'd purse her lips then laugh, the buyer withdrawing his finger to show a trickle of blood. 'Teeth like a tigress! Gait like a mare!'

If close to a purchase, the buyer would speak into the owner's ear. Then he would ask the crowd to make room, lead the buyer right up to the girl, hold his hand and lead it under her skirt.

He'd wait for the man's frown to disappear, to be replaced by a satisfied grin.

'Virgin! A virgin, she is!'

Leaving one row of girls for another, Bihzad would be called back by the merchants. 'Why? Why are you leaving? Don't you want to see another one?' Sometimes a girl would call him. 'Buy me!' Moving on, he'd speak over his shoulder. 'You're lovely.'

'Then buy me!'

'A living Shirin.'

'Then buy me!'

'A rose from the garden of Rum.'

'Buy me!'

*Buy me, buy me*, rang in his ears as he walked along the rows, nudging his way through the crowds, arriving at the very centre of the courtyard where the chief merchant sat with his box of gold. At first he looked at Bihzad with respect, with the light of greed in his eyes that turned with the passing days to pity.

*

From the slave market he went to the public baths, but he didn't stay long in the ill-lit rooms. He found the baths less than soothing. The sound of men arguing echoed and clashed under the high dome with the sound of buckets tipping over onto the marble floor. He left through the side door to avoid paying the attendant at the front.

The Tarabkhana was more to his taste. The Joy House. All of Hazari, except the residents of its heavily guarded palace, took shelter in its many rooms, the divans full at every hour. Men stood in line to enter, then jostled for a spot on the crowded divans, nibbling on opium or sipping wine, depending upon which room they had managed to enter. Within days of his arrival, Bihzad became known as the one who seldom remained in a room for too long, flitted between them, entering a wine party with a plate of majun opium in his hand, and a majun party with a bowl of wine. He troubled the cupbearers, drinking down his bowl as if it were mere water, didn't touch the bread or the meats. Amidst the wild talk he remained calm, no matter how many wagers were fought among drunks pressing bowls on to each other, his head remained clear.

Born with a jar in his belly, the other pleasure seekers said of Bihzad. At thirty he looked as if he was still a student in a kitabkhana, or a merchant's young apprentice. Too young for a spy, too clever for a soldier, the drunks agreed. There were those who doubted Bihzad's own account of his life – it seemed too full for a man of his age, changing course mysteriously from week to week. They'd wake in the middle of one of his accounts and wonder if he was indeed the same Rangila they knew from previous sessions at the Tarabkhana.

Some days, he'd pretend to be a merchant's son, a rich Persian with rotten luck. 'Unworthy of scorn, even pity,' he'd say of himself, describing how he had been forced to take on the harsh life of a trader in the desert after gambling away his fortunes. To those lying about on the divans, he'd pour out his heart, never blaming his conniving friends and servants back home for his disasters, nor the wife who lusted after his friends during his absences. 'I have lost *everything*,' he'd say with a sad face, 'except my friends,' he'd add, pointing at his audience. The majun eaters cried at Bihzad's tale, falling asleep in the fear of greater tragedies. The wine drinkers slapped him on the back, cried revenge on his enemies. The merchants among them promised to help when they were sober.

Some days he'd be a simple murid – a disciple – looking for his Sufi master. From Herat to Balkh, Kabul to Kashgar, the stories of his journeys would keep his companions awake. Even the most hardened of travellers thought him more adventurous than most, ready to sacrifice his life in the quest for his eternal companion. Baring his head and imitating the sweet voice of Salim Amiri, he'd recite the wisdom of the Sufi saints. He'd tell them about naf and fana – the travesty of desire and the purity of death. A man's wealth was no more than his friendships, he'd declare, especially the ones that were truly spiritual – required nothing but the art of pure conversation that made all other needs disappear. 'Search! Search till you find your true friend!' he'd urge the drunks. Stepping over the snoring soldiers, he'd come to sit in the middle of a small circle – like a master himself – and whisper to those who were still awake the secret of qalb, the mind within the mind. And then, just as the snoring reached its peak, he would wake everyone with his singing – loud and out of tune.

'When will you stop looking for him?' the owner of the Tarabkhana asked Bihzad.

'Looking for who?'

'For your true friend?'

'When I find him finally. Perhaps not till my last day. Seeing his face, I'll be born again, as the candle burns brightest just before going out!' He confused the poor man.

On one of his visits to the Joy House, he met the head slave merchant. Declaring himself the trusted courtier of a famous ruler, Bihzad started to play yet another role. A deserter, he thundered, was hiding among the women – a slave girl escaped with treasures from the harem.

The slave merchant narrowed his eyes. 'Treasures?'

Bihzad nodded gravely. He had orders, he said, either to buy her back, or to force the merchant to return her with compensation. His drinking companions were ready to corner the slave merchant, to detain him in the room till the girl was returned.

Could he describe the deserter, the merchant asked, trying to appear helpful. Was she tall or short, dark or fair, plump or thin, loud like a peacock or quiet like a hen?

Bihzad started, then stopped. He feigned surprise, began looking through the flaps of his robe as if searching for something. He had something, he said, which would identify the deserter for sure. He promised to visit the slave merchant with the painting.

'The painting?'

'Yes. A miniature. Of the harem – with concubines and slave girls playing with sparklers among the mirrors.' He spoke like a true courtier. 'The artist was a master. He drew each woman's face to resemble its owner exactly.'

*

There were days when he felt like the wronged merchant, the disciple searching for his master, and the courtier – all in one. Neither wine nor opium would distract him as he went stomping around the edges of the oasis, among the tall reeds and the stubborn cacti, or dared his companions from the Joy House to storm Hazari's palace to capture Haji Uzbek's pet daughter. Hilal Khan received his limp body at night, paid the driver of the cart that had brought him back to carry him to his room.

He woke everyone at the resthouse with his howling, the night after his encounter with the slave merchant. 'Don't let the angels smell his shroud!' Shirhindi's voice came down from the balcony above the tea hall. Bihzad's cheeks and eyes had turned red. Closing the door, Hilal Khan sat cradling his head like a child's, wiping his bleeding nose, watching his flickering eyelids as he tried to fathom his nightmare. Later, he returned from the kitchen with the remains of the evening's meal for Bihzad.

'Scared the slave merchant, didn't you!' Hilal Khan laughed. 'The poor man came running round here, asked to see the painting of the "deserter"!'

Bihzad smiled.

'I thought you'd started drawing again. Drawing the slaves at the market. Of course, no one here knows who you are. Sabi and Shirhindi were both surprised. A painting? A painting in the desert! They stopped quarrelling for a moment. Father Alvarez…'

'What made you come here, Hilal?' Bihzad interrupted. 'Is it true what they were saying about you in Agra?'

Hilal Khan glanced through the window. 'Is it true that I had angered Akbar, that his wives were angry with me?' He smiled at Bihzad. 'That I had become a man again? Look!' He made as if to loosen his robe. Bihzad looked away.

'Then why?'

'Because only eunuchs care for the decayed wives of the harem, but no one cares for decayed eunuchs.' Turning his face towards the dark sky, he kept on talking. 'A eunuch lives for hate. Every day of his life. Just as an artist lives for love – love for

140

his paintings. What happens when his hate grows weak? When the spirit dies, Bihzad, the whole world becomes an exile. Then it's all the same – the emperor's palace the same as the desert.'

*

'Your stepmother Zuleikha was the first to leave,' Hilal Khan kept on, even as the darkness had started to fade. His head in his hand, Bihzad listened. 'She was a wonder among the ladies. Not like any other visitor. As soon as she entered the harem, the women would call for her – they'd want to be the first to know her secrets, to try her special perfumes. The slave girls ran after her, even those in the bath would come out with their faces covered in yolk. "Make me fair! Make me young! Make my hair grow!" Some wanted her to help ward off the evil eye by joining their eyebrows with eye-black. They bought the pastes she promised would remove the crow's feet under their eyes. She'd stand in the middle of the harem's courtyard digging a hole then filling it with sandalwood and myrrh. She'd ask the ladies to come forward, one by one, crouch over the hole, clothes arranged around them to capture the fumes in their most intimate parts. She'd apply rusma to remove the hair from their bodies, she would …'

Hilal Khan paused, as if trying to recall something special. 'Everyone knew she was not only childless, but had no husband either. The Khwaja was married to his kitabkhana, and to several whores at Satan's Palace too. *She* was the artist, people said, while the Khwaja was just a courtier with clever fingers. Unlike hundreds who laboured over paintings, faithfully copying them from one book to another, she dreamt of things nobody had dreamt before. She was a magician, and everyone knew she had her own lover.'

Bihzad sat up on his bed.

'Yes. But who? Unlike the harem ladies she was free to come and go. Was it another courtier? A more powerful courtier than her husband, perhaps? She was fit to be the emperor's wife, not just the wife of a kitabkhana artist. But she didn't appear sad left alone by the Khwaja in his haveli, didn't seem eager to yield to powerful men. Like the lotus, she seemed content with her bee.' Hilal Khan smiled at Bihzad. 'A woman's love is deeper than a man's.'

'Do you know where she is now?'

Hilal Khan frowned. 'She has gone, I hear, never to return to Agra. Gone to live with her old mother in her native Multan. But she left not because of the Khwaja, or his new concubine. Not even because the harem was no longer in Agra. She left because...'

Bihzad leaned towards the drowsy Hilal Khan to catch his words.

'Because her bee had left her. Must've felt like the lotus, stale at dawn.'

*

His exile was a year old. Even after a year, he was still unused to sleeping so close to the stable, waking up in the middle of the night to a foal's neigh or a mare's grunt. Even after a whole year at the serai, Bihzad felt as he had on his first day, coming face to face with a smiling Hilal Khan. He remembered their only argument. When he had offered his sack of gold coins saved from his earnings at the kitabkhana, Hilal Khan had refused to accept. 'You are the Little Master, how can I ...'

'I am no longer an artist, Hilal, just a wanderer. But I'm not a beggar,' Bihzad had pressed on. Hilal Khan had sighed.

'You are the unfortunate one, Bihzad, more unfortunate than even a eunuch. How can I ...' He had pushed the sack aside firmly. 'Let Akbar realise his mistake and take you back. Then you can pay me. Till then let an old eunuch be your friend.'

He didn't miss his fellow artists. Nor, with the exception of Salim Amiri, did he feel the loss of a friend. If the Khwaja entered his mind at all, he appeared as in their last meeting, grim and aloof. The whole of Sikri seemed like a brilliant album full of exquisite paintings, full of faces he knew and had learned to draw exactly. The Darogha. Naubat Khan. The philosopher Murtaza Beg. Even the chameleon Adili. Turning the pages in his mind, he could see the vivid court scenes, the musical soirées, the elephant fights, the executions. He could even see his stepmother, although she had never visited Sikri, among the ladies of the harem surrounded by her garlands. For a moment he felt like the bee, unable to sleep till he had fluttered about soaked in sweat, his mind leaping over faces till he found the opening to her petals, drawn inexorably towards the tilt of her perfumed bud, till he alighted on her, the two becoming one for a brief moment.

Awake, he'd think of Zuleikha, of the last time they had met at the Khwaja's haveli.

For a whole year the soldiers kept arriving at the oasis. Hazari and Kas remained locked in an embrace of siege and counter-siege. Spies and assassins outnumbered residents in the streets of the city. Caravans waited at the edge of the desert. Then the rumours began. Hindustan's emperor was about to arrive, to settle the foolish contest once and for all. At the Joy House the visitors woke up. Men whispered in the market. Slave merchants worried over the dwindling stock of masters and slaves.

Nowroz. The New Year. The Sufis entered the oasis town playing a rousing air with flute and drums, then danced their way to the centre of the slave market. The merchants scattered to make room. *Ya Hu Ya Hadi...* Their chants drew everyone to the marketplace, from the Joy House to the serai. Bihzad joined Hilal Khan and others from the resthouse, Sabi leading the way, tripping over his untied turban in his haste to see the Sufis. Soldiers lying in the shade pricked up their ears and turned over on their sides to hear the singing.

Entering the courtyard, they saw the wandering saints who visited Hazari from time to time, especially during the New Year, appearing from nowhere and disappearing just as suddenly. The qawwali singers among them had occupied the centre. A stirring rhythm was beaten out on double-headed drums, the singers clapped, their coloured turbans swaying from side to side, dazzling against their white robes. Suddenly, without notice, the music changed, the drumming and clapping stopped. The leader's voice floated high above the reed organ. The first words of a new song took shape and descended upon the hushed audience.

> He is awake, why then
> Why then do you sleep

'Why then?' his followers repeated in a chorus.
'Why then?' the drums asked.
'Why then do you sleep?'

All is He, all is He, all is He…

Like slaves scrambling after a handful of coins, the audience leapt to its feet.

All is He! All is He! All is He…

Hilal Khan whispered to Bihzad, pointing at the man in a saffron turban, who was leading the singers. 'Sahib-i-hal, they call him. He's a master of spiritual ecstasy. He can stay suspended head down in a well for forty days and forty nights!'

*They stand in the sun, plunge into water, burn in fire to reach their god* – Bihzad recalled the Khwaja's angry words, when he had warned Bihzad to stay away from Salim Amiri, accusing him of practising the strange faith of the Sufis.

'He knows the language of birds!' Kanu could barely conceal his excitement.

Disciples among the crowd stood up one by one, bowing low, and holding out their offering. Some knelt before the leader, touching their heads to the ground. 'All is He!' cried one, tears streaming down his face, and several started to swoon in ecstasy.

In the far corner of the courtyard, another group of men had gathered around a maqalas – a storyteller's circle, waiting to hear mystical tales from another Sufi master. They seemed to be wrapped in silence, despite the singing around them, as if they were sitting in a tent.

'Even if he could stand the singing, the maqalas would certainly kill Shirhindi!' Hilal Khan laughed. The mullah, he said, couldn't stand this 'peculiar' faith, corrupting the pure with words that didn't exist in his sacred text. 'Even a small mischief is unpardonable, giving up a little means giving up the whole!' He imitated the old mullah's voice. 'Burn in God's love! He would have screamed – better to burn your dancing saints!'

The two edged closer to the maqalas.

The rich and the poor of Hazari had gathered around the master. He was going around the circle, asking the names of each. Stopping before a barber, he took the man's hand in his, then slipped a ring from the barber's finger. He raised it up for everyone to see. The gemstone gleamed.

'If you took this to the market, what would you hope to get for it?' he asked. 'If you took it to the carpenter, what would he give you?' He paused, smiling at his audience. 'The water seller? The slave merchant?' He peered into the face of the head slave merchant, who was sitting at the front. 'Probably a single silver coin, wouldn't he?' The slave merchant smiled, reached out to touch the ring.

'Maybe a friend would offer you two silver coins, not more. He might even promise to pay you later!' His audience laughed.

'But what if you took it to a jeweller? What would he pay? A thousand gold coins, no less.' He held the ring up to the sun without blinking, till a tear appeared on his cheek. Raising a finger, the leader addressed the maqalas. 'You must know Him as a jeweller knows gems, a carpenter knows wood, a slave merchant knows slaves. Only then will you know what He is offering you.'

'All is He, all is He, all is He …' The chants grew louder from the centre of the courtyard, where the singers were on their feet and were dancing, unfurling their white robes. Kissing each other, tears streaming down their cheeks, arms raised, eyes glowing. The courtyard seemed full of birds turning circles, round and round, swooping down as a flock then shooting up.

'But,' the master of the maqalas went on, 'even if the whole earth was full of seeds, each multiplying a hundredfold every year, and if each bird pecked only a single seed every thousand years, hundreds of such cycles would come and go before you came to know Him – know Him fully!'

Like foraging soldiers, the Sufis went around the market and the dark and narrow lanes, knocking on each door, calling everyone to come out and join them. They entered the Joy House too, lay down on the divans, called the cupbearers, woke the drunks.

'Wake up, my friend, there's a wonderful sleep ahead!'

'Pour your wine into my mouth, dear friend, I've lost the way to my lips!'

'Spill a drop, my friend, let the earth have her sip too!'

They troubled the attendants, drinking down their wine like

water, then won them over, filling up their bowls and urging them to drink up. The Tarabkhana resounded with the clash of broken glass. Wine ran over the carpets.

'Praise Allah for making the night long!' A roar rose from the Sufis.

'And praise the wineseller for making it seem short!' One of them had the owner of the Joy House in his embrace, refusing to let him go.

*

Even after the billowing robes had disappeared, the fair went on. Acrobats and jugglers occupied the centre of the courtyard, jumping up and down, beating their buttocks, giggling and squealing. They flung themselves into the air, then came somersaulting down. Clowns in costumes, baring their teeth, tried frightening the children, spinning around, holding their long tails in their hands.

Bihzad lay on a divan at the Tarabkhana, a thin stream of smoke curling up through his nostrils, listening to the kissa-kavan – the storyteller. The merchants and soldiers lay snoring around Mulla Assad, the fabled storyteller who was reputed to have the power to wake the dead with his stories. From Agra to Kabul he brought cheer to the grieving, sleep to the sleepless. He was a master of all four kinds of tales – love, war, power and trickery – and he had them all at the tip of his tongue. When Mulla Assad spoke, his listeners saw moving pictures even with their eyes closed, felt as if they were in a battlefield with cannon balls flying over their heads. Virtuous women were forbidden to listen to him. His tales were so seductive and dangerous, it was thought better that they should hear them from their husbands. Sometimes he became the picture himself. Even though he was a small man, whenever a king entered the story, listeners felt they were sitting before a grand monarch; when an old woman appeared, they heard the storyteller's teeth chattering.

With a pellet of opium under his tongue, Mulla Assad sat entertaining the patrons of the Joy House. His sleepy audience waited for him to reach the climax before they sat up from their divans. It was still early, and the Mulla was barely on the second night of the fifty-two nights of *The Tales of the Parrot*. He was describing the beginning of the tragedy which was to engulf the merchant's guilty wife as she waited for her husband to return from the sea, tortured by the agony of a secret affair. The sun was about to set in Mulla Assad's story, just as it was over the horizon of Hazari.

'When the sun, like the great traveller Alexander, had disappeared into darkness, and the beloved of the stars – the moon – had emerged from her bridal chamber, the flame of anguish stirred in the wife's heart,' Mulla Assad started. 'The day is a barrier to lovers, but the night is their friend. The merchant's wife was overcome with desire for her lover. She took a few hesitant steps to see if he was hiding among the trees.'

Bihzad opened his eyes. He reached into the satchel of the slave merchant, who was reclined on the couch next to him, and took out his pen and some jars of coloured ink. He tore a blank page from the merchant's ledger. Dipping the pen in ink, he started to draw.

'The wife took a few hesitant steps to look for her lover.'

Bihzad drew the woman's face without a veil. Flushed cheeks, anxious eyes like mustard flowers, a trickle of red over white.

'O, Nakshabi, what will a woman not do with a broken heart!'

He drew her with an ankle raised, gazing at a beautiful horse without its master, dressed her in the silver of moonlight.

'But before she could proceed, a voice called her from her chamber. It was the voice of her bird – her parrot – speaking as a human. Oh! Mistress . . .' Mulla Assad went on.

He drew the bird, not inside its cage, but on the branch of a fruit tree on the terrace. It had bitten off a half-ripe apple, dropping it near its mistress's feet to get her attention. The wife's face showed surprise, but her gaze remained fixed on the horse.

'Remember, dear mistress, love and musk can never stay hidden.'

In a whirl, he drew a river in the distance, a box of letters from the merchant lying at the woman's elbow, her wedding ring cast off before the tryst and flung carelessly on her bed, her present to her lover – a jewelled dagger – clasped in her left hand. And a sole witness, a maid, listening from behind the door of her chamber, an index finger poised on her lips in surprise.

The barber, raising himself on the divan, saw the painting first. Then other listeners followed his gaze. Heads crowded around Bihzad until Mulla Assad's voice fell silent.

'A masterpiece!'

The drunken soldiers woke up and exclaimed loudly. The owner of the Joy House was speechless, the slave merchant peered closely at the painting as if he was sizing up a prospect. A sigh of delight escaped the lips of Saida, the goldsmith. 'Lord! What a gem are you!'

*

The men followed Bihzad from the Tarabkhana to the serai, the barber holding up the painting and leading the others. Meeting Hilal Khan at the tea hall, they demanded an explanation. Why hadn't he told them? Where was he hiding the other paintings? The merchant from Agra, who specialised in carved boxes and ivory chess sets, held the painting up to a light.

'He paints like his namesake.'

'His namesake?' The slave merchant looked puzzled. The man from Agra assumed a superior tone. 'Kamal-al-Din Bihzad. The jewel of Herat and Tabriz. The Great One. Hazrat-i-Ustad –The Exalted Master. Nadir-al-Asar – Rarity of the Age.'

Men from the Tarabkhana looked at each other confused.

'But a lion can only be born of a lion. How can a safarchi – a tea attendant – draw like a master?' Mulla Assad asked, angry at their sudden desertion.

'He is not a safarchi.' Hilal Khan stared back at Mulla Assad coldly.

'Not a safarchi? Then what? What *is* he?'

The men started murmuring among themselves. Some remembered Bihzad telling the story of the bankrupt merchant. Others thought of the story of the disciple searching for his master. Suddenly, the slave merchant jumped up in excitement.

'He is the artist of the famous ruler who has lost his slave girl.

149

The one who drew the ladies of the harem, each face resembling its owner exactly!'

Hilal Khan shook his grey head. 'No. No. He's just a visitor, my friends. A traveller on his way. From qaf to qaf – from one end of the world to the other.'

The Tarabkhana became his kitabkhana. As much as Mulla Assad tried to win his audience back with stories of devilish jinns and ghosts with camel's feet and elephant ears, visitors to the Joy House now came only to watch Bihzad – observed him with rapt attention as he spread a blank page over a board, dipping his brush in jars of colours scrounged by the merchants from far-flung oasis towns and travelling caravans. When his fingers paused over the painting, the men sitting on the divans fell silent, cups frozen in mid air. When he looked out of the window, they followed suit, as if gauging a pattern in the fireflies' dance. Finally, Mulla Assad gave up in disgust, blaming Bihzad for the sudden fall in his popularity. 'Sorcerer! Master of evil spells!'

When his audience started to doze, laying their heads on each other's shoulders, slumped over the divans, Bihzad drew them, plucking their faces like flowers and planting them in his paintings. Sometimes he'd draw the whole lot of them as if they were dead soldiers on a battlefield. Or show them sleeping in harem rooms next to pretty courtesans. Or as athletes in swordplay under a sky full of light.

Awake, men of the Tarabkhana were struck with wonder. They'd point at each other in the painting and break into laughter. After Bihzad had applied the finishing touches, they'd start their bidding, each bent on possessing his own face, till the owner of the Joy House had to stop everyone and demand to see if indeed the bidders had come prepared with gold coins. As the winner left clutching his painting, the others went off grumbling, only to return the next day for yet another round of bidding.

From slave merchant to soldier, everybody believed Bihzad's stories now, drunk or sober trusted the varying accounts of his life.

One day he returned to the serai in the middle of yet another violent quarrel. The Agra merchant had bid highest that evening, and brought back Bihzad's painting from the Joy House to the serai, displaying it proudly at the tea hall. Sabi the fake mystic praised the merchant's noble face in the painting, with a ship behind his back.

'Look at him! He hasn't had a wink of sleep on the long journey. How happy he looks to be on shore again! But look at his son, his mind seems somewhere else.' Sabi pointed to the young man's face shown next to the merchant's.

The Agra merchant took a closer look. 'Where?'

Sabi patted him on the back. 'He must be thinking of his young wife! There's more to a man's lust than gold, my friend!' Everyone laughed, the son's face turned red.

'Gold? The emperor of Hindustan will pay more than gold for this.' The Agra merchant tapped Hilal Khan on the head. 'Think. Think hard. You and your friend could be richer than anyone in this room. Akbar knows the value of artists. He has the biggest kitabkhana in the world. His Khwaja – an Afghan – knows how to work miracles, he captures birds on paper before they can fly away. And wild beasts too – you'd be afraid to touch the painting! The emperor will capture your Bihzad and make *him* the master.'

Hilal Khan shook his head.

'No?'

'He means he's not ready to exchange his serai for a palace in Sikri!' Even Sabi's sniggering didn't seem to move Hilal Khan. The Agra merchant gave him a quizzical look. 'You mean you'd rather rot in this desert?' Then he regained his composure. 'However, there *is* a problem with the painting.'

Sitting by himself at the corner of the tea hall, Bihzad looked up from his cup.

'The artist hasn't signed his name. I mean, his *real* name.' The

Agra merchant pointed to the hull of the ship in the harbour. The word Judai – The Recluse – was scribbled on its figurehead.

Kanu the birdseller smiled sheepishly. 'That's what he asked me to write.'

'Recluse! The emperor will want to know where he is hiding. He might even think it was a fraud.' The merchant spoke with authority, informing others of the false trade in manuscripts. 'There are thieves who steal books from palaces and libraries, tear out the paintings in them and sell them in far-off places. There are men in this world who'd pay anything to own a Mirak or a Muzaffar. A Bihzad – a *real* Bihzad – would fetch half a kingdom. With such a rare signature the painting could be stolen over and over again on its way. So, the clever ones paint over a real signature, putting a false one in its place to make the painting seem like a mere copy or a fake.'

'Then how can the buyer be sure if it is indeed from the brush of a famous artist?'

The merchant gave Kanu a pitying look. 'The great ones don't need to sign their names. Who'd doubt the work of Mir Sayyid Ali, the famous Persian, signed or unsigned?'

Still drinking, Bihzad smiled.

The merchant shook his head. 'The Recluse! It'll set the emperor's mind working. Is it real or fake, he'll wonder.'

'How can he sign his real name when he knows he has sinned before Allah!' Shirhindi's voice boomed over the rest. 'It's his shame that prevents him. He doesn't dare!' The mullah started climbing down the stairs, his servant following him.

'Oh, preacher, go mind your own business!' Hilal Khan whispered under his breath. As usual, the mullah's rage struck Hilal Khan first.

'How can you expect the prophet to look upon you with favour in the midst of his enemies?'

'Who are you calling an enemy?' Sabi was most agitated.

Shirhindi pointed with his stick at Bihzad, and thundered on. 'Allah's messenger – may peace be upon him – said, thou who draw pictures will be punished on the day of resurrection. It will be said to thou, breathe soul into what you have created!'

'Breathe ...' Even Sabi seemed confused. Hilal Khan sighed. 'He's reciting the hadith of Ibn Umar. Artists will be punished, didn't he say, for failing to bring their creations to life?'

Shirhindi nodded his head in triumph. 'They shall be punished for failing to breathe life into the miserable creatures they've drawn.'

'But they have *already* breathed life into them, haven't they?' Sabi looked more confused. 'The great masters have. From the moment they complete a painting. Look!' He pointed towards the painting on the merchant's lap. 'Is he any less alive on paper than he is in person? His son? His servants? Can you not feel the river moving, the ship creaking on its sides? Can you not hear the gulls, the ...'

'Enough!' Shirhindi started to shake. 'Who is a greater villain than he who tries to create like Him?' The mullah charged at Bihzad. 'Let him create an atom if he can, a grain of wheat, the puff of a cloud.'

'Are you accusing the emperor of Hindustan of being a villain too?' The Agra merchant's disapproval was in his voice. 'How can you condemn artists when the emperor himself ...'

'Akbar! You mean the infidel who calls himself emperor of Hindustan? He has become a Hindu, haven't you heard? He wears a thread around his neck and recites the names of thirty million gods!'

'But it isn't just Akbar who rewards the artists. From Hindustan to Persia, every ruler hopes to own the best of them. Poets write verses to be illuminated by them in albums. Certainly the great Nizami, who penned the love of Khosru wouldn't stand in the way of portraying ...' The merchant rose to leave for his room.

'Then let them draw animals,' the mullah shrieked after him. 'Goats, cows, camels!'

Hilal Khan pulled out the dinner cloth, made everyone rinse their bowls and kneel in prayer. Only Bihzad kept on drinking. Mumbling to himself, Kanu the birdseller whispered to the yawning Sabi, 'But the animals too were created by Allah, weren't they? And the birds. Will he not regard the birds, regard how they were created?'

154

When he started to draw, his audience waited for the story to unfold. Even when they didn't know the story, they guessed that one was being told. Like an expert storyteller, he altered his pace, at times prolonging the painting, or bringing it to an abrupt end. But *The Tales of the Parrot* failed to hold his interest for too long. In his ear, Bihzad heard the Khwaja. *Do you draw nothing but stories? Didn't the Darogha say it's enough? Forget the parrot. The kings. This isn't Persia. We are in Hindustan. The stories here are different.*

The dozing faces of his patrons distracted him from the story he had started to draw. A horse dealer from Samarkand – wheat skinned, separated eyebrows, sheep's eyes, a prominent nose, right ear lost from a sword cut. A perfumer – upper lip touching his nose, lower lip coming down to the chin. A lama from Tibet, the crown of his head shaved to allow the soul to pass through. He felt he didn't need to borrow the faces for his stories, rather, let the faces around him tell their own stories. Like reflections in a shallow pond, they seemed both clear and fleeting, a small twitch on a face threatening to alter an entire life's account.

His patrons woke and examined Bihzad's work. But the bidding stopped, with each painting showing just a solitary face. Each one of them only wished to buy his own portrait. The poor paid as much as they could afford, the rich often paying as little as the poor. It disappointed the owner of the Joy House. He urged Bihzad repeatedly: why not leave the poor alone? They were sure to derive as much pleasure from simply watching him paint the rich. Then he'd pull Bihzad aside. Why not go up to Hazari's palace and draw the likeness of Haji Uzbek himself?

At the serai he drew Kanu the birdseller. He was an orphan, averse because of his early sorrow to common pleasures. The birds were his friends. He sat in the marketplace hoping to sell them, but actually spent all his time gazing at them fondly and listening to their twittering. Bihzad drew him – not hiding his left hand, but drawing it forth over his chest. A leper's hand, swollen, disfigured and rotting.

He drew everyone who passed through the tea hall, even Shirhindi the mullah on his way to Mecca. Bihzad drew him in his indigo hermit's gown, counting beads with one hand, with the other spreading his prayer cloth. He bade the servant to present it to Shirhindi as he was dining with the others.

The old man frowned at his servant then took a look at the painting. His face remained still for a long time, then it started to quiver. He rose from his seat, splattering the plate before him. Eyes rolling, he started to climb the stairs to his room. 'Ya Hafiz, ya Hafiz, ya Hafiz...'

On his way to the Tarabkhana, Bihzad would stop at the slave market and ask the head slave merchant to let him draw the girls. He'd offer to sit under the shade of the balcony, behind a curtain to ward off the curious.

'Why?' Even the slave merchant, who was now his friend, became suspicious. He recalled Bihzad's story of an escaped slave girl. Was he planning to capture them on paper and send the paintings back as proof? He tried to distract Bihzad, pointing at Little Moon and Big Moon, the two eunuchs, who were amusing the crowd with obscene jokes and gestures. 'Why don't you draw them?' The owner of the Joy House, he confided, was in love with them both. 'He'd pay you handsomely for a painting of his lovers!'

Bihzad pointed at the girl who stood at the centre of the circle, her tunic pulled down to her waist, breasts dripping with liquid butter.

'The envy of Busra and Baghdad.' He pointed at the girl's hair – down past her waist to the parting of her hips, made a gesture with his hand to lower the wrap. Her owner smiled at Bihzad, turned the girl around, pulled her skirt down. A gasp went up from the crowd.

'Look!'

He looked into the eyes of the head slave merchant. The man shook his head.

'Then you'll have to buy her, Bihzad.'

*

'Why don't you marry her, then?' Hilal Khan spoke with his mouth full, sitting in Bihzad's room, sharing their evening meal. 'Then I can be your head eunuch, the one who prepares her for her husband's bed! Keeps her faithful during your absences, amuses her with stories when you're tired of her kisses!'

He didn't relish his meals without Hilal Khan. No matter how late Bihzad returned from the Joy House, his friend would get up to open the door for him, lead him tottering through the dark tea hall, past the kitchen to his room. He'd see his own plate laid beside Hilal's on the dinner cloth spread over his bed. And two cups of wine. Taking his turban off, he'd sit down to eat, both speaking with their mouths full.

Usually, Hilal Khan waited till they had finished eating to tell Bihzad if he had any news of Sikri. From the travellers who passed through on their way across the desert, he came to know all the court gossip, who was conspiring against whom, which wife of Akbar had died and if poisoning was suspected.

'The emperor has left Sikri to quell a mutiny, I hear. Or maybe he has just gone off on a hunt, to scare the animals!' Hilal Khan glanced quickly through the window. 'He's headed this way, I hear. He'll be camped nearby. Soon.'

'That'll be the end of our bridegroom, then?' Bihzad winked at Hilal Khan.

'Maybe. Maybe not. The Haji might charm Akbar with his animals. The emperor might give up hunting once and for all!'

There were days when Hilal Khan didn't wait for them to finish their meal, removed the cups still full.

'Why are you in such a hurry?' Bihzad frowned.

'Because...' Hilal Khan hesitated. Then he cleared his throat. 'There was once a paintseller known as the "open ear", known for his flowing tongue. He had the entire history of the world from creation till today on the tip of his tongue. He spoke of lofty and noble things, travelled much in the company of Sufis.'

Bihzad sat up.

'While he was alive, he was a friend of the artists. He was a friend too to important courtiers. His grandmother, though, was quite another story! When his friends became more and more powerful, they left him, he was the only one to remain in a crumbling haveli.'

'Then?'

'Then ...'

Bihzad's eyes filled with tears.

'When all the pigeons had entered their cages, wings snapped, golden rings around their necks, the last remaining, the one free till the very end, flew over the ravines and became a falcon. Alone, he soared where none ...' Hilal Khan's voice broke.

*

*You possess that which nobody can destroy. Not even Akbar.* Bihzad recalled the paintseller's words. Pacing in his room, he considered his life since the time he had last met Salim Amiri. What would his friend have made of him now? The artist of the Joy House. He wondered if Salim Amiri had known all along about his secret paintings. If half of Sikri knew, how could he, the master of gossip, not have known? Why hadn't he warned Bihzad, or taught him a clever ploy to avoid blame? The more he thought about it, the more he felt Salim Amiri must have known what was coming. *What a painting shows becomes the truth. It becomes eternal.* He must have known the truth about Bihzad's love for Akbar. The master of gossip had held his tongue – before truth. He picked up a painting from his bed – the portrait of Shirhindi – and looked at it closely. In his mind, he compared it to another he had drawn years before, a portrait of Akbar. The emperor was wearing a jewelled turban, a shimmering tunic, the hilt of his sword showing over the folds of his dress. The proud and ornate emperor and the grim and bare mullah. Which was the better painting? He thought too of Sikri – the garden of gardens – and he thought of the cruel desert. Which one?

Unable to sleep, he wandered along the dark stone passages of the serai, losing his way. Curiously, after the first shock of hearing the news from Hilal Khan, his mind drew a blank. As much as he tried, he couldn't grieve for his friend, his only friend in Agra and Sikri, from the days when he hadn't applied a razor to his face to the day of his exile. It was as if his personal

158

storyteller had disappeared, and he could no longer compose a scene in his mind. As if the paintseller had left with his wares, leaving him alone with a blank page.

He circled the corridors of the serai, till he pushed open the door next to the kitchen, taking it for his own. Father Alvarez slept on his bed, a small chest at his feet, a desk under the window. A book lay on his lap, he had fallen asleep with a finger parting the pages. Bihzad walked around the bed, his eye on the book, turning his head around till it was squarely before him.

He gazed for a long time at the painting on the open page. It was a woman's face. Astonishingly beautiful. A halo above her head. An infant in her arms.

Saffron. As far as the eye could see, the fields stretched over unwatered and unploughed earth. A stalk rose four fingers from the dry soil, blooming into a flower with four petals, at its heart the orange pod. An intense smell, bringing on headaches, lingered over the field.

Sitting by their horses and behind an enormous bush, Bihzad and Hilal Khan watched a small band of soldiers strolling over the field. They had ridden for more than an hour, rising early to reach the saffron fields, hoping to catch a glimpse of Akbar. From their hideout, it seemed more like a pleasure party than a hunt. The soldiers were holding cups to their lips and laughing. They had thrown a ring around two members of their group – the only ones with twigs of saffron flower in their turbans.

'That's them!' Hilal Khan pointed at the two men, leaving the group behind and walking away towards the sun. 'Akbar and his eldest son. Salim. Named after the dead saint of Sikri.'

Bihzad rose to get a better view. Hilal Khan pulled him back with a hand to his neck. 'Shhh. They might take us for assassins.'

The father had an arm over his son's shoulder. The two seemed jovial, as if laughing behind someone's back.

'Salim. He's the first Mughal with a touch of Hindustan in his blood. Born of Akbar's Hindu wife. They're saying he's the beginning of the end for the Mughals.'

Bihzad didn't hear a word. With an artist's eye, he inspected the shorter figure of the two, the older one. Had his belly grown? Had his shoulders taken on a slight droop, or was he dragging one foot more slowly than the other? His face? Bihzad wished the two would turn back towards them.

'Salim. He loves paintings as well. Like father like son. Even has his own artists, his own kitabkhana. But he's different from Akbar.'

Bihzad caught the last of Hilal Khan's words.

'Different?'

'Yes. It's difficult, they say, to please Salim. He wants none of the court scenes and battle scenes. He wants more. Wants to see what the eye cannot see.'

What if he were to dash across the saffron field and surprise Akbar? Would he, just as at the weighing ceremony, cast his startled eyes upon him? Would his soldiers rush in, pinning Bihzad down at the foot of the emperor? Would he be taken for an assassin? Closing his eyes, Bihzad imagined his execution.

An elephant was being led to a raised platform. Bihzad's head rested on the block, his face turned up to catch sight of a weeping Khwaja. He saw his father kneeling at Akbar's feet, begging him to spare his son's life. He saw Akbar's averted face.

'Why doesn't he come this way?' Bihzad muttered impatiently.

'Shhh.'

They heard a laugh nearby – soldiers perhaps, chattering among themselves. Hilal Khan covered Bihzad's mouth with his hand. They rolled over on their backs, looked up at the sky, the smell of saffron lulling them to sleep.

\*

On their way back to the serai, Bihzad started to sulk. For days he had waited for the very moment when he'd see Akbar again. Lying awake at night, he had relived the trauma of his exile. His ears had filled with the chorus of the soldiers…*Akbar! Akbar! Akbar!* Yet, he seemed a different man in the saffron fields: Akbar roaming free under an open sky, unlike his exalted presence in the palace; an ageing father, not an emperor but a man among other men. As he rode in the morning with Hilal Khan, he had struggled with his urge to meet Akbar, had toyed even with the idea of confronting the emperor for his unjust punishment. Yet, seeing him close, the urge had given way to admiration, he had felt strangely consoled embracing Akbar with his gaze.

His trauma returned as they made their way back to the serai. When? When would he see Akbar again? He blamed himself for being a coward, for not approaching Akbar, for missing such a rare chance. *Better to have died under the elephant's foot, than hour by hour in the desert.*

Hilal Khan tried to cheer him up. 'If he had seen you among the flowers, Akbar would have called for the nuptial bed!' he giggled. 'Then what would his soldiers have thought? They would have been speechless! Akbar embracing the artist Bihzad! Not a woman, not even a eunuch, but a full man! Who'd belong in whose harem!'

The two galloped lightly, entering Hazari through the marshy oasis.

'Then your father would've been proud of you. He wouldn't have minded your secret paintings then!' As they sat down to eat that night, Hilal Khan started to tell Bihzad the story of a eunuch who had saved his father's life.

A cry came from the stable outside Bihzad's window interrupting Hilal Khan's story. The sound of sobbing. Hilal Khan stood up, pressed his ear to the wall. After a moment, he hushed Bihzad with a finger, stepping past him on the bed to take a look through the window. They heard two voices: the harsh words of an older man and the sobbing of a child. The stable seemed to hold more than the two. Then Hilal Khan turned, his face ashen. Bihzad raised an eyebrow, just as the child let out a wail.

'It's his day of blood.' Hilal Khan slumped on Bihzad's bed, shutting his ears with both hands. His body started to shake. The wailing grew, followed by the sound of a slap. The older voice rose to drown the sobbing.

'That's the owner of the boy,' Hilal Khan whispered.

Bihzad leapt towards the door, but his friend grabbed his tunic, ripping it at the neck. 'No!' He held him firmly, tears rolling down his cheeks. Then he drew Bihzad towards him, nestling his face against Bihzad's arm like a child.

A third voice started to speak in a reassuring manner, kind and friendly. The sobbing stopped for a moment. In the calm, they could clearly hear the conversation in the stable.

'Will there be any regrets?' the third voice asked. He asked the question thrice, each time speaking more slowly, pronouncing each word with care.

'That's the barber,' Hilal Khan sighed. 'He has come to do his job.'

There was no reply. Cradled in Bihzad's arms, the eunuch shook his head vigorously each time. 'Yes! Yes! Yes!'

Before the howling started once again, they heard the barber give some orders to his men, stealthy movement of feet over the stone floor, a child's cough, and the swish of a blade cutting through air.

Long after the stable had fallen silent, Hilal Khan still sat holding Bihzad's arm, his body shaking as if in fever. 'He is a monster now. Just like me. They'll take him home now to his mother. No other woman will ever have need of him.'

Bihzad raised a cup of wine to Hilal Khan's lips. He turned his face away.

'The barber will dress the wound. They'll deny him water for three days, make him walk around the room muttering to himself, "I am not a man, I am not a man." He'll feel his stomach bursting, then learn to use a thistle to relieve himself. He'll stop wetting his bed.'

'But why ...'

'He'll be denied the pleasure of the seventy virgins promised to the faithful in paradise. Only the pleasure of becoming a chair-bearer, a cook, if he's lucky, then a young princess's page – to walk before her warning passers-by, go with her to her bath. If he marries, to have a whore for a wife.' Hilal Khan sighed. 'His pain will go soon. But his hate will take years to die.'

Once more Bihzad raised the cup to Hilal Khan's lips. This time he didn't turn his face away, but drank, finishing the wine in small sips.

'He'll feel incomplete for the rest of his life.'

Bihzad kissed Hilal Khan's forehead.

'Only you, Bihzad, have made me feel complete.'

*

Bihzad woke next morning to the sound of drums. Not the Sufis' drum, but the soldiers'. His mind was still numb from the night, eyes bloodshot from the wine. He heard a shrill whistle, as if a general was calling his troops, and the sound of feet marching, running towards the door of the serai.

The tea hall was empty. The servants had not yet opened the shutters. The balconies were empty, with no sign of the Agra merchant and his son, usually busy at this hour checking their ledgers, above the din of the tea drinkers. He couldn't find Kanu, usually hovering around the kitchen in the hope of a handful of grits for his pets, a bird perched on his turban, cooing into his ear. Even the wrestlers were absent. Bihzad wondered if an inspired Sabi had called everyone out of the tea hall to the bare patch of land outside the serai to witness one of his miracles.

Suddenly remembering the night before, Bihzad looked for Hilal Khan. Then he saw Shirhindi's servant running towards the serai's door with a thick volume under his arm. Bihzad called out to him, but the boy didn't stop. The drums sounded again. He decided to abandon his search for Hilal Khan and followed the boy out to the gate of the serai.

It seemed like a maqalas, but the Sufis were missing. Bihzad saw a circle of faces. All of Hazari seemed to have arrived at the door of the serai. The merchants had left their stalls – Saida the goldsmith, the head slave merchant, the owner of the Tarabkhana. Young boys milled, laughing and running with rocks in their hands. Bihzad saw the gleam of weapons in the sun. Soldiers mixed among the men, looking more alert than usual. Their chief sat bareheaded on a slab of stone, whittling away at a strand of reed with his teeth.

He saw Shirhindi in the circle, praying in his indigo robe. He looked around for Sabi. Then, just next to a group of soldiers, he saw him – gagged, and pinned to the ground by some of the wrestlers. He saw Hilal Khan as well, sitting with his head held in his hands.

'Beware!' Bihzad heard Shirhindi's piercing cry. Only then did he see Father Alvarez, sitting on a donkey in the centre of the circle, his face turned towards the animal's rear. The priest was stripped to the waist, hands bound behind his back, a wooden cross hanging around his neck. And his book tied to a rope and dangling under the animal's head.

'Beware!' Shirhindi had finished his prayers and started to walk around Father Alvarez, pointing at the crowd with his stick.

'He's spoiling our children. Converting them without permission. Forbidding them to fast and pray.' A roar went up from the crowd. 'Only the other day, a poor girl fell into his clutches. He made her exchange God for Satan, made her forget the faith that she had drunk with her mother's milk!'

The slave merchant narrowed his eyes, spat at the donkey.

'When she returned home, what did she say?' Like the leader of the maqalas, Shirhindi went around the circle, stopping in front of Sabi. 'Like you, she made a prophecy! A little girl speaking in the voice of the devil. She said the Lord of Bethlehem will arrive at our desert to pardon the sins of Adam and his children.'

Sabi struggled to break free, foaming at his gagged mouth.

'When her mother asked her to bow to her father, she said – "I have no father but Father Alvarez"!' Shirhindi's face contorted in rage as he pronounced the Christian's name. 'When her mother asked her to study the Koran, she said, "But I am a Christian, what more have I to learn"!'

A stone landed at the animal's feet. It let out a grunt and shifted, almost toppling Father Alvarez.

'When her mother presented her with a suitable groom, she said, "No man but a Christian can be my husband"!'

'Did you wish to be her groom? Old fool!' Sabi had managed to free his mouth. Shirhindi charged at him, stick raised. The chief looked on, as if it were a trial, still whittling away at the reed.

The owner of the Tarabkhana had provided the donkey. He seemed eager for the punishment to begin.

'He must leave Hazari at once!'

Several voices joined him. 'Let him cross the desert with his book!'

'Let's see if his false gospel saves him now!'

The merchant from Agra had inched close to the chief and started speaking to him in a low voice. A frown appeared on the soldier's face. The crowd went into a lull, then resumed chanting after Shirhindi. This time he pointed his stick at the Agra merchant. 'Beware! He's poisoning the chief's mind. He's a friend of the infidels!' The merchant hastened back, raising his hands in a gesture of apology. A young boy stepped forward and struck the donkey with his stick.

Then Bihzad rose. Under the desert sun he saw Father Alvarez sitting on the donkey's back, his feet almost touching the ground, staring at the dunes. He saw his bare chest. Taking a few steps forward, Bihzad entered the circle. Walking like a drunk he approached the Father, then he kneeled. He grasped the priest's legs in both hands and collapsed at the foot of the animal, going into a fit. His body trembled violently, his mouth started to foam, he bellowed like a young camel.

The crowd fell silent with horror. Even Shirhindi retreated into a corner as if struck by an apparition. The wrestlers released their hold on Sabi, the Agra merchant held fast onto his son. Kanu the birdseller clasped his arms around Hilal Khan and started to cry.

Bihzad lay for a long time at the feet of Father Alvarez. The spectacle seemed to rob the crowd of its zeal, the merchants and the soldiers starting to leave. The residents of the serai went back to the tea hall. The chief, throwing away the reed, took one look at Father Alvarez and Bihzad, then barked out his command. 'Release!'

The bare patch at the door of the serai fell silent.

Hazari rose.
        Kas fell.

Haji Uzbek arrived at dawn at the serai and demanded to see the Lady. The painting that now went by that name, the 'Lady' that was on the tip of Hazari's tongue. His guards blocked the door lest anyone should attempt to leave. Rising from their seats in the tea hall, the residents bowed. Sabi pointed up towards the curtained balcony. Haji Uzbek frowned at Sabi, then made a gesture with his finger. A guard ran up the staircase and appeared on the balcony. He parted the curtain and revealed the Lady resting on an altar bathed in a shaft of light.

*

The siege of Hazari had ended exactly as Sabi had prophesied. After his men had fought back the soldiers of Kas, Haji Uzbek had ordered a savage massacre at the Joy House, suspicious as he was of assassins lurking there disguised as drunks. 'They'll die sleeping,' Sabi had said months before. 'Wine and opium shall save them from pain.'

Even before the massacre started, Bihzad had taken to locking himself in his room. He rarely visited the Joy House any more, choosing instead to work on his paintings at the serai. Kanu the birdseller – his 'Little Darogha' – took them to the Tarabkhana's owner when finished, returning with a few gold coins. His sudden withdrawal surprised even those who knew him well. It was as if Bihzad had taken Sabi's prophecy to heart, and stopped his visits just in time.

His room by the stable became his sanctuary, a place where

he could draw uninterrupted. Here he didn't feel the need to begin or end a painting on demand, to illustrate a favourite story, or even draw a single human face. It was as if after all these years, just as a strain of grey appeared on his temple, he started to draw for himself, picking up the brush purely for his own pleasure, not to please an emperor or a merchant.

He started to confuse everyone. Ignoring popular tales, he began to detach the viewers from the subject of the painting, so in the end they had to weave their own stories or agree that there were none to be told. Curiously, he returned to painting just like in his early years at Mir Sayyid Ali's studio. His figures grew unusually large, as if bearing the burden of the whole scene; stood isolated in the foreground, clinging to earth, refusing to recede. In painting after painting, he drew them as if to challenge the viewer. Then one day he called Hilal Khan to his room and showed him the Lady.

It was a simple face. Not a queen's or a courtesan's. Dreamy, wholly absorbed in prayer, a ring of angels at her feet. A strange light shone on her face. She was dressed simply, with just a basket of roses in her hand.

It was the happiest painting Hilal Khan had ever seen. Tears filled his eyes. One by one he called in the others. Each saw her differently, but the Lady overwhelmed them all. Clutching his left arm, Kanu started praying. Sabi laughed like a small child, running around the painting merrily. The Agra merchant's son broke down and confessed his sin – the box of gold coins he had been hiding from his trusting father. His father found relief from his troubled breathing. The wrestlers felt strangely consoled although they had lost recently to their rivals.

Extraordinary! It would have subdued the mullah even, everyone agreed, had he seen it before his journey to Mecca.

Then the word left the serai and swept through Hazari.

The slave merchant came. The goldsmith. The owner of the Tarabkhana, now Hazari's chief moneylender, offered to buy the painting. At first he treated it as a routine matter, ordering Kanu to bring it over to his house and collect the coins.

'No,' the Agra merchant stepped in, speaking in a determined voice. 'If it must go, then it must go to Akbar alone. There's no one here worthy of such a painting.' He offered to carry it back to Sikri, inviting Bihzad to join his caravan.

'No,' Hilal Khan shook his head.

This time the merchant's son showed his temper. 'Idiots! You're worse than dung-cleaners and chair-bearers.' He brought his face close to Hilal Khan's. '*Everything* has its place. The place of priceless art is among the civilised, not savages!'

'She was born in the desert and she'll stay here,' Hilal Khan said, his eye on the Lady. Sabi threw up his hands in joy, started dancing like a Sufi. No one noticed the young soldier of fortune, the one who spent his days talking to himself in his room, stepping out into the tea hall for the first time in months, gazing speechless at the painting.

*

It was decided at last. The Lady belonged to Hilal Khan the eunuch, presented to him by his friend, the artist. As the serai's door opened next morning, the tea hall was flooded. The whole oasis had come for a glimpse. Elderly women were among the first – lame, blind, struck by all sorts of tragedies. Men left their shops to come. The sick rose from their beds. Word of the Lady spread from mouth to mouth. Showing an uncanny presence of mind, Sabi had set the painting in the alcove on the first-floor balcony, far from the reach of the crowd. He had chosen the spot well – a good light shone on the Lady.

Some of the visitors offered to pay in gold to be allowed to touch her robes, even to be allowed to climb up the stairs for a closer look. The rain of coins thrown upwards from the tea hall landed back among the devotees of the Lady.

Gradually, the residents changed their habits. Morning tea was no longer to be taken in the tea hall, but in the small court-yard behind the kitchen. Wrapping blankets around themselves, the residents waited for Hilal Khan's boiling kettle, but no one complained. They took turns to guide the crowd when the tea hall was opened for visitors, separated men from women as they climbed up the stairs to face the painting's shrine. No longer interested in prophecies, Sabi became the head priest, lighting the candles and plucking out dead flowers from the offerings. The birdseller stopped visiting the market, taking on the duty of collecting the coins strewn all over the tea hall like birdseeds.

A ruler of a neighbouring oasis wrote with a special request: to borrow the Lady for a day to show her to his old mother, who was too weak to travel to Hazari. The residents of the serai conferred, then Hilal Khan said yes. 'She must go wherever she is needed.'

The wrestlers formed a cordon around Sabi and Kanu as the two carried the painting on the back of a mule, a dark curtain blocking the sun from its face. A crowd followed them in silence, forming a caravan over the desert. Bearers of the Lady took the painting to the door of the harem where an elderly eunuch carried it inside for the ruler's mother to see. The crowd waited outside in suspense. Will she be returned? Perhaps the ruler would claim the painting was stolen, and keep it for himself. The eunuch returned the painting after hours of waiting. The procession returned to Hazari following the mule.

'Why don't you paint another one?' the slave merchant asked Bihzad. 'Two, four, a dozen, hundreds of them? Then everyone in Hazari can have their own Lady.'

This time the Agra merchant advised caution. 'She must remain inside the painting. Mustn't become a goddess. Else there'll be trouble.'

'But she has already become one, hasn't she?' Sabi disagreed.

Hilal Khan patted Bihzad, sitting in the tea hall among the residents of the serai. 'Who have you drawn, my friend?'

*

A guard went up to the altar and parted the curtain, lifted up the painting and began to descend the stairs.

'Stop!' Sabi's voice rang out from below.

The Haji started climbing the steps himself. He stood facing the Lady, head tilted to one side. No one spoke. Then, he called in his shrill voice, 'Bring the artist.'

The residents looked fearfully at Hilal Khan. It was too early for Bihzad to be awake. He nodded to Kanu. The birdseller left quietly, made his way through the soldiers and started knocking on Bihzad's door. Haji Uzbek stood looking at the painting.

A door opened. Not Bihzad's door, but the one above. The soldier of fortune came out, looking dishevelled, staring at the crowd with a blank face. Not knowing what was happening, he stepped forward onto the balcony in full view of Haji Uzbek.

'Not *him*. The artist.' The ruler of Hazari took one look at the soldier of fortune, then dismissed him.

Finally, Bihzad appeared before Haji Uzbek on the balcony. After a year in the desert, his pale Persian skin had taken on a shade of mourning. Haji Uzbek examined him almost as long as he had examined the Lady. Then he embraced Bihzad, kissing him on both cheeks. 'My son!' he said several times, before ordering the guards to bring Bihzad with them to Hazari's palace.

'Son?' Kanu asked, confused.

Sabi smiled. He knew the Haji from before; he had been expelled from his court for making false prophecies.

'He means son-in-law. The Haji has chosen Bihzad to marry his pet.'

Khwaja Bihzad – Master Bihzad – he was called in Hazari's palace. From the day he entered Haji Uzbek's court, he became the chief of an invisible kitabkhana, without even a single artist to work under him. He was assigned his own pavilion, and a seat at the court, just a hair's breadth away from the Haji himself. The courtiers eyed him suspiciously – a few knew him from his days at the Joy House.

The palace was built of the same rock as the serai. The pavilions inside its walls resembled a cluster of nomads' tents, as if a temporary camp by the oasis had simply been made permanent, without much thought given to its appearance. The pavilions crowded around a flat circular plot of land protected by walls, with narrow lanes joining them to each other. The Haji occupied the largest pavilion, with his harem nearby. An enclosure almost as large as his own housed his collection of strange animals. Despite its unusual appearance, the palace compound contained all the trappings of an imperial city – mosques, an audience hall, executioner's chambers, armoury.

The tent-shaped pavilions rose above the fortified walls, their conical domes strung with flags of many colours. They had been there for so long that the residents of Hazari had forgotten how it had all begun, how, despite its exterior, the palace had become the permanent guardian of the city's coveted market, gaining from the taxes levied on passing caravans. Unlike kingdoms of the valley, the desert had raised a simple form, hiding it among its dunes, but spared little to exaggerate the interiors.

Bihzad was struck by the interiors. His own pavilion befitted a true courtier's, with slaves and servants, and guards watching over his door day and night. Surrounded by tapestries, fine carpets, a luxurious bath, he sat watching the alleys through the narrow slits cut from the rock that served as windows. The Haji's voice seemed to come from several pavilions all at once. His squeals, his shrill orders, his grunts and moans. Like an impatient child, he flitted between his wives and animals, reserving the time in the alleys to confer with his courtiers and eunuchs.

The eunuchs were the real rulers of Hazari, Hilal Khan had said, each more vicious than the other. The pet had her own pavilion, but father and daughter rarely met, each busy with their own pleasures. The Haji was tame compared to his pet, Hilal Khan had told Bihzad.

But in his first days at the palace, Bihzad ignored everyone. It seemed as if, finally, his father's dream had come true, that he had indeed fulfilled all prophecies and become a master artist. He felt a sense of triumph at spoiling the pleasure of Adili the Afghan and the mischievous Darogha. Who could stop him now? He would paint his albums exactly as he wished without having to seek the approval of anyone, or wait for permission to enter into the sight of his ruler. He felt proud, the equal of all master artists from Persia to Hindustan. A secret dream filled him. Perhaps one day Hazari's kitabkhana would rival Sikri's, perhaps the Afghan would send spies over to steal the Haji's coveted albums. Perhaps the emperor of Hindustan would come to hear of him, and invade Hazari to capture her artist. Lying awake on his bed, Bihzad imagined himself entering the gates of Sikri, not on a mule-cart but on an imperial elephant.

Despite Hilal Khan's warnings and the gossip of the market, he grew fond of the Haji. They called him a eunuch behind his back, the short, bald Uzbek, without a single hair on his cheeks. A eunuch who pretended to be a bridegroom. But Bihzad felt a strange loyalty towards the ruler of Hazari. Hadn't he chosen him as the master on the merit of a single painting, when the emperor of Hindustan had remained unmoved even after examining hundreds? He regretted the time he had wasted in Agra and Sikri, the meticulous care with which he had brought the *Akbarnama* almost to completion before his exile. He wished he had drawn the ugly Haji instead of Akbar – a hunter who had failed to recognise a lion. Alone in his pavilion, he cursed Akbar, cursed the kitabkhana. Cursed even his father for failing to choose the right master. The voice of Salim Amiri floated in over the desert air – *the pleasure of ruling is like the pleasure of sport.* Weren't the painters too a ruler's sport? Setting one artist against another, while enjoying the fruits of their pens? Making them wrestle like wrestlers, fight on the banks of the Jamuna while he watched from the jharokha window. The artist should choose his ruler, he thought, before he becomes a victim to the pleasure of others.

Watching the flickering lamp by his window, he thought again of Salim Amiri. *Much in you is a man, Bihzad. And much still a dreamer. Emperors need men, not dreamers.* That was why his teacher, Mir Sayyid Ali, had left Agra, because he couldn't satisfy the emperor's need. He saw his grim-faced teacher – his tunic pulled tightly over his chest, the sleeves pleated neatly – dreaming of triumph, of surrender, and prayer. And he saw his father – a man among dreamers, the emperor's favourite courtier. Why should an artist dream when men desired nothing but stories and vain portraits? His forehead broke into a frown, recalling his patrons at the Joy House. He remembered the biddings, and the loud praise. *Better to become a man than stay for ever a dreamer.*

*

Haji Uzbek suffered continually from stomach-aches, boils and lesions, accusing his servants of serving him poison. On his physician's advice he'd reduce his drinking, then return to his normal habit at the urging of his astrologer. The astrologer fuelled the Haji's fears, spurred on his ecstasies; some read in his predictions the scent of personal gain, but he was usually accurate. In public, the Haji appeared inscrutable. He would sit on his throne for hours without uttering a single word. A nod would be seen as a sign of great benevolence. At the advice of the

Haji's courtiers, defaulting merchants would enter his presence, heads bowed, a blade of grass between their teeth, behaving like obedient animals. The more the show of humility, the greater the prospect of a pardon. But he would turn into a different man when animals appeared before him, particularly the strange ones. His subjects knew of his interest, and presented him with a steady stream of spectacles.

He could sit for hours inspecting a gelded goat, with teats like a female, reputed to give milk that tasted like Busra honey. He'd spend a whole morning sitting patiently before a pheasant's cage, waiting for it to lay an egg – for it was most auspicious to see the egg drop. Merchants came from all ends of the desert with curious item: a turkey that changed colours when mating, a spider, its body as large as a crab, capable of strangling a snake.

From his squealing it was hard to tell whether the Haji was happy or livid with rage, ready to slaughter an animal deemed ominous by the astrologer.

Bihzad waited for the Haji's orders, sitting by his side in the court. Among the courtiers, he didn't notice anyone recording the proceedings, as was the custom in Akbar's court. He wondered if he would be asked to draw his master's life, perhaps. Which story might he be asked to illustrate? But he hadn't noticed a storyteller amusing the Haji. Secretly, he prepared himself for the likely assignment – the tedium of drawing the courtiers' portraits. From his days at the Joy House, he recalled his many successes and rare failures. Once he had drawn a Tartar, a man with flaring nostrils and clenched jaw. The man had taken one look at the likeness with its sagging double chin, and had felled Bihzad with a blow. Then he had learned to oblige his sitters, hiding the cauliflower ears, beak-like noses, scraggly moustaches, scrawny necks, and hollow chests. *You must paint their true self* – he had followed his teacher's advice to considerable acclaim.

But the Haji didn't order him to draw his courtiers, never even made any reference to the Lady. Has he forgotten, Bihzad worried. Does he take me for a snake charmer?

Then he decided to surprise the Haji. After a visit to the pavilion of beasts, he drew a short album full of the Haji's birds and
animals. He waited till the Haji was seated on his throne, then
offered the first miniature to him nervously. It was of a chinar
tree full of birds. The colony of birds seemed to be anxiously
awaiting their sovereign. A horned pheasant scanned the forest.
A quick-moving blackbird with white spots looked out from the
highest branch. Jungle fowl gazed up. Quails waited to take
flight. A pair of mountain cranes lifted their necks above the
others, drawing the viewer's gaze towards the corner of the
garden, where the peacock had just begun to unfurl its tail.

A look of admiration entered the Haji's eyes. Then Bihzad
offered the next miniature – a pair of musk deer chasing a black
antelope. A third – a huge wild ass almost the size of a lion. The
Haji snatched the album from Bihzad's hands, rapidly turned
pages, till the birds and beasts blurred before his eyes as if they
were fleeing an army of hunters. He stopped at the last page – at
the pair of fighting camels. Bihzad waited anxiously. This was
the ultimate test, he knew. Time after time, Mir Sayyid Ali had
taken out his collection of old masters from his rusted trunk and
placed them before his students, among them his favourite, The
Fighting Camels. It came from the pen of the Great One himself,
Kamal-al-Din Bihzad. Wetting his lips, the teacher would point
out the fine details – the natural folds on the hoofs, the hairy
necks, the backdrop of barren rocks that bore witness to the
beasts' fury. From Persia to Hindustan, every student learned to
copy the fighting camels. Masters returned to that scene to hone
their skills or to test the strength of their ageing eyes. *A true
artist is one who can charm with simple beasts,* Bihzad recalled his
teacher saying in Agra.

Haji Uzbek squealed, running out of the court with the
album to show it to his wives. All evening, his voice gurgled
from the various pavilions. From then on, merchants arriving at
Hazari's court had to wait until the royal artist had presented his
paintings to Haji Uzbek, and he had had a chance to calm
himself after turning pages of the album.

*

Even Hilal Khan seemed perplexed. 'Do you draw nothing but animals?' Sounding almost like the Khwaja, he admonished his friend lightly. 'There are two kinds of artists. The first draw animals and birds to fill the margins of a painting – they are the novices. The second kind – the *real* artists – might draw a horse ridden by an emperor, or a dying lion pierced by his spear. Have you heard of a master artist drawing nothing but animals?'

Sitting behind the tall reeds at the edge of the oasis, Bihzad and Hilal Khan exchanged gossip with a jar of wine and two cups before them. They met each month in the faint light of an approaching new moon, both taking care to arrive unnoticed.

The Agra merchant had died, almost on the doorstep of his home in Agra. His son, Hilal Khan was proud to say, had returned to the serai with a new caravan, after the period of mourning was over. There was not much news from Sikri any more. Sikri is dead, Hilal Khan said. Akbar had abandoned it in favour of Lahore. The palaces had fallen empty, the animals were gone, the water no longer flowed through the pretty channels of the immense courtyard. The harem had left Sikri too. The kitabkhana was empty. 'Akbar! He is a warring emperor again, not like your Haji.'

*Sikri is dead*, Bihzad thought. The faces of the artists flashed before him. Has he got rid of the Afghan too? He wanted to ask Hilal Khan if he had any news of the Khwaja, but his friend went on.

'Didn't you tell me how artists used to sneer behind Adili's back? The chameleon, they called him. The animal painter! The one without the talent to draw a human face. Is Bihzad now following in the footsteps of Adili?'

Bihzad started to protest. 'What's wrong with drawing animals and birds? They're more beautiful, a hundred times more precious than we are. Haven't you noticed their delicate eyes, their beaks, the colours of their wings? Don't you see the touch of the divine brush...'

Hilal Khan stopped him. 'To be the best you must draw the

best! Are you mad, Bihzad? What will you draw next – scorpions and snakes?'

The two fell silent for a moment. Then Hilal Khan rolled his eyes. 'Have you met *her* yet? The strangest beast in the menagerie?' He seemed a bit confused. 'But you should have met her by now. From the moment he called you his son, we all thought you'd become the lord of Hazari. The Haji's pet would be yours. You might not like what you see or hear, but you'd be the most powerful man in Hazari, for the Haji denies his pet nothing.'

'See or hear?'

Despite their distance from the town, Hilal Khan lowered his voice. 'She was seen on her way to the mosque. She let her veil drop, appearing in the market with her face uncovered. She came to the moon festival wrapped in a dress so thin that you could see all her secret parts. Shameless! Like a slave girl parading naked.'

With a quick look at Bihzad, he continued. 'She's enslaved by passion. They say women lose their appetite for men by the time they're thirty, but not her.'

'What would I see if I married her then?'

Hilal Khan started to laugh. 'Shall I speak of her eyes or her brows, her nose or her lips? Shall I speak of her cheek, her hair or her waist?' He imitated the Sufis, swaying his head. 'Shall I speak of her squint, Bihzad! Her arms – like a wrestler's – picking up watermelons with one hand!'

Bihzad thought he'd ask Hilal Khan about the soldier of fortune who had returned to the serai after seeing and hearing the pet.

'Just don't ask me to be her eunuch! I'm too old to be her love-boy!' Hilal Khan giggled.

\*

In an act of flattery, he drew Haji Uzbek among his pets – pillowed on a lion's shoulder, a leopard at his feet, a lynx and a wolf kneeling before him, an army of snowy lambs, blue bulls and deer ringing a fence around his animal kingdom. A line of calligraphy appeared below the margin: *By the reckoning of eyes he is but a man, but by the reckoning of wisdom he is the emperor of all living creatures.*

The Haji appeared unmoved by his portrait.

\*

At midnight, an attendant woke Bihzad. He led him through the guarded passages between the pavilions to Haji Uzbek's harem. Bihzad entered without blindfold, but the glittering lights blinded him. A ceiling of gold above their heads and sumptuous carpets under their feet, the Haji's wives waited for the Haji in a large room taken up almost entirely by a bed. A dozen or so women reclined on the bed in various postures, chatting with each other, their gowns and veils shed over the carpet. A young slave girl showed Bihzad to a seat at the foot of the bed, and offered him a cup of wine. He raised his eyes hesitantly, only to find the whole harem staring at him as if he were a strange animal appeared at the royal court.

He saw the Haji's chief wife, called the lotus lady – her face as lovely as the flower, sloe-eyed, lips dipped in red – reclining on the bed with her breasts uncovered. He saw luxurious hair, like a swarm of black bees, tumbling on the shoulder of another wife, her tapering thighs wrapped around a silk pillow. Moving swiftly across the room, a dancing girl stopped before Bihzad, shutting his eyes playfully with her palm. When he opened them again, he saw the eyes: demure and brazen – each distinct yet tinged by the same desire. The dancing girl motioned him to finish his drink. Raising his cup to his lips, he stopped, unable to restrain his eyes from darting all over the room like a black-bird's. He spilled the wine on his tunic, inviting more laughter.

The Haji came into the room from his bath, holding a cup of wine. The slave girls undressed him, teasing and fondling him as if he were a little child, while he kept on drinking. Between sips, he examined his wives with the cold stare of a merchant. When he finished his cup, he turned to the lotus lady and asked for more. But she refused him, inviting him instead to join her and the others on the bed. It made the Haji angry. Stepping onto the bed, he grabbed her from behind, scratching her back with his nails. She bit and scratched him too, none daring to separate them.

Bihzad watched, the skin on his back beginning to crawl.

With the sound of ripping silk, the Haji turned into a crab, folding his legs around his mate's body, bringing up his feet to her navel. He seized her wrists and uncurled her limbs, lunging his head forward hungrily on her breast. A wild duck cried out, followed by the shameless yammering of a quail. In a moment, he unfastened his grip and just as his mate started to quiver, he caught hold of her hair and struck a love blow on her rear, stifling her cry in her throat.

Like a hungry man trying to swallow all his food in one gulp, he didn't stay with any one of them for long. He pounced like a tiger on another one of his wives, gripped her around the waist and bent her forward, making her stand four-footed with both palms flat on the carpet.

Bridegroom! *Man's burden is made tolerable by the brief moments when he becomes a beast,* Bihzad recalled Hilal Khan saying.

Like a blind animal, the Haji plied her with thrusts, then gripped her ankles suddenly, almost toppling her over, and fastened them like a chain behind his neck. Bihzad watched as the Haji imitated his pets one by one – the tusker stroking the arched back of a consort with his head, grinding into another like a boar, mounting a third like a proud stallion. Then he became still, lying on his back like a dying tortoise, drawing in his limbs, withdrawing his senses. He lay like a monk. The head servant – the one who had prepared his bath – came over to the bed. She moved slowly, as if wounded, her gait unlovely. Pushing aside the lotus lady and the other wives, she climbed on top of the bridegroom, sitting like a queen on her throne. She began to churn, head flung back, then without breaking her rhythm stooped to fasten her teeth on his neck.

Bihzad watched, his throat dry despite the wine.

The Haji raised himself up in the bed, the servant still above him, his head at the monkey tufts under her arm, and stared at

Bihzad. He pointed at his feet, to a stack of paper and a row of brushes and colours. With his fingers he mimed holding a brush over a painting, then collapsed on his bed once again.

A slave girl knelt at Bihzad's feet, placed a sheet of blank paper in his lap, and handed him a brush. From their play on the bed, the women stared at him again. The Haji – now in the pose of an archer with a slender slave on his lap, her breasts crushed against her thighs – squealed, spurring on his women towards Bihzad. Leaving the bed, they stood crowding around him, admiring the colours in the jars, exhibiting themselves openly before him, urging him to view their charms, begging him to capture them in his painting. One raised his cup to her breasts, dipped in her rosebud. Another stretched her leg to touch his, raising an eyebrow. Bihzad's hands shook as the women stood before him imitating the Haji's motions on the bed, pretending to be his mare, feigning pleasure. In one ear, he heard a sharply drawn breath, harsh panting in the other.

The Haji had been testing him with birds and animals, he thought. He closed his eyes. Akbar! He imagined the emperor in his own harem.

The throaty sobbing of a woman distracted him from his thoughts. She sat inside a cage at the far corner of the room, her limbs in shackles. A red streak ran down her back. But she was sobbing not from pain but from the denial of her pleasure. The Haji stopped for a moment, gave her an angry look, then resumed. He was now the only one standing, erect over the bed, the lotus lady clinging to his neck. All beasts were in him – at full gallop. 'Son!' he screamed at Bihzad.

A bead of sweat formed on Bihzad's forehead, and dropped on to the blank sheet in his lap.

*

Never in the three decades of his life had he suffered so before a blank page. Not since his first day at Mir Sayyid Ali's studio had he been so struck by the absence of a story to illustrate. Even at the Joy House, he would glance briefly at a sleeping face, then conjure his own story, borrowing lavishly from the ones read aloud to him by Zuleikha when he was still a child. Despite Hilal Khan's ire, he felt a certain comfort drawing the birds and animals. Unlike the human faces, he sensed no urge to hide their imperfections, relished drawing the sharp claws of an eagle, or a tiger's fangs. Never, since he had started drawing at the Khwaja's haveli in Agra, had he felt inept faithfully recording a scene that was enacted before his eyes.

But the harem was different. It was as if his fingers had rebelled against his sight. As much as he tried to compose a scene, the lines refused to flow. The forms that he saw cavorting before him, seemed like Mulla Assad's ghosts – invisible on close scrutiny. After several false starts, he went back to the early discipline of a novice. *Start with the immovable*, he whispered to himself, drawing the lavish bed with ease. For balance, he added the cage at the other end of the room. He drew his own seat and the stack of paper next to it. Then, he closed his eyes. *Imagine the central figure and the key purpose.* With Akbar it had been easy. The emperor on his throne receiving a visitor. The emperor in a hunt. Opening his eyes, he couldn't find the Haji amidst the profusion of limbs. He searched in vain for the central figure and its key purpose.

He thought of the days when they had sniggered at Mir Sayyid Ali's painting of a bathing princess. Shirin, naked to her waist, a lotus floating on a lake, breasts half-submerged in silver. The students had wondered what their grim teacher had felt when he added a touch of blush to her bud. He raised his pen to draw the lotus lady, the young slave girl, the head servant, but the figures refused to take shape. What, he thought, could make his paintings crow with the pleasures of the harem?

The Haji looked surprised when Bihzad presented him at the court with his next album – another parade of birds and animals. He looked up a few times at him, shaking his head. Then he made a gesture with his fingers as if holding a brush over a painting.

*

He became a favoured intimate, one for whom the harem was

always open, women no longer covering their faces before him. He would enter before midnight while the Haji was still in his bath and draw the women. He drew them gossiping around a marble fountain folding piles of embroidered napkins, laughing and chatting, refreshing themselves with sherbets. He drew them coming out of their own baths throwing water at each other. He drew the lotus lady, smoking a water pipe as she listened to a singer, the head servant trying on a chagtai hat while the other women looked on in contempt, a slave massaging another slave, the look of love in both pairs of eyes.

'You have become a eunuch,' Hilal Khan said with disgust. 'That's what eunuchs do – accompany their master to his bed-chamber. Wait, they'll start calling you names. The women will tease you. Come here, my dearest, tailless, hairless one! Come here my love, whose prickle is the size of an ant, whose sting can barely pierce the skin!'

He warned Bihzad of a more serious danger. 'What if you were to draw one of the wives more often than the others? You'd make them all jealous, and nothing's worse than a jealous woman. One day you'll wake to find the Haji's death sentence on you!'

Bihzad confided in him his failure to draw the harem in full vigour. Hilal Khan understood. 'I don't blame you, Bihzad. Artists are men too. Can you imagine what others would do? Your teacher would have died of shock. Your father would have pleaded with Akbar to spare him. Even make him the Chief Executioner instead! The artist understands love, understands its purpose. But this isn't love.'

'Then what is it?'

'It'd be easy to call it madness.' He shook his head. 'No ...' Then he returned to his jocular self. 'I bet he wants you to make his sword look longer than it is! Maybe he'll distribute your paintings among his courtiers, to tempt their wives!'

Some days, Bihzad told Hilal Khan, the Haji wouldn't be interested in his women at all, only in their jewellery. Even when the dancing girls accosted him, lifting up their dresses, he'd continue to inspect an earring or an armband without any sign of emotion on his face. There were days when he did nothing but drink. The slaves who undressed him would ask for gifts, usually receiving a yes, hardly ever a no. It was enough to refuse him a drink of wine to drive him to tears. To dry them, they had only to fill a cup to the brim.

Hilal Khan did not pay attention to Bihzad, but kept on staring into the dark sky as if searching for a solution. Then he turned to face his friend.

'There are a few artists who know how to draw these scenes.'

Bihzad waited for him to continue.

'But we must go veiled to see them.'

*

By a clever stratagem, he succeeded in pleasing the Haji. It was a common trick, turning the inanimate into the living – a tree in the shape of a man for instance, or a cloud resembling an angel. The masters would use the trick to add a touch of life to a scene that was weak in purpose.

Bihzad drew the palace of Hazari in the foreground and a giant flesh-coloured mountain looming above it. With its cracks and ravines, it resembled a crouching woman, its flanks suggesting her ample proportions. A pair of boulders jutted out proudly from its flesh-toned slopes. Ridges ran down to a deep nook, into the dark cave between her thighs, hinting at a bed of wispy grass. The glacial peak was about to melt, a gorging stream about to flood the parched minarets of the palace.

*

He was woken at midnight. Out of habit, he started to walk through the passages towards the harem. But the eunuch nudged him towards the Haji's bath. Slave girls washed and chafed his skin, darkened his eyes, waxed his brows, then slipped a crown upon his head. He carried a sheaf of arrows and a strung bow. His bride followed him into the wedding hall, as was the custom, drawing a veil over her face.

Bihzad saw Zuhra.

For three nights after the wedding, Bihzad slept alone on the floor of his wife's pavilion, as was the custom. On the fourth night, Zuhra appeared – named after the flaming star born in the first hour of the night. She didn't ask him to extinguish the lamps. Covered from head to toe, she appeared more naked than anyone he had ever seen. As if by magic, the veil dropped at the right moment, and he saw her eyes – a sparkle of malice in one, a vacant brilliance in the other. An attendant looked discreetly away.

She led him out past her armed guards and servants, and into a smaller pavilion, her bathchamber lined with blue tiles and mirrors. He tried to stroke her velvet bodice, but she slipped past his embrace. A voice came from the bath. A soft and ravishing voice, the voice of a young boy. Bihzad sat next to her beside a marble fountain, listening. The song lulled them both. She beckoned her attendant to bring her favourite black water from the Bosphorus. Sipping it, her lips turned dark, and a bitter smell from the boiling liquid filled the air.

Then she rose to embrace the singer. The boy, twelve or thirteen years of age, had the face of a young girl, a pair of rosebuds on his chest and gently rounded hips. She embraced him, her eunuch boy, then started the kissing game. The two went over to a divan, sitting face to face, eyeing each other like two wrestlers, eyes unflinching, moving their cheeks from side to side, moving closer then moving back. Bihzad sat drinking his wine, watching the game. The first to catch the other's lips would be the winner. Eyebrows arched and nostrils flared, Zuhra lurched forward,

186

missing by a breath, pursing her lips in disappointment. Then, she unclasped her velvet bodice, shook her hair free from its silky knot, loosened her waistband. Her breathing turned violent as the boy tried to distract her by sticking out his tongue.

Bihzad watched intently.

Her back, turned towards him, was patterned with henna. She started to rock on her cushion, a bubbling cry rising in her throat, the two now lashing at each other like hooded serpents.

She was first to strike, throwing the boy off guard with a sudden raising of her arms, seizing his lips in her teeth. Then she started to laugh.

Turning, Bihzad saw a trickle of blood on Zuhra's lips. Setting down his cup, he reached out to hold her, to stroke her back, to kiss her, but she denied him. She spoke not as a demure bride or a brazen courtesan, but as his wife.

'Do you want to play the kissing game now?'

A desire greater than lust entered him.

*

His wedding was not like the weddings he had seen as a boy in Agra. He had expected his wife to live with him, just like the Khwaja and Zuleikha. But after the first four nights in Zuhra's pavilion, he was led back by her guards to his own. It puzzled Bihzad. He resumed his life in the Haji's court, visited his master in his harem, then stayed awake till late waiting for Zuhra's call, for her guards to come and escort him back. When he did return to Zuhra's pavilion, he had to search for her on her terrace, in her bath, everywhere, as if he had arrived unannounced, and his wife wasn't expecting his visit.

Wandering from room to room, he'd come upon Zuhra and the eunuch. She would be applying colour to his nails, braiding his hair, like mother and daughter, or applying a burning paste to his body to remove his hair. The boy screamed as she spread the rusma, then scraped it off with the sharp edge of a mussel shell, threatening to rip off the erring strands with her teeth.

She appeared unblemished by beauty itself. There was nothing extraordinary about her, in her eyes, her lips, or in the lustre of her skin, nothing alluring in the turn of her neck or the arch of her waist. Her gait wasn't as graceful as a swan's, her breasts not as firm as a slave's in Hazari's market. Yet she tempted by her urge, in moments transformed to a seductress, her spirit sparkling in her eyes, blending with her breath, adding a dancer's spring to her steps. Like a blank page, she seemed open to a painter's brush.

He'd see the eunuch's glowing eyes on her, as the boy undressed her, applying henna to her back and navel. He'd leave a mark on her breasts, like a peacock's foot, with his nails. The constant murmur of water surrounded them, and the muffled sound of voices. She'd order the boy to sit in the cave of her thighs. He'd become a suckling calf, or a blind man picking a fruit from a tree. Calling Bihzad over, she'd ask him to join them, offering the boy or herself as his prey. They'd become a starfish with several fangs, or a pyramid turning itself over and over. From languorous to violent, she'd make Bihzad hover on the brink, wouldn't let him recede. Sensing the boy's urge, she'd hold up a pillow for him to bite and rip, to strike his head against and growl. Then, still in Bihzad's embrace, she'd twist her face away from him and, without breaking their union, kiss the eunuch boy.

*

They strolled over the terrace at dawn – Bihzad and Zuhra, freeing themselves from the sleeping boy. She rested her head on his shoulder, turning her face to the moon. He pointed out the stars to her, speaking into her ear.

'One day they'll come to visit Hazari from all the planets and stars, from all the empires of the world. They'll come to see her kitabkhana.'

'And what will they see?' she asked, her face still turned towards the sky.

'The most magnificent paintings! Better than Persia's Mirak, Hindustan's...'

'You mean they'll come to admire dead men, dead animals, dead flowers.' She seemed unimpressed. 'Is that why you've come here? To trick everyone? To make a desert seem alive?'

He ignored her words, started to tell her the stories he had heard from Mir Sayyid Ali, and from his friend Salim Amiri. But Zuhra stopped him, pointing at the sleeping boy on her bed.

'He is a *true* artist. A master. Look! He's clad from head to toe in his art. But it's different from yours.'

Bihzad felt angry at the boy – stealing a man's love by pretending to be a woman, and a woman's by pretending to be a man. 'And what will your master artist draw when he wakes?'

She spoke as if she was teasing him, but there was a sting in Zuhra's voice. 'Nothing. Absolutely nothing. The pleasure he gives would fill album after album, unlike the fool who tries to please long after the hour of pleasure has passed.'

'What must an artist do then?' He stared into her eyes.

Her words seemed misty and disconsolate. 'Art is dead life.'

Bihzad shook his head vigorously. 'No. The great masters breathe life into their paintings, just like the Creator. They make them ...'

'Nothing but a fake. A mirror doesn't hold a face, a lake can't capture the sky. A painting lives *only* in the act of love. It dies on paper.'

She seemed less alive that morning, unhappy with how the night had ended, unhappy with Bihzad. To please her, he held up a drawing of her face. She turned away. 'Don't flatter me,' she said. To rile her and break her sullenness, he began to tell her the gossip he had heard, what men said about her at the market and the Joy House, how she appeared in the eyes of the drunk. 'As if you had entered the market with your breasts uncovered!' She looked at him, as if she was troubled by a loss greater than that of her veil. He started to tell Zuhra about the Haji and his women.

Her face remained clouded, as they strolled at dawn on the evenly lit terrace.

*

When the guards didn't arrive to fetch him for long periods, he'd blame himself for upsetting his wife. He'd murmur his apologies, sitting by himself in his pavilion. Then, he'd be unable to resist, charging out into the narrow passages, wailing like a child.

'Zuhra.........................................................!'

His servants would grab him before he could reach her, bring him back. Ignoring the Haji's call, he'd curl up with a tael of opium and jars of wine.

*

Why? he'd ask Zuhra when they met again. Why hadn't she called for him for so long? Why did she disappear from time to time? Why didn't she want to see his paintings or ask him to draw her portrait?

'I am a breeze,' she said, 'never remain still. I am a desert breeze, never leave my mark. I belong to none, no one belongs to me.'

*

He felt pain, as if their intimacy was yet to touch a secret but vital part, despite ravishing with pleasures. Which fold, which orifice was left to discover, he wondered, which one would reveal her finally?

Never since he had left Zuleikha's bed had he felt such dismay. He lived in constant fear, feared she would go away never to return, feared her rejection.

He'd spend a whole morning watching the Haji teach his parrot to speak. His master would hold up an imaginary pen, order him to draw the bird. He'd seek an excuse to leave, but the bird would speak to him in the Haji's voice. 'Kiss me, you rotten tart!'

He thought of Zuhra every moment, planning his escape from the court and the Haji's harem. When he did manage to enter her pavilion, he'd find it quiet, the maids cleaning her bath and chatting in whispers, with no sign of Zuhra or the boy. He'd enter her bedchamber at midnight to find the eunuch asleep on her lap, and a faraway look in Zuhra's eyes. He would not be able to wake her then, not even if he paraded before her as a stallion, imitated a rutting bull, or charged about madly flooding the carpet at her feet with his seed.

He grew jealous of the boy, denied the pleasure of seventy

virgins in paradise, but inseparable from Zuhra's pleasures. The eunuch has married Haji Uzbek's pet, he thought, always ready to possess, deceiving her, yet keeping her alive in her fantasies.

Zuleikha's perfume wafted in from his memory. Why couldn't he capture his lover, hold her still within a painting? He railed at his fate, blamed his luck.

\*

'Ziadi. The witch!' Hilal Khan heard Bihzad in silence. 'She has bewitched her father, and now she has bewitched you! What do you see in Zuhra? You must be a mad Majnun to see your Laila in her!' He shook his head. 'It's her opium, her wine, the black water from the Bosphorus. You're not yourself since you have been with her and her boy.'

He told Hilal Khan of the kissing game – of the only time he had played with her and won. Then she had become a wonder of wonders, truly like the flaming planet.

'A man in love has no use of advice,' Hilal Khan sighed. 'Ask her, Bihzad, what she does with her eunuchs when they become unfit for intimate service.'

'You mean when they grow old?'

Hilal Khan nodded his head. 'Or sick.'

The boy seemed ageless to Bihzad, his voice like a newborn thrush. What would she do with *him*, her husband, he wondered, would he suffer the same fate as the doomed soldier of fortune?

'It'd be too easy to call her mad,' Hilal Khan frowned.

'Then what is she?'

'You are the artist, aren't you?' Hilal Khan smiled. 'Why don't you draw her *true* self?' He handed Bihzad a black veil and slipped one over his own head. Bihzad looked surprised.

'Didn't you want to draw the Haji at play?' he reminded Bihzad. 'You know how to depict a proper love – the blush on a virgin's cheeks, the eyes of secret lovers even. Now you must learn how to depict a shameless love.'

The two huddled down the narrow lanes of the market, and crossed the slave merchants' courtyard. Passing the stables, they felt the soldiers' gaze on their shapeless forms. Hilal Khan spoke under his breath. 'There are artists who draw these shameless scenes. The infidels.' He motioned with his eyes towards the village isolated from the others among the dunes. No one from Hazari ever went to the infidels' village, except the Sufis. No one came from there, except children stolen and sold as eunuchs and slave girls. Once a year, a great fire covered the village in smoke, as if a corpse was being burnt. It was the custom of the Hindus to burn their dead, and also to mark the end of the year with a fire. Mullah Shirhindi would silence with his eyes anyone who spoke of the idol that guarded the village among the dunes.

Hilal Khan hushed Bihzad with his finger. They kept to the back of the mud-thatched homes as they entered the village. The veils were essential, Hilal Khan had explained; if detected they'd be taken for women of Hazari secretly visiting a sage for magical potions. Otherwise they might be chased – mistaken for spies, or slave merchants looking to steal their children.

Hilal Khan peered in through the windows. He seemed to be looking for the right hut, moving quickly, dismissing at first glance. Then he stopped, motioning Bihzad to come over.

Bihzad saw a man sitting with his back to the window, a half-finished painting propped up on his knees. Bihzad peered in over the man's shoulder.

The artist had drawn a lover. A courtesan, alone in the night, arms raised, pining to embrace the dark sky, walking through a forest in languid steps. Her arms were outstretched, as if the sky was her lover, the moon scorching her, the breeze ruffling her modesty.

They moved over to the next window.

Another artist sat drawing the same courtesan. She had lost her way in a dark grove, brushing against her lover by chance. Her fingers touch him furtively as he holds his silence, teasing her by remaining still. Unashamed, she gazes openly at his body, draws in his smell, tastes his skin with the tip of her tongue. Her lover watches, amused. Finally aware, she becomes a trembling butterfly beating her wings against his chest.

It was as if the whole colony of artists had chosen to depict nothing but the lovers, each adding a stroke to their fire. Peering

through the windows, Bihzad saw the artists with their lovers –
women reclining on beds of leaves waiting for their own love
play to begin.

'For whom do they draw these scenes?' Bihzad asked Hilal
Khan in a whisper.

'For their god. The god of love. For them it's an act of
worship. Just as a Muslim prays on his knees ...'

He saw the infidels' god, Krishna, adorning the women with
flowers, embracing one while fondling another, playing hide and
seek with many hands touching him, holding a pair of swaying
hips like an earthen jar. Krishna whispering secrets into a courtesan's ear, making her blush. His face and body bore the marks of
a lover's teeth. In one scene he appeared on the branch of a tree,
shooting arrows at the women, setting fire to their veils.

Hilal Khan looked at Bihzad, gave him a knowing smile.

*If not love, then?*

Returning, they glimpsed the idol at the village's centre – a
carved black stone in the shape of a pig's head.

*

She came to him, she left him, she returned. He never succeeded
in keeping her. As usual, violent games preceded their mating.
Her pavilion came alive as soon as she returned from her mysterious absences. She made sport of his jealousy, never waiting
for him to arrive to begin her evenings. 'Whether it pleases you
to come or not, we are content and thankful!' she'd say, a cloud
of smoke above her head, lips blackened by the black water that
kept her awake at night, and made her hallucinate. He'd see
fresh marks on her body.

He started to burn and wash away his paintings. *A painting
lives in the act of love* – Zuhra's voice chased him as he wandered
through her pavilion from room to room. He burned the portraits he had drawn at the Joy House, those that his patrons had
refused to buy. He burned the sketches he had made of his friends
at the serai, Kanu and Sabi. After a hard look, he drowned the
slave girl he had drawn at Hazari's market despite the refusal of
her owner. The rose from the garden of Rum. He had drawn her

glistening face, melting butter splattered all over her breasts, thighs parted at her owner's command. He took one last look then drowned the painting in a pond for goldfish. From his stack of meagre belongings, he recovered a portrait of Zuleikha – one of many he had drawn while lying on her bed listening to her gossip. His stepmother. He took a long look at the Khwaja's wife, then burned her too. A true artist, he whispered to himself, doesn't wrap his paintings in silk. No amount of care could save them, they were bound to die after the hour of pleasure had passed.

Besides the Haji, his animals and his harem, he painted little else. For the first time in his life, Bihzad felt like a true kitabkhana artist, his urge going no further than a Darogha's orders. He felt relief, dipping his brush in colour simply as a matter of course, like a clerk counts coins at a mint. After quite a few hesitant starts, he learned to master the Haji's love play, drawing the limbs, the intricate geometry of desire without any heed to purpose, till the viewer's pleasure required not even a dash of imagination.

Living with and without Zuhra, he ceased to be the artist his Persian father had willed him to be, the one named after the Persian eagle. Only Hilal Khan kept on, nagging him whenever they met by the oasis, reminding him of his genius, cajoling him to begin the grandest of albums that the world would remember him by. Bihzad avoided discussing his paintings with his friend, gradually avoided bringing up the Haji in their conversations, even his woes with Zuhra. Their meetings by the oasis fell silent. Living by his master's whims, he became a true courtier, a willing prisoner of the Haji's court, till, on the day of the second feast of Ramadan since his arrival in Hazari, he drew a scene in black and white, without a touch of colour, leaving it for his absent wife in her empty pavilion.

A stag and a doe grazed with their young foal over a carpet of grass that stretched to the foot of a mountain. Suddenly, a flood rushed in, drowning the stag and the young one. He drew the doe escaping into the woods without once looking back.

*

'Drink not the heart's blood.' Hilal Khan fixed him a hard stare.

In the years Bihzad spent in Hazari, Akbar marched from one end of his empire to the other. After only fifteen years in his new capital, he returned to the life of a nomad. Sikri, abandoned, became a ghost town. But the cheering in Agra was muted. He didn't return to see his favourite elephant fights on the banks of the Jamuna. First Bengal, then Kabul and his rebellious half-brother, he busied himself quelling unrest, going on to capture his birthplace in Sind, sweeping into Baluchistan and Kandahar further west. The fear of an attack from the mountain warriors of Central Asia – warriors much like his own Mughal ancestors – had drawn him out of Sikri, his courtiers surmised. His court followed him reluctantly, forced never to spend the feast of Ramadan in the same land twice. He was intoxicated by the wine of conquest, they grumbled. Like the great Alexander, he too would die weeping with no more worlds left to conquer.

He succeeded where his ancestors had failed. Hindustan – the vast plains between the mouth of the river Indus and the cradle of the Ganges – became truly his, secure between the mountains and the sea. *As brave as Akbar! As fortunate as Akbar! As wise as Akbar!* his subjects rejoiced. Still, he pressed on, southward over the Deccan plateau, with his drunken sons dying one by one of their father's ambition. The emperor's pleasure was like the noonday halt under a shady tree, never to be prolonged, his generals grumbled.

He fell in love with Kashmir, despite the arduous journey from Lahore, and travelled often to the valley, building roads and resthouses along the way. His harem stayed behind in Lahore, while Akbar strolled alone in his private garden.

There were those who believed the emperor was fleeing another enemy – his son Salim, impatient to inherit Akbar's throne. Poisoning was suspected if the emperor suffered from an attack of colic; if his gun misfired during a royal hunt, the entire gunnery fell under a shadow. At sixty, he was considered old enough to die. He is spiting his son by staying alive, the inner circle whispered.

During the years Bihzad spent in Hazari, caravans ferried rumours about the emperor's faith. Travelling merchants spoke of his delight on receiving illuminated albums with pictures from the gospel of the Portuguese. Pictures of a holy mother with a newborn child. A man gazing down at his followers from a cross. Travelling saints described Akbar's House of Worship – the lively debates, the squabbles between Christians and Jews, Shias and Sunnis, all vying for the highest honour from the emperor. The ruler of the soil now wishes to rule over the souls of his subjects. There were rumours that he was after a new faith – his own faith. Allahu Akbar! God is Great! There were those who gave a new meaning to that age-old cry of the devout – Akbar is God, God Akbar!

Not everyone approved of Akbar's views. Some said he was unfit to be a true Muslim, surrounding himself with luxuries and wine. How can he be called a Christian, serve one god and one wife, unless he renounces his harem? How can he be a true Hindu when the blood of the impure flows in his veins?

Then the decree of infallibility came from the emperor. Only Akbar would convey the words of God to his subjects. Not the learned men or the priests, not his religious advisors, or the head of the mosque. He would rule over *all* matters in his empire. None could refuse or sanction an act of faith in Hindustan. Only Akbar.

*

As they crossed deserts and mountains, travellers felt safe under the gaze of the warring emperor. Whenever he heard of an attack on a caravan, soldiers were despatched in pursuit of the bandits. The guilty were duly hanged, and stolen goods returned. Nearly half of the world's commerce passed through Hindustan, inspected and haggled over by merchants under the cool arches of the bazaars. Even her neighbours flourished. Oases, the likes of Hazari, grew prosperous, suffering only from periodic droughts and sieges, or when the harvest of poppy failed, driving up its price and replacing the golden Akbari coin with taels of dark opium.

During the time Bihzad spent in Hazari's palace as Haji Uzbek's son-in-law, Hilal Khan's serai suffered an unexpected upheaval. In the Persian month of Faridun, commencing with the day of the spring equinox, the Lady went missing from her shrine in the alcove on the balcony. Few recalled anything unusual in the days leading up to the theft. The serai's doors opened every morning, men and women streamed in, separating at the foot of the staircase into two rows, each making its way up to the top of the flight for a look at the painting. Sabi had lit candles and plucked the dead flowers from the offerings that morning. As he counted the coins in the hall below, Kanu had looked up and seen a man, a litter-bearer, bowing before the Lady. He had begged Sabi to be allowed to approach the painting, then placed his head on the floor in the manner of the infidels who worshipped their idol in the village hidden among the dunes.

It wasn't unusual, Hilal Khan had remarked later. Men and women of all faiths came regularly, rubbed shoulders on the staircase, exchanged gossip as they waited for their turn. Sabi too hadn't noticed anything alarming. But Kanu, from the hall below, had noticed a difference. The man had stared long at the painting. His eyes weren't those of a devotee praying for an ailing wife, even of a litter-bearer. They were the eyes of an artist.

'He was copying the lines from the painting in his mind,' the birdseller said later when they discovered the theft.

'But their paintings are different,' Hilal Khan had protested. 'The Lady and their dark god? Who'd be consort to whom!'

Every visitor came under suspicion. The residents of the serai pointed to the merchants' greed in the marketplace. The travelling saints, even the Sufis, fell under a cloud. 'The Lady is their rival,' Sabi said. 'No one wants to hear the mystical tales any more or sing and dance along with the qawwali singers. The sick, the wronged, the covetous – all have become the Lady's disciples. *Anyone* could have stolen her to keep as his own.'

A massive search of Hazari yielded nothing. From the stables to the slave market, every inch was scoured, till the only suspect left was the infidel artist. Word reached Haji Uzbek's soldiers, and a band of them set off for the infidels' village to rescue the Lady. They went from hut to hut, kicking the doors open, emptying the contents and laying them out in a huge pile before the idol at the village's centre. Stacks of paintings lay scattered, jars of paint were broken to pieces. The soldiers sifted through everything as if looking for missing treasure. Men were paraded naked, the folds of the women's dresses were loosened by force and peered into. Animals were driven out of the pens, which were then searched. A fire was set to the pile, smoke covering the village just as it did during its new year celebrations. A swinging spear struck the black stone, crushing the head of the idol on its pedestal.

The artists watched their paintings burn.

*

Still the Lady remained missing.

The serai's residents and regular visitors turned their suspicions on each other. Perhaps Sabi was the guilty one, hiding the painting so he could fulfil his prophecy and produce it at a suitable hour. The owner of the Joy House, before it was burnt down, who had offered to buy the painting from Bihzad, was accused too. 'Who'd buy the Lady?' he protested. 'What fool?' Perhaps the thief has sent it to the Shah of Persia or to Hindustan's emperor, he said. Forced into a corner, the man pointed at Kanu. 'It's him!'

No one thought of going up to Hazari's palace with the mystery, for the Haji was rumoured to be on his deathbed.

Confusion over the Lady's disappearance had muted the stories about the bridegroom's rapid decline. He had been suffering from fever from the month of Muharram, his physician regularly drawing his blood, but his court astrologer had held his tongue. Then doctors were summoned from other oases. A Khurasani gave him watermelon in accordance with the custom of Khurasan, a hakim from Agra advised that he should leave the desert for the mountains to cool his brain, a dervish – reputed to be a sorcerer – suggested abstinence from the harem.

In his last days, he barked like a dog, his face swollen and lips black. His favourite animals were brought out one by one and paraded before him, but he showed no interest. His wives squabbled with his courtiers, demanding that he be moved to the harem. He seemed unable to move even a single limb without help. His time had come, and after a decade on Hazari's throne and just under a month on his sickbed, he went to God's mercy.

*

'Bihzad!'

Hilal Khan called out to his friend as he reclined in his pavilion, an empty cup in his hand. He had broken his promise to himself, never to set foot in a palace again, bribing a guard to let him enter.

Bihzad opened his eyes.

Hilal Khan had come to ask a favour of his friend, although it was a long time since their meetings by the edge of the oasis had stopped. As Hazari convulsed with the mystery of the Lady's disappearance, Hilal Khan worried about what was yet to come. He had heard the faltering words of Kanu and seen the soldiers' eyes light up in rage. He had sensed their dark mood, returning empty-handed from the infidels' village. Sitting beside Bihzad, he nudged his arm and smiled, made as if to fill his cup. Then, he brought his face close to Bihzad's ear and whispered his request: a new portrait of the Lady to replace the one stolen.

Bihzad remained silent.

'Just one more. Then you can stop being an artist.'

Bihzad pretended not to hear, raising the empty cup to his lips.

For a while, Hilal Khan tried to humour his friend, flattering him with praise, reminding him of his genius. This new Lady, he said, wouldn't remain in Hazari. It would go with the Agra merchant's son to Akbar's court in Lahore. He hinted at a possible reunion between the emperor and his artist, conjured by the magical portrait.

Bihzad remained silent.

Then, Hilal Khan decided to tell the truth. He told Bihzad about the missing painting, the failed searches, Kanu's suspicion, and his own fears about the festering rage of the soldiers.

'You remember the infidels' village, don't you?' He mimed the two covering themselves in veils. 'The village has been attacked. The soldiers thought the infidels were hiding the Lady, they went to free her by force.'

Hilal Khan's voice grew urgent. 'They've burnt their homes, burnt their paintings. But they couldn't find the Lady. The soldiers are certain the infidels have stolen her and smuggled her out of Hazari. Might even have sold the painting to a travelling merchant. Now they'll return to the village and torture the artists one by one, force them to tell the truth.'

Bihzad's face remained impassive, he closed his eyes. Catching hold of his chin, Hilal Khan shouted at him. 'You are an artist. You must save the artists.'

Freeing himself from Hilal Khan's hold, Bihzad raised his arm and pointed at the door.

'Go!'

Sheeshmahal. The Glass Palace. Bihzad found Zuhra in her rarely used dressing room. The walls of its chamber were studded with mirrors, and its dome glazed with Persian tiles. A spray fountain at the centre sent a shimmering waterfall through marble channels on the floor. The servants had lit lamps, the light seeping through delicate lattice screens.

It reminded him of Sikri, the screens around the emperor's harem, that allowed the ladies to see without being seen. He remembered the row of dark eyes and the whispers. 'The Little Master!' It used to make him blush.

The glittering Sheeshmahal also reminded him of the weighing ceremony, when he had entered Akbar's sight for the first time. The play of light and darkness surrounding the emperor's throne, and the carefully drawn patterns on the walls, as if the builders had tried to calm the burst of energy radiating from the centre.

But the Sheeshmahal was different, it seemed to arouse and pacify at the same time. He looked for a pair of eyes. After weeks of absence he hoped to find his wife behind the screen.

When Zuhra appeared, she looked like a storyteller's Asman Pari – an angel. She wore a transparent red veil, red flowers, her forehead marked in red like a newlywed bride. She appeared as the shamsa – the sunburst. Seeing her, Bihzad's heart flooded with relief. He followed her into the Glass Palace.

Late at night they lay with the boy between them, like parents cradling their child. She rested her thigh on her angel, her wonder of the world, turning to face Bihzad, her breath still sharp at the end of their games. For the first time, he spoke to her about Zuleikha. He started to tell her everything about his stepmother, from her perfumes to her stories of the harem, her haughty and aloof air, her views on the Khwaja and his kitabkhana, even the rumour he had heard from Hilal Khan about her departure from Agra. For the first time, he confided what his friend Salim Amiri had suspected years ago, his love for his stepmother.

'I was her bee...'

'But you left her, didn't you?' Zuhra interrupted. 'Why didn't you stay with her, forget the kitabkhana...? You weren't in love with her at all, but with the magic of your fingers.'

Laying his head on Zuhra's arm, Bihzad started to sob.

'It's not what you love, but what you love most... above all else, that matters.' Sipping her dark cavee, she continued in her distant voice, making no attempt to soothe Bihzad. 'Your gift is your curse. Your defect. It'll make you suffer. Even if you wanted to escape, it wouldn't spare you. It'll cripple you, even if you flee, it'll seek its revenge.'

He felt her breath on his face. 'Even if you did love her, you couldn't have her, could you? Art is all that remains for an artist, like the unhealed wound that takes him to his grave, becomes his final lover.'

She kissed her sleeping boy lightly, then she freed herself from Bihzad and rose from the bed. Taking off the silk cord that held her gown together, she passed it around the neck of the eunuch. With a quick look at his face, she tied a knot, then climbed over his frail body. Leaning her elbows on the pillow, she brought her face close to the boy's, then tightened the knot.

Bihzad saw crimson bursts on her face, her neck, streaks running across her eyes from her pupils as if she hadn't slept in many nights. The boy woke with a start, staring straight at Zuhra, his nostrils flared, his lips starting to shake. Like a tigress on her prey, she pressed harder. As the cord cut deeper into his flesh, the boy's face flooded with blood. An inaudible cry passed his lips.

How many? The thought ran through Bihzad's mind. In a

flash he remembered the words of Hilal Khan. *Ask her what she does with her eunuchs when they grow old or sick, unfit for intimate service.* And he remembered Zuhra's own – *Love is destroyed by love.*

What would happen when the hour of pleasure had passed, he had often wondered. He had feared for Zuhra. Just as he had grown used to his wife's absences from Hazari's palace, he had grown used to the boy's constant presence between them. His early jealousy had waned, he had learnt to ignore the childish pranks, the whimpering and wailing, the readiness with which the eunuch feasted on Zuhra's flesh like a foraging beast. Between women they create hate, between a man and a woman, love. After his hate had spilled out during their nights of love, bursting and sapping everything in its blind path, he had started to feel a certain fondness for the boy. He who lives only to adore, the monster forever ready to be enslaved.

It was a game, he felt, yet another one before they were entwined as intricate threads of a woven cloth. Another of Zuhra's fantasies perhaps. Perhaps she was trying to scare him. He remembered the soldier of fortune at the serai. What had he seen? He too must have lain next to a dying eunuch, then spent the rest of his life crying at night, sleeping no more than a watch and a half, whimpering. *Maybe he has seen what none should ever see.*

In his mind, Bihzad saw the two together in the cold morning light: an angel embracing a mortal. A naked, warm body in the clasp of Zuhra, sleeping in the arms of the corpse. Which was the angel, and which the mortal?

'One who has given pleasure will appear before Him in paradise,' Bihzad heard her whisper. He felt the body stirring. Raising himself, he seized the dagger that hung at Zuhra's waist at all times even when she was naked, and cut through the silk cord at the boy's neck, leaving a faint streak of blood over his pale skin. The boy lay still – still as death. Then he woke with a start. Pushing Zuhra aside, the boy ran from the Sheeshmahal.

\*

Under a sky full of light, he saw her on the terrace. She turned to face him. He saw her eyes. In one – pity. Hate in the other.

# Tasveer

## portrait

*

Shatter the goblet
Fall for the glassblower's breath

RUMI

The moon started its eclipse. From beginning to end, it lasted till five watches into the night. Several months before, two heavenly portents had appeared in the sky above Hazari: a pattern of stars in the south that resembled a pot boiling over a fire, and a comet in the north, streaking towards the constellation of Libra. The monsoon had failed that year, and the famine was blamed on the mischief in the sky. Hazari started its penance – the rich distributed alms, the peasants lit fires of precious wood, soldiers tattooed the evil eye on their horses to drive away the omen. Everyone worried over the court astrologer's strange verdict. A weakness will arrive, he had said, remarking on the comet's path, among all who lived in the desert.

Five watches into the night, as the moon was about to emerge, an unearthly cry rose in the desert. In the blink of an eye, the palace was reduced to rubble as the earthquake struck. The walls of the compound crumbled, exposing the pavilions inside to public view for the very first time, before the parting earth levelled them too. The palace's minaret snapped in half. In the armoury, barrels of gunpowder exploded, lit by sparks from falling torches. The tall canopies of the pavilions burst like balloons, flags flying up into the night sky.

From a distance, the city's inhabitants watched the fireworks spellbound. It was as if an invisible enemy had ambushed and set the palace on fire, without even a touch of mercy. Then the invisible enemy struck the city with the same pitiless fury. At the marketplace, the earth sank, sucking down the merchants' stalls, burying their animals. The earth shook more than a dozen times, as dust rose like a cloud over the courtyard of slaves. The walls of houses parted effortlessly, the rubble from their collapse blocking roads, sending shockwaves through the streets. The Tarabkhana lay shattered. The public bath resembled a cemetery, its marble fountain strewn around in bits like gravestones.

There were some who escaped unhurt, thanks only to God's mercy. After the first shock, the survivors emerged from their crushed homes, clutching their dead and wailing for the missing. A few started to run towards the open desert, others huddled beneath the balconies surrounding the slaves' courtyard. Some knelt in prayer, thanking Allah for their lives. When the aftershocks came, the survivors were tossed around, flying through the air like jinns, coming down to earth with a thud. This time, there were no cries, just the silence of death.

In the days that followed, the remaining inhabitants fled. Most of them left their few precious possessions behind in their haste. Hazari's court astrologer had marked the unusually long tail of the comet, like the trail of a vast army. The last of Hazari fled the devil's army. Men escaped in panic without their wives, mothers without their children. The few travelling merchants who were still alive prepared their caravans with a feverish speed, desperate to go before calamity struck again.

In the terrible aftermath, bubonic plague swept into the city. Like the ghosts of the dead, the wind of pestilence spared none, sweeping away Hazari's soldiers and their chiefs. More than a hundred of them lay dying with buboes in their armpits, their colour changed to black. The sufferers begged for water, but none of those left untouched dared to go near them for fear of contagion. The cries of the sick and starving became more horrifying than the disease itself. Men died with the word 'bread' on their lips. The streets were clogged with corpses, as the living didn't dare to bury the dead. The Zenana Rauza – the women's graveyard – lay deserted.

\*

Bihzad fled. Awakened by the first tremor, he had seen the

pavilions crashing around his own, seen them going up in smoke. He heard the howling of the animals in Haji Uzbek's menagerie.

His only thought was to escape. His wife had disappeared soon after their last meeting at the Glass Palace. She had vanished before, but never for so long. Without Zuhra, without the court, and without his regular attendance at the harem, Bihzad had been confined to his pavilion, drinking and dreaming. Now he ran for his life.

He jostled with the survivors in the dark passages, among them frightened eunuchs, guards entering the charred pavilions and stealing whatever was remaining, and soldiers carrying their injured over their heads. He saw prominent courtiers being pulled out of the rubble by their servants, cursing the Haji's astrologer as they gasped for breath, as if it was he who had brought on the calamity. Outside the harem, he saw the lotus lady, a eunuch weeping beside her. He saw the empty cage, tossed upside down. A slave girl came rushing from the crumbling doorway, then let out a scream at seeing him, and ran back. He saw a dead cat from the Haji's zoo wrapped around his neck, its blood splattering his tunic. Running through the drifting smoke with the smell of burning flesh in his nostrils, he searched for a way out, then fled through a breach in the palace's walls, leaping over mutilated bodies – faces twisted and deformed, and bones scattered among the felled trees.

When he arrived in the city, Bihzad could not at first make out the familiar streets, going around in circles before he arrived at the ruins of the Joy House. He saw shadowy forms grieving in throngs, eyes glued on the rubble, waiting for a twitch to send them into a flurry of activity. Their faces covered in dust, he couldn't tell one man from another – just a blur of limbs digging out corpses only to bury them back.

Bihzad left the men and entered an empty street, walking along till he came upon a woman beating her breasts before a burning house. When she saw Bihzad, she pulled on his arm, and pointed to her husband, who was twitching like a dying insect under a pile of rubble. Suddenly a swarm of bats, wings flaming, flew out from the smouldering house, screeching and blind, smashing into the remnants of its walls and crashing to the ground. He stood frozen to the spot, surrounded by stillness and flight, then started to run.

A familiar voice called after him. 'Alive! Thank God you are alive!' He recognised the goldsmith's voice. Saida stood before his crumbled home with a sack over each shoulder. He had managed to save his precious jewellery from the ruins of his shop, but he had lost his entire family. His eyes were full of fear as he glanced around and whispered into Bihzad's ear, 'Run! The bandits will arrive soon – to kill off the dying. They're worse than the rotten earth.' Together, they made their way towards the slave market. Arriving at the square, Bihzad saw a row of young boys staring down at one of their friends who lay with his skull shattered. The girls ran around the square, heads uncovered. The quake had freed them finally, but from their screaming Bihzad couldn't tell if they were happy or as frightened as the others.

He left the goldsmith and, skirting the edges of the oasis, made his way towards the serai. It seemed to take almost an eternity to reach it, and when he finally arrived he found the main gate was open. In the tea hall it was dark as usual, the early light of dawn yet to clear the cobwebs over the tall shutters. The thumping in his chest started to slow, he began to feel calm. His eyes, accustomed to familiar bends, brought him easily to the kitchen. He hoped to find Kanu. The birdseller would be awake now, sitting among the cages, parting the covers to wake his pets, fill their water pots and seed racks. He went in expecting to hear Kanu's friendly voice chattering with the birds.

From the empty kitchen, he came to the foot of the staircase. There was no sound, not a cough, not a snore, nor the muffled voice of someone talking in his sleep from the rooms up by the balcony. Hesitating, Bihzad started climbing the stairs. Perhaps Sabi would be awake. Pleased to see Bihzad, he might start welcoming him in his high-pitched voice, waking the others. He passed by the soldier of fortune's door. It was open and the room empty. He pressed his ear to one door after another.

The Lady was missing from her alcove, but the shrine seemed still to be in use. He saw half-burnt candles, dried bouquets, a row of incense burners, and saw Sabi's hand in the neat arrangements, but the priest himself was missing. Retracing his steps, Bihzad returned to the tea hall, his mind made up to visit Hilal Khan himself and to offer his apologies for his rude behaviour at the palace. He entered his friend's room.

He saw his friend at once.

'Hilal!'

Hilal Khan sat on the floor with his eyes open, facing the door as if waiting for someone to enter. Bihzad saw the neck slit from end to end, and the dried blood on his chest and arms.

'Hilal..........................................................!'

He ran out of the room, running through the tea hall screaming, up the stairs then down, banging on all the doors, kicking them open. In each room he saw the hand of bandits, the dawn now revealing the jumble of smashed chests and ripped quilts, the floors strewn with objects left behind in haste. He saw signs of vain struggles – a clump of hair, a severed ringless finger, dark vomit in the middle of a room where a resident had been tortured to reveal his hidden treasure.

He ran back to his friend's room and embraced the cold torso. 'Hilal!'

In his mind, his friends at the serai were protected. He had trusted the power of the Lady. Although the goldsmith had made him nervous, he thought the serai's isolation from the city would shield it from the threat of looting. He stared in anguish at the shock of grey hair on Hilal Khan's head. A smooth chin and blubber lips above the body of an old woman. His friend, the monster, once the keeper of Akbar's bed, the faithful guardian of the loveliest women in Hindustan. 'Day of Blood ...' Bihzad whispered.

\*

He entered his own room by the stable, shutting the door behind him. It seemed just as before, as if his friend had kept it vacant, waiting for him to return. He removed his turban, and started to unwrap the folds. Then he took off his blood-splattered tunic. In the silence of the adjacent stable, he heard the desert wind. He searched for the barber's stool under his bed, taking it out and wiping off the dust. Bihzad remembered the first time the barber had come to the serai to cut his hair. 'Beware! Don't let him cut anything more than your hair!' Hilal Khan had joked. He stood facing the window for a moment, then wrapped the turban around his neck, front to back, fumbling with a knot at the back of his neck. He threw the long end of the cloth over the beam that hung below the roof, and tied the two loose ends of the turban together. Then he stood on the barber's stool and faced the blank wall. As he flew from his perch, the knot stiffened, sending a rush of blood to his head. The wall changed colour, becoming a headless torso gurgling to him through a vessel of blood.

The door opened. He saw a blurry form before him, blocking his view of the wall. Then it moved and came towards him in a few quick strides. He felt a hand holding him up and freeing his neck from the cloth.

The pair of powerful arms raised his limp body like a child's, and laid it down on the bed. Then it disappeared for a few moments, and returned with a bucket of water, splashing it on his face. He felt a gentle rubbing on his chest.

Through the film of water, Bihzad saw a man in white, kneeling by his bed. Father Alvarez.

Qaf to qaf. From one end of the world to the other. Leaving Hazari, Bihzad joined the travelling merchants. Wherever their caravans went, he went. It didn't matter if they were visiting a city famous for its market, or returning home empty-handed. It didn't matter if his fellow travellers spoke his language, or merely gestured with their arms. He travelled in all seasons – in the dead freeze of winter, and under the scorching summer's sun. He visited the lands that lay between the Sea of Arabia to the south, the Great Central Asian Desert to the north, the river Indus to the east and the Persian empire to the west. He crossed and re-crossed the formidable Hindukush, travelling through mountain passes and avalanches, spent months on barren plateaus, rested briefly in the desert oases. From market town to fort, he went to cities known for their pious men and mosques, crossed the line between warring kingdoms, sneaked in and out of a tyrant's reach. He went everywhere. Except to Hindustan.

The merchants, of course, knew he wasn't one of them, but they believed in his stories at the beginning. He'd pretend to be someone else, making up stories like he had done at the Joy House. The story of a courtier or of a wandering prince. Halfway through the journey, his fellow travellers would guess the truth – that he was neither a courtier nor a prince. The rest of the journey would be spent in conjectures. His discreet nature matched that of a spy. An assassin? But he carried no weapons. From his speech, some took him to be a learned man. 'He knows the names of every constellation in the sky!' 'He knows where

Hindustan ends and Persia begins!' 'He knows a fake ruby from a real one!' 'He acts like a wealthy nobleman.' 'Silly! Have you seen anyone abandon his riches to toil through a desert?'

From his piercing eyes, the master of a caravan took him to be a physician. He called Bihzad to his tent, and urged him to burst a boil on his leg. Taking his refusal as an unkindly streak, the angry master had the impostor thrown out at the caravan's next stop.

He was a mystery to his companions, always ready to offer advice. Years in Agra and Sikri, and then in Hazari's palace, had given him a sharp eye. Smelling a vat, he could tell the difference between musk and damask rose. He could sift real borax glass from fake, and value silk by guessing where it had been woven. He'd sit with the merchants in their tents at night, or in rest-houses along the way, advising freely, except when someone delved into a sack and asked him to pronounce on a painting. He'd refuse politely when someone asked him to judge if an album was worth the price quoted by a thief who had stolen it from the house of a nobleman, or if indeed it was the work of the eminent artist claimed by its seller. He'd gently push the album away and shake his head.

The merchants were confused. How could a learned man who knew so much about silk and gems be ignorant of art? They urged him on, promising a share of their profits. A real Mirak or a Muzaffar would certainly tempt a rich buyer. One that had flown from the pen of the Persian Bihzad might even be worth more than a season's crop of poppy.

\*

Wherever he went, Bihzad saw the same men. Their faces, colours and names changed, but he recognised them instantly. Among the merchants and generals, beggars and saints, he saw the same urges. What would make a merchant different from another, when the same greed flowed in them all? How could one tell one thief from another? A murderous general from his rival? What was the use of drawing a face with minute care, when it was no different from another face? Finally, as his old teacher had taught, Bihzad saw their *true* selves.

Everywhere he went, in the markets and in the resthouses, he heard the same tales over and over: treachery and might. Greed and surrender. Tales of false miracles. He worried about artists, condemned to find beauty in an ugly world. What could they draw that was truly graceful? The human artist must copy in miniature what the supreme artist has created – he recalled Mir Sayyid Ali in his Agra studio: *He is the first artist who revealed the power of light, adorned an album with leaves of the universe.* Did He adorn the despots as well? The soldiers blinding their prisoners? Which colour and brush had He used to draw the executioners, the spies who lived simply to betray others, the men who stole children to sell as slaves? Bihzad held his hands before his eyes. From his childhood he had been told of the genius of these fingers. He examined them one by one. Of all the paintings they had touched, he couldn't think of one that was free of the lies he had learned as a child. 'He has drawn an imperfect universe,' he whispered to himself. 'Better never to draw than imitate His strange pleasure.'

*

More alone than ever, he sat in his caravan tent and recalled his childhood. The painter of kites appeared before him. He chuckled, remembering the neighbours' dismay and his father's anger. Then, he opened the album of Bihzad, went through the scenes of his own life one by one. He saw the first page, a boy drawing monsters from stories read out to him by his stepmother. Next, he saw him sitting in Agra's kitabkhana, painting to meet the Darogha's requests. Then he saw the face of a young courtier in Sikri – full of ambition, waiting anxiously for the emperor to bestow honours upon him. He kept on turning the pages, more scenes flashing past his eyes: Bihzad the artist of the Joy House, Bihzad the creator of a goddess, Bihzad the painter of strange animals, Bihzad the artist of shameless love.

Words of praise rang in his ears from each of the scenes. Yet every page seemed full of rebuke, resounding with angry words.

Bihzad heard the Khwaja scolding him for drawing from his mind, throwing down his painting of the Simurgh, and of the landscape that showed the sun's mischief at dawn. *You must please the emperor by drawing his face…*

And he heard Zuleikha… *Now it's your turn. To follow your father, to please the emperor, become what you are not.* His lotus had shut her petals, leaving him, the bee, to live outside, alone.

For a brief moment, he found comfort remembering his friend the paintseller. Only Salim Amiri had been forgiving of his moods. *It doesn't matter, Bihzad, who you draw or how. As long as in your heart you paint no other face than His.* But even Salim Amiri had remonstrated. Like a blind man, he had pleaded with Bihzad, *You must see, then show us…*

Shutting the album, he sat wondering why he had failed to please those who mattered to him most. What good was his genius, after all? Why couldn't an artist be like a barber, his art designed to please all? He blamed himself for the suffering of others. If only he hadn't been an artist, but stayed back with Zuleikha in Agra. He blamed himself for his stepmother's loneliness, blamed himself for his father's shame – forced to examine his deviant son's album – and for his sorrow at his exile. If only he hadn't painted the Lady that was to result in the carnage at the infidels' village. Perhaps he could have saved his friend's life, had he remained in the serai, if only he hadn't charmed the Haji with his animals and become the Khwaja of Hazari. He blamed himself for Hilal Khan's death. Then he thought of Akbar. The album opened again on pages he had overlooked, had passed over in a hurry. He saw the artist painting his lover in secret. Why had he failed to please Akbar? What unknown suffering had he inflicted on his beloved?

*Your gift is your curse*, he heard the voice of his wife across the vast desert. *It'll make you suffer.* Bihzad recalled the time when he had resolved never to touch the pen again, after his exile in Hazari had started. Despite Hilal Khan's vigorous disapproval, he felt he had been cured then, with none to praise or rebuke his work. He had forgotten that he was an artist, content to live as an ordinary man among ordinary wanderers. Then he frowned, thinking of the relapse into his old urge. He cursed himself for having started again, foolishly depicting Mulla Assad's story at the Joy House. Yet it wasn't the admiration of drunks that he had sought, but that curious disease returning just when he was on the verge of a cure. *It'll cripple you even if you flee...*

What had made him draw, despite his father's refusal to teach him when he was a boy? What made him draw hundreds of paintings, stop then start again? He sat with his head in his hands. A question kept hovering over his mind, kept on hovering for days. How could he free himself from his urge, lift the curse for ever?

*

His merchant friends noticed his sullen mood. He seemed sad, not quite himself, not ready as usual to examine their wares. Perhaps he is missing his family, they thought. Perhaps his stock of gold coins was running low, causing him to worry.

The merchants tried to cheer him up with wine, with stories about foolish buyers and foolish sellers. Failing to lift his mood, they talked about strange spectacles they had witnessed on their journeys. One of them described the ruler of the land they were passing through. He was a strange man, with a passion for discoveries. He wished to know the mystery of the stars, and of all living beings. He was known for his ingenious schemes, none more unusual than the experiment that was now being conducted in a retreat called the Gung Mahal – the Hall of Silence.

Gung Mahal. It was a lofty building carved of stone. Far from other dwellings, it seemed quite new, as if the masons had just struck the final blow. Bihzad had felt curious listening to the story of the strange experiment being conducted there. The ruler had imprisoned a dozen newborn babies, orphans, in the building. Right from birth they were reared without ever hearing a human voice. The women who attended to them were prohibited from speaking, either among themselves or to the children. Not even a word. The ruler, Bihzad had learnt, wished to prove a point – if the children remained dumb as a result of growing up in silence, it would prove that the power of speech was simply a trick learned young, not a gift of divine inspiration.

Bihzad entered the Gung Mahal, managing to arrive and enter the building unnoticed. It was dusk; the children were about to rise from their afternoon nap, their attendants still dozing in their own quarters. He stepped into the room where all the children were sleeping, and opened the windows. As they woke, they observed him in silence. Bihzad watched them too – a whole room full of children, silent as a graveyard. It couldn't be true, he told himself. Perhaps there was a trick...Something must make them talk, squeal aloud or cry. He started to imitate birds, cooing and whistling as if they were returning to their nests at the end of the day. He cried the shrill cry of a peacock, feigned the soft moaning of a dove. The children listened in silence, following him with their eyes as he darted from one end of the room to the other as if playing hide and seek with himself.

He clapped his hands loudly, laughed out loud, raising his voice to a crescendo, rising higher and higher. Bringing his face close to each one of the children, he called them by various names, speaking in many tongues – Farsi, Turki, Chagtai, Uzbeki.

The children remained silent. Dumb. Their eyes widened with each new trick.

*

Bihzad sat on his mule-cart and thought about the Hall of Silence. Silence had robbed the children of the power of speech. He frowned, attempting to solve the riddle. Could blindness then…? What would make the artist forget? What would kill his urge, destroy the magic of his fingers? He played with the edge of his turban, taking it off, still lost in thought. Then he tore off a piece of the white cloth and tied it firmly over his eyes.

The world grew dark. Although he couldn't see the faces of his fellow travellers, from their voices he knew of their surprise. They surrounded Bihzad after the driver of his mule-cart had run to the caravan master and informed him of the 'ghost' with no eyes. They didn't think he was a trickster, putting on disguises for fun. Was he ill? Did his eyes hurt? Were they brimming with tears for no reason? One of them made as if to examine him, trying to take off the blindfold, but Bihzad pushed him away, and he landed on the sand with a thud. Then they started whispering to themselves. Maybe it was his head not his eyes. Perhaps he has gone mad, or the devil has possessed him. They recalled rumours of travellers who had seen fearful apparitions in the desert, then kept their eyes shut for ever, fearing to see them again. Maybe he has seen what none should ever see, they thought.

He remained with the caravan for a few more days, until the merchants began to feel uneasy. They worried that word would leak out of the strange man travelling with them. He might become a greater attraction than their goods, they thought. Some of their buyers might even take him for an evil omen, and refuse to trade with the caravan. He could be taken for an assassin, casting suspicion on the innocent merchants. Although he still paid for his meals, and for his place in the caravan, the travelling merchants started to talk of moving on without Bihzad.

When they stopped at a small market town at the foot of the Hindukush, the caravan master came to tell him their decision.

Bihzad didn't answer. Since blindfolding himself, he spoke rarely in any case, and only to ask for help feeding himself or getting down from his cart.

'We must leave now, Bihzad. From now on, this market will be your home.' The master waited for a reply, then cleared his throat. 'God knows why you've chosen this path. I pray He takes you where you want to go.'

One of the merchants, who was closer to Bihzad than the others, led him to a seat under a tree in the centre of the town's marketplace. Tying Bihzad's sack of coins firmly around Bihzad's neck, the merchant told him about a resthouse nearby where he could find a bed at night, and foodstalls that stayed open till late. He also warned him to leave the marketplace before dusk, because of bandits. Then he collected a band of urchins around him, gave each one of them a coin, and told them to keep an eye out for the one without eyes.

*

After the initial burst of curiosity, the stall-owners got used to him. They were used to strange men – strange in appearance, speaking in a strange tongue, or offering strange items for sale. Living in the nearby resthouse, Bihzad would arrive in the market at dawn and leave at dusk, holding on to a helping hand. But from his seat under the tree, he couldn't tell one stall from another, didn't see any of the faces that addressed him. His ear still alerted him to days and nights, but he was unable to mark that special moment when the sun inched up over the horizon and started its mischief. In the early days he often hurt himself, slipping and falling, or dipping his fingers into a boiling pot. It made his face take on a perpetual frown, frozen grim around the jaws. In the early days, his stomach growled with hunger as he made his way around the foodstalls at midday, circling round and round till he was forced to swallow his pride and call someone for help. His head felt heavy from the constant swaying, scanning the world with his ears, following a trail with his nose.

His face showed no emotion as a band of guards flogged a

man right before him for stealing from the stalls. He remained still as a swarm of lepers danced around him, jangling their bowls, earning suitable curses from the onlookers. The lepers started a fire, casting off their garments into the pit, begging for a new set of clothes. Someone threw them a coarse woollen sack, followed by a scramble.

From his seat, Bihzad held out a coin, then dropped it unnoticed on the ground.

Sometimes he'd ask a boy to lead him to the mosque near the market, entering through the back into a small garden where he sat before the tomb of an infant. No one knew who the dead child was. Travelling saints came at sunset and recited from the Koran. Bihzad would doze with his back to a tree trunk, listening to the prayers, till awakened by a rain of alms on his lap.

The urchins followed him wherever he went. Prancing before him, they would raise an alarm, as if he was a leper capable of infecting others through his blindfold. At the resthouse, men asked him questions. Why? Was he a culprit, his eyes put out for an unpardonable crime? Men seemed more curious about his crime than his condition. Had he sinned against his family – jealous of his wife's love, had he slit his brother's throat? Was he a rebel? Had his eyes seen what none should ever see? Had he peeked into the emperor's harem? An old palace guard described the horror of the punishment Bihzad must have undergone. A drop of poisonous herbs on the pupils. The eyelids stitched up, or a hot iron passed before the eyes, causing a pain beyond all comparison. The men at the resthouse flinched. Bihzad remained silent.

There were those who thought he was pretending to be blind so that he could steal when others had shut their eyes to sleep. 'Pretending to be blind but watching everything!' Perhaps he was doing penance for someone or something, punishing himself like the infidel monks, the living dead, who strode into the desert without food or clothes, ready to die of hunger and thirst.

'Why would he be wilfully blind?' a visitor to the resthouse asked.

Others pointed to his head, made faces. 'To the sick man, sweet water tastes bitter!'

There were days when he was pushed into an alley, eager hands going through his saddlebag and the flaps of his robe. He'd try to thwart the thieves, flailing his arms, clutching the coin purse to his chest, but they'd push him against a wall, ripping open his tunic, bloodying his face if he screamed out for help.

The stall-owners looked at him with pity, but they didn't try to nurse his wounds. If one of them came over to where he sat slumped under the tree, still bleeding, the others would call him back.

'Leave him alone! It's his choice.'

'A man shouldn't choose his own fate. If he does, then he's bound to suffer.'

'He's fine! Can't see his blood, can he!'

Sometimes, soldiers passing through the town made fun of his helplessness. Bored by sieges that lasted too long, they had little to do to while away their time. Even the whores were afraid of them. Bihzad would hide from them in the resthouse, paying the bazaar urchins to bring him his meals. Sometimes the urchins would give him away to the soldiers.

Then the fun would begin. The soldiers would make Bihzad stand in the centre of the marketplace. Insults would be hurled, he'd be asked to chase a ball, soldiers kicking it around. He'd be asked to point to their officer, who would constantly change position, and he would be slapped for his mistakes.

In one such show, a wolf was brought out from a cage. It was a mountain wolf, trained to obey the officer's orders. It started to stalk Bihzad, sniffing at his robe, then suddenly made a growling sound and knocked him over. Mounting him, it started to hump, cheered on by the soldiers. A tear seeped from the patch over his eyes.

*

He saw the qamargah in his dream. The imperial hunt. A forest lay under siege. The soldiers had trapped the animals within a tight circle of hunters. The courtiers sat on royal elephants – the Khwaja and the Darogha, Sikri's Chief Executioner, the Royal Physician, and the veena player. He saw the artists perched on a nest in a tree – a tired-looking Mir Sayyid Ali, his weary face held high. Another artist cast his hungry eyes over the animals from an elaborate tree-house. Adili. He saw the priests lined up before the courtiers: a dour Shirhindi counting beads, Sabi pleading with the soldiers to be allowed into the circle so he could bless the animals. He saw Father Alvarez on his knees, staring above the line of men and beasts. Kanu ran around the dancing peacocks, imitating their shrill cry. To the beating of drums, and the sound of firing muskets, he saw Akbar enter the qamargah, his sword raised. He was stalking a strange animal, just a solitary one in the circle, its eyes blindfolded. He saw the emperor's sword strike the neck of the animal.

*

As his coin purse started to thin, as he started to lose more from theft than from paying for his bed and his meals, Bihzad had no choice but to live as a poor man among the poor. From the rest-house, he came to the gholurkhana – the soup kitchen with a stable by its side. The owner of the kitchen allowed beggars to share the stable with his animals.

Unused to sleeping on the floor on a bed of dried leaves, he'd stay up all night, his constant shifting keeping the other human inmates of the stable awake. In the morning, they would shower him with curses and order him to leave. He'd spend the day searching for another place to sleep.

Unused to the taste of rancid meat and stale bread, he'd starve for a few days, then splurge when luck found him a freshly cooked meal. He'd sit motionless in the market before a stall selling delicacies, without even a drop of saliva wetting his tongue. From other beggars he learned to wait by the foodstalls next to the mosque before the evening prayers. Sooner or later a rich man would arrive and throw a bag of coins to the owner, asking that the poor be fed in his name.

Like a beggar, he lived with beggars, living by begging, never once questioning the wisdom of his decision following his visit to the Hall of Silence. In just a few months, his skin cracked, like the skin of rotting vegetables, breaking out in lesions attracting flies. His hair grew all over his face and stuck out like a comic's wig. His stooping frame made him seem older, his eyeless face forever sleepy. The stained robe flapping in the breeze made him look like a torn kite, rattling its streamers after its fall from the skies. The urchins held their noses when he passed by. 'Lord of Filth!' they teased him.

He lived too by the generosity of strangers. A man, a postal runner, took him to the small hut which he shared with his wife in a nearby village. Whenever an imperial message came, or a merchant sent a letter to another, he'd run and deliver it to the next runner who lived a few miles away. The man was illiterate, like Bihzad, but he had learnt to recognise the seals on the letters he delivered. He didn't know who the letter was meant for, or what it contained, only that it should reach the next runner in a hurry. Bihzad sat with the postal runner before his hut, waiting for the letters to arrive. His wife cooked, and the man filled a pipe with coarse tobacco for the two of them. They sat chatting over the affairs of the town and its neighbours, never discussing the letters or their senders.

From the embossed seal of a lion, Bihzad could tell if it was an order from the emperor of Hindustan. From his days in Sikri, he knew the seal's power. The power to exalt a courtier, promoting him in rank or offering him the guardianship of a famous city. The power to bring relief to a battle-weary general, ordering him to return to the capital. Perhaps it was meant for his father, the Khwaja, elevating him to even loftier positions than before. He knew the power of an order to punish with exile or death.

His host gently pried the letter from his fingers, then started to run.

Some days, they'd receive a bundle lovingly wrapped in silk. The runner's wife would come out of the hut and turn it over in her hands, admiring. A present, perhaps, from a high official to his betrothed. Bihzad thought of the presents he wished he had sent but never did – presents to Zuleikha in Agra when he was still deemed master of Sikri's kitabkhana. He imagined her in her room, calling her maid Nikisa over to unwrap the bundle, imagined her pleasure at receiving a present from her own Bihzad, then imagined her reply as well – a couplet, perhaps, from the pen of Jami or Hafiz, which would certainly have required a read by his friend Salim Amiri.

The runner's wife would smell the bundle of silk, holding it under Bihzad's nose to share its perfume.

For a few months, he felt the warmth of friends around him, almost as if he was living in Hazari's serai. Then a letter came for the postal runner himself, from a local lord, ordering him to leave his village and desist from ever touching a letter. An important order, it read, had been stolen while on its way from the sender.

The man and his wife brought Bihzad back to the market town, then left to go wandering off. The urchins welcomed him back with curses.

*

As days passed, Bihzad saw his paintings in a new light, the paintings he had completed since taking up the pen in Agra. Hundreds of them. As if they were his only memory of the time when he could see and act like the others around him. He started to examine them in his mind, viewing them as a teacher would view a junior artist's work, his forehead in a perpetual frown.

'What is he frowning at?' one of the urchins surrounding him in the market asked.

'He's frowning at your snot!'

'No! He's frowning at your round belly, full of worms!'

'He's frowning at your open fly, silly!'

He examined the face of Farhad that he had drawn in Mir Sayyid Ali's studio. Farhad carving the face of Shirin on a piece of stubborn rock. Why hadn't he tinged his face with sadness? Didn't he know that the peasant would fail to win his love? Shouldn't an artist prepare his viewers, leave a hint about how the story would end?

226

He examined his portraits of Akbar. Even the ones from his secret album. In one of the paintings, he had drawn the emperor as a bridegroom, engaged in the rites of a secret betrothal, receiving burns on his forearms from his lover. He dwelt on the painting for a long while. He had drawn Akbar's calm face, unmoved by the wounds, when indeed it should have shown marks of pain, not from the glowing tip of the knife, but from the thought of parting from his lover.

Bihzad passed his waking hours imagining himself as the Darogha, a monocle over his blindfolds, subjecting his paintings to minute scrutiny, noting errors, grimacing over omissions, flailing the artist for misjudging the purpose of a scene. Gradually he started to see a trick, chuckling to himself. He knew what would finally kill his urge. If only he could exchange an artist's heart for an executioner's, replacing his dreams with contempt.

*

The Sufis brought relief. Relief from the interminable squabbles between buyers and sellers, and the regular beatings of thieves that did more to enervate the guards than reduce the complaints from the shopkeepers. A rumour had been going around about a possible invasion from the north, raising everyone's anxiety. The Sufis brought much needed distraction, gathering the town under the roof of a giant prayer hall. Then the music started.

They danced and sang for three days and nights. 'Don't hand him a cup, pour it into his mouth – for he has lost his way!' the Sufi master cheered as Bihzad entered the hall. He danced and drank with the Sufis, his body in the air, swirling like the dervishes, his face covered with tufts of hair and beard. The old tunic open at the chest showed the last patch of pale skin.

'All is He! All is He! All is He!'

He felt one with the ecstatic dancers, crying like children and kissing each other. For the first time, he felt as if he was one of them – the travelling saints, who cared for nothing more than to die in the embrace of their beloved. Like them, he too had stood in the sun, plunged into water, burned in fire.

Between the chantings, he listened to the maqalas. The leader welcomed him, pointing him out for the crowd to see. 'I see a free man sitting on the ground. A king in a beggar's garb. A giant wave from the mightiest sea.' He started to tell the assembly the story of Maulana Rumi – 'our master'.

'Rumi met his friend, Shams of Tabriz. The two drunks spent months together without any human need. Their friendship became one of the great mysteries of the world.'

'A friend's embrace is sweeter than a century of prayer!' a man called out from the crowd. The leader nodded. 'Yes. With a friend you may truly become a man. Without a friend, you will remain an animal. What will you sacrifice for your true friend?'

'My head!' the crowd roared.

'Rumi became a poet, pouring out his love for Shams in line after line. "My life is not mine," he wrote. "But your life is mine!" Then his beloved disappeared. Rumi mourned the loss of his friend.'

Someone screamed out madly – a friend's name, a lost or dead friend. The hall started to wail in chorus.

'He searched everywhere. "Alas! My eternal friend is hidden." Rumi wrote poems of repentance and sorrow.' The leader stirred up the crowd's mourning.

Suddenly a Sufi, bareheaded and drunk, caught hold of Bihzad's arm, and peered into his face. 'Aren't you the artist of Hazari?'

A few in the crowd stopped to take notice. 'Artist?'

'No, he's just a beggar,' a beggar who shared Bihzad's stable said.

'Lost,' said another.

'A convict punished for his crimes.'

'Aren't you Bihzad, the artist?' The bareheaded Sufi held fast to Bihzad's arm.

Now the leader stopped. Pushing Bihzad to the front of the crowd, the bareheaded Sufi started telling them about an artist he had met once – an artist with a rare gift, a Persian perhaps, or an émigré from Hindustan. He was known all over the desert, rich men had their portraits drawn by him. He could illustrate all the stories known to man, although he couldn't even read a single word. *The Tales of a Parrot. The Adventures of Amir Hamza.* He could draw with his eyes closed, paint an entire album in his sleep!

Bihzad remained silent, his head drooping. A blank page was pushed before him, a pen thrust into his fist. The leader beamed. 'Then let him draw this assembly.' Even the drunks woke up then, straightened themselves on the floor.

'It is *he*!' The Sufi who had recognised him patted his head, trying to wake him from his stupor.

'What! An artist?' The stall-owners were confused. 'But that's impossible. How can a blind man draw?' The owner of the stable where Bihzad slept teased them. 'Maybe he wasn't blind before. Maybe he has become blind seeing how you rob innocent men!'

Bihzad sat with the blank page before him. As the pen dropped from his hand, there were whispers and laughter.

The storyteller smiled at the bareheaded Sufi, then resumed his tale. 'Then word came of Shams. From Baghdad. Rumi sent his son to beg his friend to return. When they met again, they fell at each other's feet.'

Bihzad rose with the others, and started to dance the dance of mourning and reunion.

*

Drunk and sick, he moved from one stable to another, begging for alms during the day, drinking the cheap brew of the market behind the stalls at night. He'd hear voices around him in the dark, drunken endearments. He'd feel hands groping below his robe, from the coarseness of the fingers try to imagine his lover.

*

He became a pawn. Two women sat before the entrance to the mosque near the market, one on each side of the road, charging a fee to visitors for watching over their shoes. Each had a beard on her chin, warrior-like, and not the least bit of pity for her rival or for the visitors. One of them brought Bihzad over to sit by her side, hoping that people might be drawn to the spectacle of a blindfolded man. The pilgrims started to arrive, breaking their journey to Mecca with a day or two in the market town before they joined another group to travel onward. The stall-owners were busy, the mosque flooded with visitors. The shoekeepers thrived as well, but Bihzad's owner was the more successful, showing off her prized mascot. 'Leave your shoes with the blind man! He'll watch over them!' Amused visitors flocked around him, and he sat all day like an island surrounded by a sea of shoes.

The other woman became jealous. She tried to entice Bihzad over to her side, slipping him a loaf of bread or a tael of opium when he returned to sleep in his stable at night. She offered to look after him, wash and sew his tunic, give him a roof over his head. Bihzad's owner increased her attention too, allowing him to keep a few of the coins, or a pair of old shoes. When the war heated up between the two, the women would stalk him at night, pulling him by his tunic into a dark passage, murmuring their love for him. They'd tempt him, drawing his hand in theirs under their skirts, up the folds of the rolling thighs.

One day, as he sat among the shoes, the rival shoekeeper came up, demanded that Bihzad move over to her side of the road. The two women got into a violent fight, with visitors crowding around them. The rival claimed the blindfolded man was her husband, complained bitterly about the 'man stealer'.

'Husband! Your eunuch, you mean. He can't even husband a bird, leave alone a woman!'

The rival jumped on Bihzad. 'Let me show you my husband's…' She tugged on his robe, started to drag him away. The other resisted, spurred on by the crowd. Both women pulled him towards them.

'Bet he has fun with them both, the sly fox!' The crowd watched intently.

The rival seemed the stronger of the two. Carrying a frayed Bihzad over her shoulder, she managed to land him in the middle of the road, halfway to her own pile of shoes. In a desperate attempt, his owner lunged at him, biting his thumb with her toothless gums. 'Thief!' she barked at him, pointing to the string purse around his neck.

Within moments the crowd descended on them, separating the women and showering Bihzad with blows. 'Thief!'

'Robbing a poor woman of her dues!'

'Playing one against the other!' someone spat at him.

He sank under a mountain of shoes.

The birdwomen saved him. Swooping in from nowhere, they disappeared with him from the market town. They fled along secret passes, soon leaving behind the dustbowl at the foot of the Hindukush as they climbed up the slopes. Carrying Bihzad in a sack hanging from their backs, they dropped down into gorges, made their way around dangerous bends, and arrived eventually at the foot of the pigeon house. Infrequent visitors had given that name to the steep hill that had numerous caves sunk into it from its foot to the top. The caves were joined by passes, often as narrow as a dwarf's grave, and in parts high enough for small animals to be hidden. It looked like a giant bird's nest. Crawling into one of the caves at the foot of the hill, one could follow the passes and reach the cliff in a few hours.

A stream separated the pigeon house from a valley of rocks. It was an unusual sight. Perhaps a hill had exploded, spewing rocks all over, some landing on top of each other, smashing the trees, turning arid what had once been a gentle valley. The stream ran deep in parts, but its waters didn't join a sea, sinking into sand and the dust of stones.

Here, in the land of rocks, there were no villages or caravan paths with resthouses. No emperor sent his emissaries here. Passing soldiers avoided riding through the valley on their horses. Even fugitives didn't come this far. Greedy merchants on the lookout for a gem quarry or a forest of fragrant wood stayed away, fearing a sudden avalanche.

It was rare to see animals, but birds of all kinds nested among the rocks, laid eggs and raised their young, then flew away to other lands. They came from the northern lakes to escape the harsh winters, and from the southern swamps when the sun dried the lakes in the summer. Parrots came in large numbers in the hot season when the mulberries ripened. The northern swallow came – called the Chughurchuq in Turki, the Sharak in Hindustan – slender and red around the eyes. The pheasants grew fat in the absence of hunters. There was the wild fowl, the partridge from Arabia, named Shakrak after its child-like cry, the crane, smaller in body than the rest, but longer in the neck. Buzzards, mallards, magpies – birds known by different names in different tongues. Crushed eggshells turned the banks of the stream white.

Bihzad lay sleeping in the largest cave of the pigeon house. He slept without pain or nightmares. In the few hours that he was awake each day, he heard the birdwomen around him. He knew about these women from his travels, and from the gossip in the marketplace. They were so named because they lived among the birds in the pigeon house, sold birds' eggs in the markets, and themselves resembled a flock of birds that flew from perch to perch at will. These women, he had heard, were the only ones who were totally free, unlike the harem women and their slaves. They lived outside the cages that men had built. They were women of great courage drawn from all over Central Asia, Hindustan and Persia. Among them were women from Kalmuk and Turkestan, dark Abyssinians, women from Tartary and Kashmir. Some were of tall Circassian stock, some small and delicate like the Armenians; there were foul-mouthed Mongols, peasant women from the plains, and from the islands to the south. Their lives had been full of sorrow. Quite a few had been stolen and sold as slaves, abused by their masters and left for dead. Others had raised a knife to their masters' hearts. There were withered wives, cast out of their husband's bed and forced to beg in the streets, women who had been harem servants and had fallen foul of their masters, simple peasant women whose husbands had been slaughtered or taken by force by marauding soldiers, women whose children had been thrown into wells before their eyes.

Like an army they swarmed over the rocks, collecting eggs from the nests, saving injured birds, feeding young ones whose mothers had flown away. Besides the eggs, the birdwomen collected feathers that they sold as turban-aigrettes at market towns, as well as the beaks and claws of dead birds to use in potions.

The stall-owners called them whores, but they were jealous of them. Whenever the women arrived, they drew the buyers away. A small fossil in a woman's palm would attract a crowd, ignoring the precious gems for sale on the stalls. They disregarded the rules of the market, emptying their sacks at the gate and throwing out the contents. A bunch of peacock feathers. A necklace of claws. Mountain honey. The dark wine of cacti. They made the buyers anxious, showing their wares for a brief moment, then wrapping them back in their sacks. A purchase demanded swift completion, without the usual rounds of bargaining. The stall-owners were jealous, and surprised at how easily the birdwomen emptied their sacks, emptied their buyers' pockets, while they themselves needed cups of tea and flattery to rob their customers.

Any attempt to drive them away usually ended in disaster. Without a quarrel, they'd leave the market and alight in the courtyard of a resthouse, drawing the entire town with them. The guards too were helpless against the women. These weren't the normal sort, but mad. A hidden dagger could well slice off a merchant's nose, or a finger poke nastily into his eyes. Without homes or stalls of their own, the guards couldn't hold the women to ransom, unlike the merchants' wives forced to gaze out through the bars of their cages.

They left the market usually with more than their sacks full of coins. Like scavengers, they picked up the rotten in their beaks: orphans, or a child abandoned for the sign of the devil – six fingers on its palm, or a baby cast away by its mother for crying in her womb.

*

At the pigeon house, the women spoke in a jumble of tongues, as did the children. It didn't take long for Bihzad to learn the meanings of the different words and sounds that he heard from his cave. Rushing water in the mornings meant that the bathing cave was busy. He heard the tranquil drops from a bucket, and the soft thud of clothes clashing against the washing stone. Then, he heard the splash of the children, the squeals and gurgling, and the sharp notes from their adoptive mothers. He heard the laughs from the kitchen cave, mixed with a crackling fire. He couldn't tell how many of the women were inside, but the clash of pots and the whistling steam would keep him awake all morning. In the silence of the afternoon, when the women left with the children to collect eggs or to visit the market towns, he strained his ears to catch a single note. He hoped someone might have stayed behind in the pigeon house. He'd hear only a bird's call or the wind, raising himself on his bed, hoping to speak with his visitor.

Even in the years of his deprivation, his normal speech, learned as a child on the steps of the kitabkhana, hadn't deserted him. He had learned to speak in the manner of a courtier, precise in courtesy, without undue familiarity but a touch fancifully with a sprinkling of verse. 'A true Persian tongue!' Zuleikha would tease him. 'Their speech is their disguise,' she'd sigh. Even at the Joy House or at Ḥaji Uzbek's palace, he surprised them with his words, so distinct from the jumbled vocabulary of the desert. His speech was as responsible for the respect he commanded in Hazari as his fingers were. During his real exile, beggars and merchants would be struck when he asked to be led to the mosque or back to his stable. The words seemed to come from some place other than the frail body and the smelly tunic. At times, Bihzad would be treated to a decent meal by someone moved by his gentle manners, taken for a highborn fallen on hard times.

He would raise himself on his bed hoping to speak with his visitor. Perhaps a birdwoman had returned earlier than the others. He'd take the silence as his own fault. Perhaps he had been too forward, put the lady in discomfort. He'd try again. Perhaps she was used to a different tongue. He'd try again.

In the evenings, he heard the women all around him. He heard the sound of coins stacked up and divided, sacks emptied of food. Every now and then, he'd catch a familiar word or two. Some days, he'd hear a young voice, that of an orphan, rescued and brought back from a slave merchant's tent, as she told the story of a young life. Whatever the language, the birdwomen listened in silence, the cave filling with sighs.

Most nights he slept alone. Occasionally there'd be a sick child sharing his cave. Rarely would he wake at night, except when a woman in labour was brought into the infirmary. He'd hear frenzied whispers, the rush of water being emptied from a bucket, soft whimpers and the birdwomen singing in soothing chorus. He'd wait and wait, till the cry of release flew from the cave like a bird.

*

Twins – Jamal and Jamil – became his shadow, the boys appointed by the birdwomen to be his guides when he was fit enough to move about outside the pigeon house. Bihzad took his first hesitant steps with both boys holding his arms and guiding him over the loose rocks. With the two by his side, he crossed a humpbacked boulder, gliding past its jagged edges and slowing down to turn his body through a narrow pass. On the very first day they took him down to the stream, and helped him to cross over on a bridge of stones. Once on the other side, the twins discovered the nest of a rare bird, slipping the eggs into Bihzad's hand.

They called him Tana – the sapling. It was absurd to call a grown man by that name, but the boys explained to the birdwomen: like a sapling, he was frail. The gust of a storm almost blew him away, and the boys had to hold on tight to his flapping tunic. The ends of his blindfold danced in the breeze over his ears like a stalk. He *was* a Tana, wasn't he, growing stronger every day, making fewer mistakes, needing less and less help coming down to the stream or climbing up?

He didn't relish his meals if his young friends were absent. If they went with the women to visit a market, he'd lie in bed all day. He wouldn't leave the cave, not out of fear but out of sadness. His sack would remain empty. The boys had taught him to discover the nests, tell the eggs from the smooth round stones. In the beginning, he'd sit at the foot of the pigeon house while the boys went about their search. They'd bring their catch over to Bihzad, surrounding him with pyramids of eggs. Then they'd teach him which came from which nest, which kind of bird – partridge or pheasant, heron or owl. They'd laugh at their pupil, unable to comprehend the birds' names. How could a grown man not know the Chughurchuq, the Shakrak, the Kitlik? Dancing around, they'd brush against a pyramid, smashing the eggs on his tunic.

*

'Jamal!'

He screamed. The rumble of a huge rock grew, hurtling towards them like a meteor.

'Jamil!'

He stood on a high boulder, waving his hands madly, shaking violently like a stalk about to snap. He felt the hill bursting into pieces, shooting up towards the sky and raining down. He feared the rock would catch the boys unaware, smashing their young skulls, smashing them like eggs in their nests.

'Jamal ...! Jamil ...!'

They came running to him, held his hands, made him sit down, his heart pounding as he heard the rock splash down on the stream.

Poor Tana, he couldn't see, could he, that it was harmless, sliding down on the other side of the stream, far from them?

*

'Chughurchuq?' Bihzad frowned. He recited a list of birds, imitating their calls, but the boys said no. It wasn't one of them. 'Then what is it?' He asked Jamal to draw the bird on the ground with a stick. The boy started, Bihzad holding his elbow to follow the strokes, as he drew the head, the beaks, the bulge of the neck.

'Ah! The Sharak.' He let out a sigh of recognition.

237

'Sharak?'

'Chughurchuq in Turki, Sharak in the tongue of Hindustan,' he explained to the twins.

Then they drew the Shakrak, the Kitlik, each time breaking into laughter as Bihzad pronounced a different name. It became a game. First one of the boys would raise a stick over the ground and start to draw, Bihzad holding on to his elbow. The boy would draw a bird's head. Then, just as he was about to draw the wings, Bihzad would jerk his elbow along, making his hand move away from its course, coming up with a different creature altogether.

'Name it!' he'd challenge the twins.

'No. You name it!' they'd roar back.

The boys would pass the stick to Bihzad, ask him to draw a bird while they guessed its name. Caught up in the game, he didn't think twice, drawing rapidly on the ground. They were amazed how quickly Tana drew. He had the power to confuse them with his creatures: the monster wolf Karkadann, Hizabr the lion, or the mythical bird Simurgh. Pir Janwar, they called him. Saint of Animals. Saint of Birds.

Playing in the valley of rocks, sometimes they'd hear the sound of distant voices. They'd fall silent, hiding behind a boulder, looking up towards the top of the cliff. The voices came mixed with the rush of the breeze and the clomping of horses' feet.

'Soldiers!' Jamil whispered.

Bihzad asked the boys to look carefully. Which way were they going? How many were there? Were there flags – did they see any flags?

The boys looked out from their hiding place. It took a while for them to spot the general's canopy.

'His flag is red and green.'

'Green?' Bihzad shook his head in confusion. 'Look again.'

It was green, both boys said.

Who was invading whom, he wondered. He tried to remember the colours of the imperial flag. The great Mughal army on a march to the western fort of Kandahar? Rebels retreating to the safety of the impregnable Hindukush? Would they stop here, climb down to their stream? His heart raced.

*

Their Tana could see, Jamal and Jamil told the birdwomen. Crossing the field of thorns with them, he stopped abruptly and stared at a fire of dry leaves burning before a patch of red flowers. The apricot trees in blossom distracted him from the task of collecting eggs. He seemed to admire each egg, each a shade different from the others. A gasp escaped his throat when they passed a jumble of stones that resembled a human face. In winter, the dead vines spread out like vipers' hoods would make him frown. It was as if he saw everything – the forms and colours speaking to his heart without the distraction of sight.

*

Leaving the pigeon house with the boys at dawn, he'd face the rising sun. He watched the artist painting his scenes with obvious relish, like a child, changing the course of all creatures by his whim – turning young this ancient world, destroying too, with pleasure, the loving craft of his hands.

His teacher's voice floated in over the Hindukush: *Remember, Bihzad, an artist is closest of all to the Creator.* He felt close to the Creator – the one who sees without sight, the one who creates unmindful of rewards, the one who is unable to stop. Through his blindfold he saw the mischief of the sun, repeating itself over and over each day. From Agra to the pigeon house, he felt the truth of the artist around him. Felt that indestructible urge.

*

He would argue with the birdwomen if they left him alone. 'But you can see now!' they laughed. Perhaps he too would come with them to his old market town, returning to visit his stables and the mosque. What would the stall-owners think, seeing him among the birdwomen? The shoekeepers? They laughed, sending a shiver down Bihzad's spine. He was well now, well enough to give up his favoured spot next to the fire to the limp

239

form the women had brought back after their last visit. A man –
a postal runner – lay among the sacks, almost lifeless. He had
been accused of spying and beaten by soldiers. His hut was
burnt, his wife raped and killed, and the man given up for dead.
He was a postal runner, not a spy as accused, an illiterate too.

Bihzad lay next to the runner. He ran his fingers over the
man's face at night. He was the same one. Bihzad's mind
returned to the few happy days they had spent together in his
hut. The man would live, he was told by the women, but he
wouldn't be able to run again.

The runner recognised Bihzad when he woke. They talked
about their days together, without once mentioning the letters.
The whole world was in a turmoil, he told Bihzad. The great
Mughal army was in retreat in the south, and the mountain sol-
diers were threatening to swoop down yet again from Central
Asia. The local lords were conspiring against each other, and
even tiny market towns had started to fear a sudden catastrophe.
The emperor of Hindustan, he said, lay on his deathbed in Agra.

**1605** of the Christian era. Year 1014 of the Hegira. The sun was in Aquarius. Emperor Jalaluddin Muhammad Akbar lay on his deathbed in Agra. He had returned to the old capital after an absence of three decades, but the residents had more reasons to mourn than to rejoice. The previous year, the emperor had resolved to tame Salim, his rebellious son, by proceeding in person to Allahabad, but his ship had run aground in the Ganges. His mother had died the year before, as had his youngest son, from incurable vices. His own illness had started with a congestion of blood. At first, the royal physician had refrained from treating him, trusting the patient's iron constitution to heal itself.

For forty years, ambition had ruled Akbar's passions. His life had been dedicated to conquest. But he was more than a warrior – the richest merchant of them all. He had built pleasure palaces in the blink of an eye, then deserted them after just a few nights of pleasure. The caliphs of Baghdad, the sultans of Turkey, the shah of Persia, even the Son of God from distant China, couldn't match his hoards of treasure. But he was an emperor and a merchant who was never far from God, known as a believer among infidels, and as an infidel among believers. A Muslim, a Hindu, a Jain, a Christian, a Zoroastrian – he was all in one. He had even founded his own faith, but never raised his sword to convert his subjects.

The same Akbar who had once wished for a body as large as an elephant's, 'so that all the world might feast on it', lay speechless on his bed, servants dripping water into his mouth. A trusted general stood with a jewel-studded dagger by his bed, his face white at having shed the emperor's blood at the physician's command. His courtiers waited outside the room. The plot to supersede Salim on the throne had failed; ministers awaited the arrival of the rebellious son to his father's chamber. The poets had gathered, the artists. The House of Worship wept outside the closed door. *When a man's sleep is better than his waking, then it is better that he should die.* Abdullah, the court poet, now old and senile, started to recite from the great Nizami – 'I am like a corpse with the soul of a man, journeying alone without my caravan.' The zajal singers, brought to entertain the patient, had been sent home. In the streets of Agra, his subjects had started to whisper the posthumous title of their emperor: Arsh Ashyani – the one whose nest is on the divine throne.

*

Bihzad entered Agra on his mule-cart. Travelling in one caravan after another, protected by friends of the birdwomen in every town, he returned to the city of red hewn stone after almost as long an absence as Akbar's. Agra, no longer the watering hole of invading armies, but the much spurned, much adored capital of Hindustan. He asked the mule-cart driver to stop outside the western gate. The man helped him alight, then he took a few steps towards the old house that had once been his teacher's studio. Although he could no longer see the window that allowed the sun to enter Mir Sayyid Ali's room, he raised his nose to smell the resin and the paints. A slap landed on his face, he heard his teacher's voice: *Who do you think you are? A clerk? A convict under oath? Speaking the truth and nothing but the truth?* Bihzad smiled, then asked the driver to lead him back to the cart.

As they went through the market, the driver drew the curtain around Bihzad, to ward off curious onlookers who might be drawn to the sight of a blindfolded man. He could still hear the traders, especially the one who sold kites. From the tinkling of ankle-bells, he knew a courtier's wife was doing her rounds, her maids following her with bundles on their heads.

Soon they left the bustle and trotted over an open patch of

ground. He felt the river's breeze through the curtain. The Jamuna. The quiet surroundings reminded him of his favourite ruins by the river. He wondered if the palace was still standing, the halls and the courtyards, the crumbling harem, the night tower. His driver had been told to take him to the imperial quarters. Approaching the courtiers' homes, the driver slowed. He came to a stop before a giant arch, then turned back with a questioning glance.

'Where do you want to go?'

Bihzad kept silent. He toyed with the idea of visiting the kitabkhana – the old kitabkhana. Then he changed his mind.

'To the Khwaja's haveli.'

'The Khwaja?' The driver was young; he must have been born after the artists had left Agra.

'The haveli of Shirin Qalam – the Persian master.'

Still, the driver didn't know. He left Bihzad alone in the cart and went to ask others, then returned to take the cart slowly down narrow lanes, before coming to a stop. He left his seat to help Bihzad alight.

Bihzad stayed sitting, ignoring the man. Why had he returned to the Khwaja's haveli after so many years? In his mind, he returned to the first page of his album. He saw monsters, wingless birds – but much as he tried, he couldn't conjure up his father's face. This time he didn't raise his nose to smell the perfume. Turning to his impatient driver, he asked to be taken to the emperor's palace.

The palace guards let him proceed to the Commissioner for Complaints, as was the custom, taking him for a subject who had travelled from afar to bring a grievance before the court. He met Murtaza Beg – the Commissioner – the man he had known as the philosopher during his days at Sikri's kitabkhana. The chess player who was reputed to know more than ten thousand moves by heart, a friend of the artists, a man of universal curiosity. He recognised Bihzad.

'At last!' Murtaza Beg led him into his room. Closing the door, he scolded Bihzad for not having returned earlier.

'It's *you* Bihzad! What took you so long?' Didn't Bihzad know that his sentence was no longer in effect? Didn't he know that Akbar had repealed his order of exile after hearing Bihzad's story from the lips of his spiritual friend Father Alvarez? 'The priest told him about the Lady, your Lady. He said it wasn't simply the ultimate proof of an artist's genius, but that of a man's dedication to God. Akbar regretted his order then, he sent emissaries to hunt you down and to bring you back. But by then you were lost …' Murtaza Beg sighed. 'Did you have to wait for his last days to return?'

Murtaza Beg seemed to know all about him, from the day he had left Sikri to cross the desert, to his days in Hazari's serai. Merchants and spies, entrusted with keeping the emperor informed, had brought word about the recalcitrant artist of Hazari, and of his marriage to Haji Uzbek's daughter.

'Then we lost you. You were lost to the world.' Murtaza Beg spoke of unconfirmed reports of Bihzad spotted in far-flung market towns. He seemed to be the same man, the spies reported, except that he no longer drew or painted and covered his eyes with a cloth.

'The emperor was curious,' Murtaza Beg said. 'Why would someone wilfully blind himself?' The courtiers suggested several reasons, but Akbar refused to believe them. 'Not unless he wishes to see none but the one most dear to his heart,' Akbar had said.

A shiver went through Bihzad.

'You were his favourite artist. No one came close. Years after your exile, he'd ask to see your paintings. He would look at them carefully, sighing often. He was sad after he had signed the order banishing you from his empire, didn't speak a single word to anyone for a whole day. His courtiers were worried for him. He was sad, Bihzad, not for the Khwaja, or for his kitabkhana. But for you.'

Bihzad turned his face to the open window.

Then, speaking each word slowly, Murtaza Beg told Bihzad of the Khwaja's death. 'He died in his mint. He wasn't completely himself after Zuleikha left him, and after your exile.' At the pinnacle of his success, he regretted not being an artist any more, he felt he had betrayed his forefathers in Persia. 'What once belonged to Persia is now Hindustan's,' the Khwaja would say in his last days. 'The Mughal artists are now superior even to the Persian masters.'

Like an old uncle, Murtaza Beg went on telling Bihzad about the demise of Sikri, Akbar's mad rush around his empire, the rise and fall of prominent courtiers. He told him about the gossip that was sweeping Akbar's empire – the gossip about a son trying to murder his father. Then he stopped and asked Bihzad, 'Why have you returned to Agra?'

He kept silent for a while, then replied, 'To see Akbar.'

*

A trusted general stood with a jewel-studded dagger by Akbar's bed, his face white at having shed the emperor's blood at the physician's command. The sword of the Mughals that hung over the royal bed had been removed. The emperor had announced his succession, passing on the sword and the imperial turban to his son Salim. Guards hushed the visitors who were arriving for a final look at the emperor. He was sleeping, the door to his room was shut. Murtaza Beg was allowed to come forward, leading Bihzad by the hand. All eyes turned to the blindfolded man, dressed in a pilgrim's robe. They waited outside the emperor's room for a long while, then the physician came out and gestured to the guests to enter one by one.

The two stood before Akbar, who was resting on his bed with his eyes open. Murtaza Beg whispered his praise for the emperor, then started to narrate a story – the story of an unpardonable crime. He told Akbar of an unfortunate artist, born of a master and himself a genius, who had displeased his emperor. But his crime was a strange one ... Akbar stopped him with a raised hand. He asked Bihzad to come forward. He approached with a few measured steps, and started to recite a prayer. Facing the bed, Bihzad prostrated himself with his forehead touching the ground.

The emperor rose from his bed. Holding Bihzad's shoulder, he brought his face close to his, staring at the patch over his eyes.

In a swift move – one with which he'd sever a deer's neck in a hunt – he flung open the blindfold.

Bihzad saw the green jade cup full of Akbar's blood. He saw the mole on Akbar's cheek, now a dried cherry. He started to cry.

The emperor held his face, tears running down his hands. 'You are not an artist,' Akbar told him. 'You are a saint, Bihzad. Only a saint is truly blind, seeing none but the God inside him.' He raised him from the floor, drew him towards his bed, made him sit by his side. He kept on looking into his face for a long time. Then he spoke, still in the voice of the emperor.

'But I want you to turn into an artist for the last time.'

S ama. The final dance. The dance of ecstasy and death. The Sufis danced in a garden under the moon, arms raised, faces glistening in the light of stars. It was the night of the chosen one. At the centre, he drew Akbar dancing in a trance, his hair swirling around his face like a small cloud. The emperor as the prophet, flaming in golden fire as he ascended to heaven, not on a horse but on his feeble feet. Every inch of him illuminated, casting not a shadow before the blinding sun. He drew Akbar like the dark god of the infidels, the god of love, cavorting with his consorts, setting fire to their veils. With every stroke of his brush he healed the wounds of a sick emperor, turning him young again.

*

And so it is written in the books of Hindustan that when the day of his death arrived – the eve of Thursday, the thirteenth of Jumada – the emperor asked to see his artist. Before his soul was given over to the creator of souls, he sat before his portrait, the artist by his side. He embraced him, then tied a string around his wrist – not one made of pearls, but a simple thread, as was the custom among friends. He thanked Bihzad.

'If every hair of my body were to become a tongue, still I would fail to express one of a thousand thanks to you.'

'Jamal…! Jamil…!'

He ran up the slope from the stream to the pigeon house, calling aloud for his young friends.

The birdwomen peeped out of the caves. The orphans came running to meet him. They stopped, seeing Bihzad, laughing, with an egg in each hand. His sack seemed full too. Stepping over a pile of rocks, he threw the eggs at them, smashing into the walls of the caves.

It took a while to get used to him again. He *was* their Tana, but different – not afraid of falling rocks, swaying no longer in the breeze like a stalk. He didn't need a hand coming down the slopes or crossing the stream. He could see.